The Devil on Lammas Night

The Devil on Lammas Night

SUSAN HOWATCH

STEIN AND DAY/*Publishers*/New York

First published by Stein and Day/*Publishers* in 1972
Copyright © 1970 by Susan Howatch
Library of Congress Catalog Card No. 72-94532
All rights reserved
Published simultaneously in Canada by Saunders of Toronto Ltd.
Designed by David Miller
Printed in the United States of America
Stein and Day/*Publishers*/ 7 East 48 Street, New York, N.Y. 10017
ISBN 0-8128-1534-3

The Devil on Lammas Night

I

Nicola was dreaming. She was alone by the sea and before her stretched miles of empty sands. There was no sound. Even the waves made no noise as they rolled across the sands toward her, and because there was no sound she was acutely aware of the emptiness of the sands and the brilliance of the light. She walked and walked until suddenly she realized that she was no longer alone.

Evan was ahead of her.

He had his back to her and was a long way off, but she knew it was Evan because she could see his dark red hair and recognize the set of his shoulders. She called his name but when he did not turn to face her she ran across the sands toward him. She had to run for some minutes and after a while she could hear her sobbing gasps for breath, the only sound in that silent landscape, but no matter how far she ran she came no closer to him. Finally she stopped, and as she stared ahead of her Evan faded away into nothingness to leave her alone once more on that wild lonely stretch of shore. She tried to shout to him; the breath stuck in her throat but making one last effort she managed to scream his name at the top of her voice.

She awoke, still screaming, a second later.

"Oh, for heaven's sake, Nicola," said her roommate crossly. "I wish you'd never met that wretched man! Can't you dream about someone else for a change?"

It was five o'clock. When Nicola wandered into the living room a minute later the sun was rising across Hampstead Heath, and London was emerging from the night into a pale April morning.

Nicola sighed. She knew she would not sleep again before her alarm sounded at seven-thirty, so presently she resigned herself to her wakefulness, lit a cigarette, and went into the kitchen to make herself some coffee. In the bedroom Judy was already asleep again. Judy had no worries. If she dreamed at all she would dream of her fiancé or the job she enjoyed or the entrancing potential of her future. For Judy life was turning out exactly as it should and luck was inevitably, tediously, on her side.

"I'm not surprised," Judy had said complacently the previous evening. "These things go in cycles and I'm in a good cycle at the moment. Maris told me that this would be a marvelous year for Capricorn subjects because Jupiter would be coming into the ascendant, and . . ."

But Nicola did not believe in astrology.

"Oh, but Nicki, how silly! I mean, it's like saying you don't believe the earth is round! Now if you went to see Maris—yes, I know she's peculiar but she's a genuine Hungarian gypsy, and gypsies are so clever about all those sort of things— No, don't be insular, Nicki. Just because she's not English—"

But Nicola was skeptical of all fortune-tellers, even the English ones, and saw no reason why she should have any special faith in Maris whom Judy had met at some bohemian party in Pimlico. Maris owned a Hungarian restaurant off the Fulham Road and was a small mysterious woman of uncertain age with a carefully preserved accent and a wardrobe of eccentric clothes. She was reputed to do nothing, even selecting the menus for her restaurant, without first consulting the stars and making the appropriate astrological calculations.

"Well, if you ever do go to Maris," Judy had said with maddening confidence, "and if she predicts your future and if she turns out to be dead right, don't say I didn't tell you so."

But Nicola had no intention of consulting the stars. She knew exactly what the stars would say.

"You are passing through a difficult and unhappy phase but—courage! Venus will soon be entering your House and Venus in conjunction with such-and-such means that Love and Happiness are without doubt on the way ... Five guineas, please."

The trouble with me, Nicola thought as she sipped her coffee and watched the sun rise over London on that April morning, is that I'm a cynic.

But she had not always been a cynic. Less than two years ago she had been as carefree as Judy; the company for which she worked had just promoted her to be secretary to the managing director, she was still savoring the independence of having her own home in London, and at long last Evan was showing signs of taking more than a friendly interest in her.

But there was no point in thinking of Evan now. Evan was no longer part of her present. The present now consisted of a job that bored her, a city that had grown jaded with familiarity and a roommate who was getting married and would have to be replaced. Nicola hated the dreary task of finding a roommate, and had recently been toying with the idea of living alone, but it was too easy to be lonely in a big city, particularly when one's social life was going through a bad phase, and irritating though Judy was in many ways, she did at least stave off the loneliness and oil the rusty wheels of Nicola's social life from time to time.

"Nicki, you just can't sit at home night after night! It's so—so wasteful! You can't give up just because one beastly man walked out on you—heavens, he's not the only man in the world! Listen, we'll give a party. You must be launched back into circulation."

Judy had tried very hard to help her roommate recover from Evan Colwyn. Nicola could only wish she had been more interested in recovering.

9

Six o'clock came. Then seven. London was wide awake now, and from her position by the living-room window Nicola could see the postman progressing slowly down the street while the milkman trundled along behind him in his electric cart. It was time to get up. After drinking some orange juice she returned to the bedroom and began the dreary task of dressing for what she already knew would be another dreary day.

On her way to work she bought a paper at the tube station and glanced at it as the train careened south from Hampstead into Central London. She was about to skip the society gossip page when she saw the picture of Lisa.

"Mrs. Matthew Morrison, wife of the millionaire industrialist, at the charity ball held last night for the benefit of the starving children in Africa. . . ."

Lisa's diamonds, thought Nicola, could have paid for a year's supply of food for at least a dozen of the starving children. But Lisa wouldn't have thought of that.

Nicola checked herself with an effort. She supposed it was natural for her to resent her father's recent marriage to a young and glamorous socialite, but while acknowledging the resentment, she must take care to keep it in control. Lisa could have been much worse. Well, perhaps not much worse, but worse anyway. Nicola smiled wryly to herself. Perhaps the plain truth of the matter was simply that she was jealous of her stepmother. Lisa was only five years her senior and yet she had been married twice, had indulged herself in numerous romances between marriages, and had lived in half a dozen different countries before settling down near London with Nicola's father, who happened, by a most providential stroke of good fortune, to be a millionaire. Nicola could not even pity her for being childless, for Lisa had two attractive children by her first marriage. Lisa had everything, and the most maddening part of all was that she was still only twenty-nine.

Nicola wondered how much would happen to her in the five years that separated her from her twenty-ninth birthday. Very little, probably. She had a sudden picture of herself still working at the same job, still her boss's faithful Miss Morrison who reminded him when to send flowers to his wife, still looking on while the latest roommate left the flat to get married.

Somebody bumped into her as she left the train and stepped onto the platform.

"I'm so sorry!" someone said in a throaty voice which Nicola realized dimly that she had heard before, and then the someone exclaimed, "It's Judy's friend! Nicki! It *is* Nicki, isn't it?"

It was Maris. Maris of the astrology and the palmistry and the zodiac signs and the Hungarian restaurant off the Fulham Road.

"Darling," said Maris, clutching Nicola's arm in the middle of the platform of Holborn-Kingsway station and sounding like a bad imitation of one of the Gabor sisters, "how strange I should meet you like this! I had a dream about you—"

Oh dear, thought Nicola.

"—a very strange dream—I had seen Judy, you see, and she had mentioned you, and my mind—all subconscious, of course—"

"Yes, of course," said Nicola. "How are you, Maris? What a surprise to bump into you like this."

"Well, darling, obviously it was destiny, wouldn't you think? Listen, have lunch with me today. I'll tell you about my dream. It was a very strange dream—"

"Maris, I don't think I—"

"Darling, do you know a man with red hair—dark red hair—and blue eyes, a very strong, masculine sort of man—"

The train was drawing out of the station. The crowds and the noise and the dust were intolerable.

Nicola thought: Judy's put her up to this.

But supposing Judy hadn't?

"Yes," she heard herself say. "That sounds like someone I used to know."

"*Most* interesting." Maris patted her dyed coiled hair in satisfaction and allowed her eyes to assume a dark inward expression. "Darling, we have to have lunch. Twelve o'clock

11

at La Belle Époque—you know? Please—as my guest! You'll come?"

"I . . . yes, all right . . . thank you, Maris—"

"Lovely, darling," said Maris serenely and the next moment she had vanished into the crowds and Nicola was left wondering if the entire interview had been a hallucination.

II

"You were at the seaside," said Maris three hours later in a private corner of the little French restaurant east of Russell Square. "It was a very pretty seaside, sandy with big waves. Perhaps there were cliffs. I don't remember. But there was no one there. That I remember clearly. Just you and the young man with red hair."

The waiter arrived with the entrées. As Nicola automatically picked up her knife and fork, half her mind was telling her she was without doubt going mad while the other half was trying to remember all she had ever read about extra-sensory perception.

"Darling," said Maris sympathetically, "don't, please, be cross. Judy, being your friend and being worried about you, did, it's true, tell me a tiny bit about your troubles, but—"

So that was it. Judy had described Evan and recounted every detail of Nicola's relationship with him before asking Maris naively for advice from the stars. But that still didn't explain the coincidence of the seashore.

"Did you really dream this bit about the seashore, Maris?" she asked curiously.

Maris at once became mysterious. "It was—in a sense—a dream. Yes. In another sense, no, It wasn't."

Nicola felt too confused to be irritated. She cut a piece from the escalloped veal on her plate and tried to sort out her thoughts.

"Never mind," said Maris grandly, "what kind of a dream it was. It was a dream. You and your young man were on this sand by the sea—"

"—and when I walked toward him he disappeared?" suggested Nicola in a crisp practical voice.

"Not at all," said Maris severely. "Quite wrong, darling. You walked toward him, yes. But he stood still, calling your name and you didn't answer. You walked right past him. He begged you to notice him but you didn't even hear. You walked past and eventually disappeared."

Around them the restaurant hummed with conversation and the discreet clatter of plates. Nicola found she was still staring at the piece of veal speared on the prongs of her fork.

"Of course," said Maris, sampling her ragoût de boeuf, "the meaning is perfectly obvious."

There was a pause. "Yes?" said Nicola at last.

"But yes! Of course! You mean you don't see what it means?"

"Well, I—"

"Obviously, darling, you are going to recover from your—your—"

"Infatuation," said Nicola dryly.

"—involvement," said Maris, "with this young man. You are within reach of a time when you walk past him without even noticing he exists. He may plead with you, but he will plead in vain. It will be over. Finished. You will be free," said Maris, very European suddenly, "to love again."

"I don't believe it," said Nicola before she could stop herself, and then, embarrassed by her own rudeness, added in a rush: "I'd like to believe it, but Evan's been away in Africa for a year now and I find I'm still thinking about him as much as ever. I just can't believe a time would ever come when I'd be completely indifferent to him."

"I am very seldom wrong about these things," said Maris.

"What are the odds on the prediction coming true? Surely there must be times when you're mistaken."

"May I see your palm for a moment?"

"Palm?"

"You wanted to know the odds, darling! I must have some sort of guideline!"

"Oh, I see—which palm?"

"I'll look at the left first."

Feeling absurdly self-conscious, Nicola laid down her fork and extended her left hand across the table.

"I am not an expert on palmistry," said Maris. "Never have I pretended to be an expert in a scientific sense. But sometimes there are nuances—impressions—you understand? I am very sensitive to nuances." She took Nicola's palm in both hands and examined it for a moment. Presently she released it. There was a silence.

"Yes?" said Nicola, suddenly nervous.

"Let me see the right palm now."

There was another pause. Maris' face was expressionless. Nicola wondered in panic if her lifeline were severed at an early point in time.

"Hm," said Maris. "Your left palm, as you probably know, shows your potential. Your right shows what you have made of it."

"I suppose I haven't made very much of it yet," said Nicola, trying to speak lightly.

"You haven't yet fulfilled your potential." Maris returned absentmindedly to the ragoût de boeuf. "You are a passionate person," she said at last. "You are emotional although you try to hide it. Your Evan may have been the strongest love of your life so far, but he won't be the last. No. Definitely not the last. So that persuades me that my dream is an accurate prediction—you will forget Evan and love again."

Nicola was acutely aware of Maris' impassive expression. "Is that such bad news?" she inquired uneasily.

"No, no," said Maris with a careless shrug of the shoulders. "Not necessarily. But perhaps yes. Who can tell? It depends on many things. But tell me one thing, Nicki. You're not attracted to dark men, are you?"

"Dark?"

"Dark hair, dark eyes."

"Not usually, no." She found herself remembering Evan's red hair with a pang.

"Lovely, darling," said Maris, relaxing with a smile. "In

that case you have nothing to worry about. Now, how is your escallope de veau? The cooking here is usually good, not like so many French restaurants who think they can disguise a poor cut of meat by saturating it with a fourth-class wine . . . You must come to my restaurant one day! You like Hungarian food? Good! When you fall in love with this new exciting man, I want you to bring him to my restaurant and I'll give you both the best dinner our kitchens can provide."

"I'd love to—if I ever meet him. Thank you, Maris."

"Of course you'll meet him! Haven't I just told you so? Soon you'll have forgotten your Evan ever existed and you'll be content for him to spend the rest of his life in Africa."

All Nicola's skepticism came flooding back. After the meal was over and she had parted from Maris, she found herself wondering with that familiar bitter longing where Evan was at that moment and whether he ever thought of her.

III

Evan Colwyn was working in a remote strip of Africa administered by the French and largely unmarked by twentieth-century progress. On the day that Nicola lunched with Maris in London he was holding his mobile clinic in one of the primitive villages and administering the injections and medications which the World Health Organization made available among the disadvantaged peoples of the underdeveloped countries. The villagers were not obliged to offer any form of payment to Evan for his services but he usually returned to his house in the capital with several chickens which his patients had offered in gratitude for the help he had given them. The nurse who assisted him on these expeditions, a strong silent Frenchwoman called Genevieve, disapproved of the chickens and regarded them as a source of infection, but Evan did not want to insult his patients by refusing their gifts and he overrode Genevieve's disapproval.

On that particular day a woman whose child he had treated for one of the eye diseases prevalent in that part of

Africa gave him a different kind of present, an intricately carved necklace, and told him in the strange French which even Genevieve had difficulty understanding that it was a gift for his wife.

"But I have no wife," said Evan in his Parisian French with the English accent, and Genevieve had to translate his words again because the woman could not understand.

The woman said that in that case it must be for his future wife since obviously one day he would consider marriage.

"Thank you very much," said Evan, trying not to think of Nicola. "It's a beautiful necklace. I'll take good care of it."

The next patient walked up for attention. And the next. And the next. It was very hot. Evan felt his shirt sticking to his back and the sweat darkening his hair, and his thoughts turned longingly to sea breezes blowing through the grounds of his father's house far away, to light rain falling from pale northern skies, to the frost and sleet and snow of a climate far from the Equator.

It was time to go home, he knew that now. His year with the World Health Organization would soon be completed and he would have the option of either signing on for a second year or returning to Britain to make the long-postponed decision about his future. His year of exile had at least enabled him to decide that he did not want to remain an exile for the rest of his life; on his return to England he thought he might join the staff of one of the big London hospitals or try private practice. Before his visit to Africa the current lack of incentive for doctors in Britain had made the idea of emigration to America attractive to him, but while his father was still alive and his sister was an invalid he had felt himself obligated to resist the temptation to emigrate. However, the temptation had been strong, and Africa had been his way of compromising between his duty to his family and his urge to go abroad. A year in Africa was a different proposition from a lifetime in the States. He had been able to say truthfully that the job would give him some valuable experience in tropical medicine, and despite his obligations at home he knew his family would tolerate his departure in the

16

knowledge that his absence would be only a temporary state of affairs. Meanwhile Africa would prove to him how well he could settle in a strange environment and give him the necessary perspective to make the right decision about his future. He had been in a muddle before he had left England.

"I don't know what I want," he had said to Nicola. "I've got to get away and think about it."

Nicola would have married him, he realized that now. But he had been muddled about her, just as he had been muddled about everything else. If he had married Nicola he would have had to make a decision about his future and he had felt incapable of making a decision at that time. His father had wanted him to marry Nicola and, illogically and unfairly, his father's very approval had made him shy away from her. It was principally because of his father that he felt himself tied to Britain. Of course his father wanted him to marry Nicola! Marry, settle down, sink roots, forget all notion of emigration . . .

"I do love you," he had said to Nicola, "but I can't marry you. I've got to take this job in Africa."

"If you loved me," Nicola had said, "you wouldn't even be considering going to Africa."

"That's just a woman's way of looking at things."

"Romantic nonsense, you mean."

"Oh, for God's sake, Nicki . . ."

Evan winced. Better not to think of Nicola. It was all right to think of England and his home in Wales because he would soon have the opportunity to assuage his homesickness, but it was no use thinking of Nicola. She'd probably found some other man by that time anyway. It was all over with Nicola and it was no use thinking of her any more.

"The witch doctor wants to see you," said Genevieve, returning to the tent with some fresh vials of penicillin.

"Oh God . . . I suppose I'd better see him now. Is he outside?"

"Yes, but shouldn't you attend to the rest of the patients first? Why do you have to drop everything to see him?"

"Because he's a big man in the village and he's always been

17

friendly and I want him to stay friendly." Evan's voice was abrupt. He disliked it when Genevieve tried to tell him what to do. "Show him in, would you, please?"

"Very well, doctor." Genevieve assumed her habitual expression of disapproval and departed.

The witch doctor was a powerfully built man in the prime of life with the superiority of a natural autocrat. He had hooded bloodshot eyes, a calculating smile, and an unexpected knowledge of intelligible French.

"Good-day, M. le docteur," he was saying grandly to Evan. "What a pleasure to see you again."

"It's a pleasure to be here."

The formal politenesses, Evan knew, would seem unending but his months among the people of this remote French possession had taught him not to give in to his usual impulse to speak abruptly and plunge into the heart of the matter before the proper preliminaries were concluded. The unreal phrases, enriched by the formality of the French language, were patiently recited, the insincere compliments meticulously exchanged. Evan did not like the witch doctor, whose psychological influence over the community he deplored, and the witch doctor did not like Evan, whose medical miracles threatened to reduce his hold on the village, but each respected the other's power and was intelligent enough to stave off an open confrontation. The witch doctor had long been spreading the rumor that he was responsible for Evan's visits and that each cure Evan achieved was by benign permission of the witch doctor himself; it seemed the wisest way of dealing with the threat Evan presented to him, and none of the villagers had so far given him any serious trouble.

"When may we expect you again, M. le docteur?" he inquired politely, watching Evan's blue eyes. He had long wondered if blue eyes saw colors differently, but he knew it would be a tactical mistake to ask point-blank; he did not want to mar his reputation of knowing everything. "Next month as usual?"

"I expect so, but I may not see you the month after that. In June I'm returning home to my own country."

The witch doctor knew this, since news traveled fast and he had an excellent information network, and he had been worried about it for some time. A new doctor might not be so easy to get on with. There might be a confrontation and he might suffer a loss of face with the result that his entire power over the people would be irrevocably weakened. Ever since he had heard the news of Evan's pending departure the witch doctor had been praying for a revelation which would encourage Evan to reverse his plans.

The revelation had taken some time coming, but it had been presented to him the previous evening during a perfect trance and afterward he had been highly pleased.

"I have news for you, M. le docteur," he announced sonorously. "News which may make you decide to stay with us."

"Really?" said Evan, scrupulously polite. "What news is that, sir?"

"Do not return to your homeland. The devil waits for you there. If you return, the devil will harm you and bring you close to death. Perhaps you will even die."

After a moment Evan said gravely: "And if I do return—how may I recognize the devil when I meet him?"

"He will be white."

Evan had suspected this; he knew the black races visualized the devil as white, just as the white races believed him to be black.

"He will be white," repeated the witch doctor, "but he will manifest himself from time to time as an animal. He will be at his most dangerous when he manifests himself as a black horse."

Evan suppressed a sigh and carefully avoided asking himself whether some of the world's more primitive peoples would ever emerge into the twentieth century.

"I understand," he said courteously to the witch doctor. "It was most gracious of you to advise me on this matter, sir, and you can be sure I'll give your advice every consideration."

The witch doctor was pleased. "It is always a pleasure to

19

help a valued friend," he said, preparing to leave. "Au revoir, M. le docteur. I look forward to your visits to this village for many years to come."

IV

When Evan returned to his small house on the outskirts of the capital two days later after visiting several other villages in the interior, he found two letters waiting for him, one from his father, Walter Colwyn, the other from Evan's sister, Gwyneth. After telling his servant to unpack his luggage and his cook to go ahead with preparing dinner, Evan returned to the living room with a glass of beer, switched the air-conditioner to high, and settled down to absorb his weekly glimpse of home.

He opened his father's letter first. The main item of news was that Gwyneth had been ill again with a mystery ailment—news which made Evan snort in disgust and reach for his glass of beer. He knew perfectly well that his sister was a hypochondriac who made use of a genuine history of minor heart trouble to become ill if and when she thought it was necessary. He had never had much patience with Gwyneth, but she was the apple of their father's eye and Walter took every fluctuation in her health very seriously.

". . . so when Gwyneth became ill again," Walter had written to Evan in his delicate handwriting, "we asked this herbalist to try to help her. Mr. Poole is the most charming young man, a little older than you perhaps, who has been staying in Swansea while looking around for a house which he can use as the headquarters of his organization, and we happened to meet him by chance one weekend . . ."

Herbalist! Evan snorted again, finished his beer and slammed the glass irritably down on the table. Why was it that old men and impulsive young women were always so eager to put their faith in quacks?

". . . and he absolutely cured Gwyneth," Walter had written. "Wasn't that wonderful?"

Psychological mumbo-jumbo, thought Evan. Psychosomatic illness. Given the right circumstances, even the witch doctor could have cured her.

"... so I invited him to stay at Colwyn Court while he tries to find his headquarters for the Society for the Propagation of Nature Foods ..."

"Good God!" cried Evan and leaped to his feet to get another beer. When he returned to the living room he pushed his father's letter aside and turned to the envelope addressed to him in Gwyneth's willowy handwriting.

Gwyneth seldom wrote to him; as he unfolded her letter he wondered if he could guess why she had become excited enough to pick up a pen.

"Dearest Evan," he read, "What do you think! At last a little excitement has come to Colwyn! I know Daddy has written to tell you about Mr. Poole and how ill I was, but don't worry because I'm *miraculously better!* Mr. Poole is an expert on herbs, and I know you'll say it's just a lot of old wives' tales and worthless folklore, but all I can say is that I haven't felt so well for years. Mr. Poole makes up the medicine himself and I take one tablespoonful three times a day. I've asked him several times what's in the recipe, but he won't tell me. However, he's promised to teach me a little about herbs when he has some spare time. As you can gather, he's rather a super sort of person, and—"

Evan flung down the letter, hurled himself out of his chair, and grabbed his writing paper from his desk. As his second beer stood untasted on the table behind him he filled two pages with respectful admiration for the unknown Mr. Poole's healing powers tempered with tactful warnings that it might be best to leave Mr. Poole well alone.

At least his months in Africa had taught him self-restraint. Evan, surveying the skillfully diplomatic tone of his letter, wondered what they would have thought at Colwyn Court if he had simply written: "This man is probably a fraud, no matter how charming he is. Some herbalists may do good but the genuine ones recognize their limitations and would not expect to work miraculous cures. Don't trust him too much.

21

don't rely on him too heavily, and whatever you do, don't give him any money for the Society for the Propagation of Nature Foods . . ."

V

Evan's letter reached the village in South Wales four days later and was carried from the post office at Colwyn to its final destination at Colwyn Court by the local postman on an elderly red bicycle. The mail for Colwyn Court that day was substantial; as well as Evan's letter and several bills from nearby tradesmen there was an envelope with a Cambridge postmark, and then, quite apart from the letters to Walter Colwyn, there were the letters addressed to Mr. Tristan Poole, Managing Director of the Society for the Propagation of Nature Foods.

Colwyn village was intrigued by Mr. Poole and his society. One rumor, inspired by the word "nature" in the society's title, hinted darkly that Colwyn Court was about to be turned into a nudist camp. A counter-rumor protested that although Walter Colwyn was now well over sixty he was by no means senile enough to abandon all sense of decency, especially while his young unmarried daughter lived at home, and insisted that the society was nothing more than a collection of amateur botanists whom Walter, himself a keen botanist, naturally found congenial. Another rumor suggested that Mr. Poole and Walter's daughter, Gwyneth, had fallen in love with one another and that this explained why Walter should have invited Mr. Poole to stay for a few days at Colwyn Court. On the whole this was the rumor which found most favor among the female population of the village, and everyone was waiting with bated breath for the engagement to be announced.

Meanwhile the possibility of his daughter's and his guest's falling in love had never occurred to Walter. It was not simply that he was getting older and more absentminded and less

22

interested in the people around him than in the flowers and shrubs and trees on his estate; it was not even that he had so many worries—the nagging anxiety that Evan might choose not to return to England, for example, or the secret dread of a twilight future or the more imminent fear that he might have to mortgage his family home to pay his bills. Walter had not imagined a romance could exist between Gwyneth and his guest because there had been no signs of such an entanglement to spark his imagination. Mr. Poole had been friendly and pleasant to Gwyneth but nothing more, and Gwyneth herself, although enthusiastic about Poole's powers as a herbalist, had shown no sign of looking lovelorn. Walter had a vague idea that young women in love wandered around sighing, reading poetry, and evincing a general lack of interest in food and all practical matters. But since her recovery from her mysterious illness Gwyneth had been eating voraciously, answering her letters from pen friends in ten different countries, and devoting herself as usual to her enormous record collection, her files of trivia on pop music, and her library of pop art posters. Gwyneth, in short, was exactly as she had always been. If she were in love with Poole she was savoring the fact in secret, and why would she want to do that? It did not occur to Walter that for Gwyneth the world of imagination had long been more rewarding than the world of reality; in reality, Mr. Poole might show a mere platonic interest in her welfare, but in dreams he could speak to her in the voice from the record player and promise her unbelievable delights, and with the door locked and the curtains drawn she could live exactly as she wished in the brilliantly colored world of her own creation.

But Walter knew nothing of this. To Walter, Gwyneth was still his little motherless daughter, nineteen now but still a child with her naively enchanting interest in all those alien, absurd modern art forms. The very idea of her falling in love would have seemed incongruous to him, so strong was this image in his mind that Gwyneth was too young to play a leading role in the romance which the villagers of Colwyn busied themselves in inventing over interminable cups of tea.

Walter had never understood either of his children. He had loved them and marveled at their existence, but he had always thought of them as stereotypes acting out their lives in cliché-ridden situations. He still thought of Evan as the "son and heir," all set to become a "brilliant surgeon" one day, and of Gwyneth as the "delicate daughter" who would one day make a "perfect match" to a young man from one of the local county families. This two-dimensional vision of his had even extended to his dead wife; he had married late in life when he had inherited the estate with a view to "settling down" after years of travel on botanical expeditions, and had chosen a "society girl" ten years his junior to be his wife because she was bright and pretty and filled his concept of the sort of wife he ought to have. She had left him a year after Gwyneth had been born and had died two years later in the south of France. The odd part was that he had always been convinced she would be the "dutiful wife" and return to him in the end, and for a long while he could not reconcile himself to the fact that she was dead. He had gone on his way, becoming a little more absentminded each day, a little more devoted to botany, a little more absorbed in the book he was writing on the wild flowers of the Gower Peninsula until one day he was able to look back on his marriage, realize that it had been unhappy, and make a mental resolution to remain a widower till the end of his days.

"You never like to look at the truth, do you, Father?" Evan had said once. "You're always so much happier playing the ostrich and burying your head in the sand."

It had been a terrible shock when Evan had gone abroad. It had been an even bigger shock when Evan had flung out defiant hints of America and implied that as far as he was concerned the sun didn't rise and set entirely either on a small village along the south coast of Wales or on an estate which had been in Colwyn hands for six hundred years. Every time Walter received a letter from Evan he was frightened to open it for fear it would contain news that Evan had decided not to come home.

The letter which arrived that morning in April was no exception. Walter picked it up and looked at it and turned it over and felt so nervous he could not begin to eat his breakfast. But as usual his fright was all for nothing. Of course the tenor of the letter was a little severe—all those warnings about Mr. Poole were quite unnecessary—but the boy meant well and that was the important thing. There was even a sentence at the end of the letter saying Evan expected to be home in June and would soon be booking his flight. Walter put down the letter with a sigh of relief and attacked his eggs and bacon so heartily that it was some minutes before he remembered he had another letter to read that morning.

It was the letter with the Cambridge postmark, a note from Walter's cousin Benedict Shaw who was a professor in classics at the University.

"My dear Walter," said Benedict's handwriting with its cross-scratchy strokes of the pen. "How are you after all this time? No doubt you will be surprised to hear from me out of the blue like this but I was hoping you might be in a position to give me some advice. I'm planning to write a thesis this summer after the commencement of the Long Vacation, and very much fancy the idea of retiring somewhere far from the madding crowd for two or three months. Do you know of any places for rent around Colwyn? Jane and I wouldn't want more than a small cottage, and I thought you might know of someone who rents such a place to summer tourists. Any ideas? If you know of anywhere quiet, comfortable, and secluded I'd be most anxious to hear of it. I hope Gwyneth is well. When does Evan return from Africa? Jane sends her love and says she hopes to see you soon—a hope which I, of course, share. Yours, Benedict."

Walter finished his eggs and bacon slowly and read the letter again. He could not make up his mind if Benedict were angling for an invitation to stay. The letter gave no hint that Benedict expected an invitation but surely in the circumstances he would think an invitation would be forthcoming. The words "if you know of anywhere quiet, comfortable, and secluded" at once suggested Colwyn Court to Walter, and he began to feel guilty. It was not that he disliked his cousin; although they seldom met nowadays and had little in common, they had always been on good terms. But if Mr. Poole decided to relieve Walter of his current financial worries by hiring both wings of Colwyn Court for the society there would hardly be much room left for Benedict and his wife.

"Dear, oh dear," said Walter aloud and gazed with unseeing eyes at his half-finished toast and marmalade. "Dear me, how very awkward."

The door of the dining room clicked softly. Smooth shoes sank noiselessly into the carpet and a faint draft from the hall made the curtains shiver by the open window.

"Awkward?" said Walter's guest in his warm, flexible voice. "Tell me about it, Mr. Colwyn! Perhaps I'll be able to help you."

VI

He was a tall man with a face which people found hard to remember because it was capable of so many different expressions. His eyes were deep-set above high, broad cheekbones and a wide, mobile mouth, and his hair, though thick, was short and neat and parted in a conventional style. He wore a conventional dark suit, a conventional white shirt, and a conventional conservative tie, but the impression of the conventional English businessman, so meticulously created, was blurred by his hands and his voice. He had beautiful hands, the fingers long and tapered, and, contrary to the habits of many conventional Englishmen, he wore a ring on the third finger of his right hand, an intricate un-English ring inscribed with odd patterns and cast in some dull, silverish metal of uncertain origin. When he spoke his voice was so easy on the ears that at first it was hard to decide why it too should fall short of conventional English standards, but after

26

a time, when the ear became attuned, a listener could detect the inflections of a foreigner in the occasional ambiguous vowel sound or choice of words. Mr. Poole seldom used any of the more obvious Americanisms, but with an occasional short "a" in the wrong place and a rare un-English use of a preposition it became clear he had in the past spent some time on the other side of the Atlantic. It was hard to say how old he was; Walter thought of him as the same age as Evan, who was thirty, but to Gwyneth he was closer to forty, cosmopolitan, experienced, and immeasurably sophisticated.

"Perhaps I can help you," said Tristan Poole to his host. His glance noted the pile of unopened bills beside the letters from Evan and Benedict, and he wondered how severe the financial troubles were. It was probable that they were a mere temporary inconvenience. The house was well kept and filled with valuable possessions; the estate was large; if Walter Colwyn were at present hard pressed for ready cash he would still be a long way from bankruptcy. "What's the trouble? Nothing too serious, I hope."

"Oh no, no, no," said Walter, turning to his guest in relief. Really, it was amazing how soothing it was to talk to Poole . . . "Help yourself to eggs and bacon, my dear fellow . . . No, the trouble is simply that—" And in his rambling way he explained the contents of Benedict's letter and all the complications inherent in Benedict's request.

Poole poured himself some tea and made a mental resolution that as soon as he was living at Colwyn Court on a more permanent basis he would insist that coffee—real coffee—was served at breakfast as well as the inevitable pot of tea.

". . . so anyway I thought—can I pass you something, my dear fellow? Salt?"

"No, thank you," said Poole.

". . . yes, well, I don't know *what* I thought, except it's all most awkward. You see, I would indeed like you and your society to come here, but . . . well, Benedict . . . very tricky . . . I ought to issue an invitation—"

"But surely," said Poole, "there's a very simple solution,

Mr. Colwyn? Don't you have that cottage down by the beach which you've been renting to summer visitors for the last two years? Why don't you simply rent the cottage to your cousin this summer—or offer it to him rent-free? That should satisfy Professor Shaw since he'll be living in your grounds even if not in your house, and I think he'll find it quiet enough to suit his tastes. Besides, couldn't you be mistaken in thinking his letter is a hint for an invitation to Colwyn Court? It would seem to me he had the cottage in mind, not the house."

"Oh, Benedict doesn't know I've been renting the cottage these last two summers," said Walter vaguely. "My old chauffeur used to live there, you know—I let him have it for a nominal rent when he got too old to drive—and then when he died—"

Poole was thinking of the cottage. It would be better for it to be rented to a professor absorbed in his work than to a series of families on holiday with a stream of inquisitive children. "Have you rented the cottage yet?" he inquired when Walter paused to recollect his original train of thought. "Is it still available?"

"No, I rented it in January to this very nice family—"

"Ah, but surely your cousin must come first!"

"Yes, but I don't quite see how I can—"

"Surely," said Poole, "your cousin must come first."

"But what shall I say to—"

"Leave it all to me. I'll handle the matter for you. If you'll give me the address of these people I'll write to them and explain the circumstances."

"Well, I . . . hardly like to trouble you—"

"It's no trouble at all," said Poole with his wide, charming smile. "I'd be delighted to be of assistance." He took a sip from his cup, forgetting that it contained tea, and grimaced as the strong flavor dragged at his sense of taste. "Tell me about your cousin. He's a contemporary of yours, I take it."

"Benedict? Well, no, actually he's only about forty-six. My mother had a very much younger sister who married . . ."

Poole listened patiently and buttered a slice of toast. The toast was cold. Why did the British always have cold toast? When he was at Colwyn Court on a more permanent basis . . .

". . . married a girl of twenty-seven," said Walter. "We were all absolutely dumbfounded, of course. Let's see, how old is Jane now? I forget how long they've been married. About five or six years, I think . . . no children, unfortunately . . . she's rather a nice girl, quite pretty, very pleasant—can't think what she saw in dear old Benedict who was one of those crusty sort of bachelors . . ."

One professor absorbed in his work, thought Poole, one woman probably absorbed in her husband, neither a threat.

"How very nice," he said to Walter in his warmest, most interested voice. "They both sound delightful. I'll be looking forward very much to meeting them . . ."

VII

"Of course," said Benedict Shaw crossly to his wife at breakfast two days later, "Walter must be either mad or on the verge of destitution or both. Imagine letting some crack-pot society have the free run of one's own home! And imagine charging me rent for that nasty little cottage where his chauffeur used to live! How dare he charge me rent! Me! His own cousin! It would be an insult if it weren't so patently absurd. He must be on the verge of bankruptcy, that's all I can say. Maybe when Evan comes home in June I ought to have a word with him about it."

Jane Shaw said vaguely: "Is Evan definitely coming home then?" She was trying to work out how many calories there were in one slice of toast liberally covered with butter and marmalade.

"According to Walter's letter, yes, he is." Benedict was polishing his glasses furiously. "God knows what Evan will make of the situation! Society for the Propagation of Nature Foods—my God! Ridiculous!"

29

Two hundred and twenty calories, thought Jane, I really mustn't. She tried to think of something else. "I expect Walter does find Colwyn Court very expensive to run," she said reasonably. "I know you always think of Walter as being rich, Benedict, but what with taxation and the rising cost of living nowadays—"

"My dear," said Benedict, "you don't have to remind *me* about the monstrous iniquities of taxation and the rising cost of living."

"I suppose not," said Jane and almost reached for the forbidden slice of toast. How hard it was to be strong-minded sometimes. "I know you know much more about that sort of thing than I do, darling."

Benedict smiled. He had a sudden smile which smoothed away the irrascible lines about his face and made his eyes twinkle behind his thick glasses. When Jane leaned forward and kissed him impulsively he took her hand in his and squeezed it before rising to his feet. "One of the best things about you, my dear," he said, "is that you always say all the right things."

"But that sounds as if I never mean what I say, and I do!"

"I know you do. Far be it from me to accuse you of sycophancy."

"What a funny word," said Jane, not sure what it meant. "Benedict, are you going to accept Walter's offer of the cottage? I know it *is* rather strange that he's charging you rent, but—"

"Most unlike him," said Benedict, cross again. "Not at all the done thing in the circumstances. And as for this crackpot society at Colwyn Court—"

"—but the cottage is in a lovely position, isn't it, and of course it would be so quiet and peaceful for your writing—"

"Quiet and peaceful? Surrounded by a bunch of nincompoops eating nature foods?"

"I don't suppose you'd see anything of them at all. I'm sure they wouldn't bother you at the cottage."

"You want me to go there," said Benedict, very fierce, "don't you."

"Not unless you want to, darling, but I think it might turn out quite well if you did."

"And to think I was half-hoping for an invitation to Colwyn Court itself!"

"You wouldn't have liked that really," said Jane. "Walter would have got on your nerves and Gwyneth's never-ending pop music wouldn't have given you a moment's peace."

"But to pay Walter rent for this miserable hovel—"

"You'd have had to pay rent anyway if we'd taken a cottage elsewhere," said Jane practically, "and the 'hovel' is actually rather nice. I went inside it once with Gwyneth when she was taking the old chauffeur a present for Christmas. And think how soothing the sea is, Benedict! You know how well you work by the sea."

"Hm," said Benedict. "I see I have no choice in the matter." He roamed moodily over to the window and gazed at the tiny garden which Jane tended so carefully behind the house. "Maybe I should go down to Colwyn, if only to find out how senile Walter is. Maybe this wretched society's swindling him." He turned, flung himself down in his chair at the table again and toyed with his empty cup. "Is there any more coffee?"

Jane poured him another cup. "You don't really think Walter's in financial difficulty, do you?"

"Wouldn't surprise me. Walter always was a complete fool about money. And of course a big house like Colwyn Court is an absolute white elephant these days. He ought to sell it or turn it into flats or something."

"But Benedict, he couldn't! His ancestral home!"

"Such sentimentality," said Benedict, "is out of place in the latter half of the twentieth century."

A thought struck Jane. "Maybe Walter's planning to sell Colwyn Court to this society!"

"Good God!" cried Benedict. "He couldn't do that! He wouldn't be such a fool!"

"But if he's desperate for money—"

"Money," said Benedict. "I hate all this talk about money. Money, money, money. Money's so depressing."

31

"Yes, dear. But useful."

"Take that brother-in-law of yours, for instance. Whenever he's mentioned in the papers it's always: 'Matthew Morrison, the millionaire industrialist'—why don't they simply say: 'Matthew Morrison, the industrialist?' Why do they have to drag in the 'millionaire' label all the time? Does the word 'millionaire' make Morrison a different breed of homo sapiens?"

"Well, it does make a little difference," said Jane. "I mean, if you're a millionaire you don't live in quite the same way as the local butcher."

"Naturally!" said Benedict. "We all know your sister would hardly have married Morrison if he'd been a mere butcher!"

"Darling, isn't that a little bit unfair to Lisa?"

Benedict had the grace to look sheepish as well as defiant. "Can you see Lisa marrying a butcher?"

Jane couldn't but would not allow herself to say so. For one long moment she thought of her sister. Lisa. Twenty-nine years old. Poised, glamorous, effortlessly smart. Lisa who had everything from a selection of mink coats to two beautiful children . . .

Jane reached for the last slice of toast and had buttered it before she realized what she was doing. "Lisa's very romantic," she heard herself say levelly. "She probably would marry a butcher if she fell in love with him."

"Fiddlesticks," said Benedict. Instinct told him to veer away from the subject. "What's Morrison's daughter doing nowadays? Is she still working in London?"

"Yes, she's still living in Hampstead and doesn't go home too often. Lisa said she hadn't seen Nicola for ages."

"Hm," said Benedict, and wondered if he could guess why Nicola no longer found her father's house appealing.

"It was such a pity Nicola's romance with Evan didn't work out," Jane said, taking a bite of toast. Two hundred and twenty calories. Maybe she could skip lunch. "It would have been so awfully suitable if they'd got married."

"Suitable strikes me as being a very apt word," said

32

Benedict dryly. "The way things are probably going with Walter, Evan would need to marry an heiress."

"Oh darling, I'm sure Evan wouldn't marry anyone just for their money!"

"Money," said Benedict. "That dreadful word again."

"But Benedict—" Jane stopped. Better not to remind him that he had introduced the subject. On an impulse she pulled one of the morning papers toward her and began to thumb through it. "Heavens, I almost forgot to read my horoscope! Maybe there'll be some hint about whether we should take Walter's cottage or not."

"I've already made up my mind to take it," said Benedict. "I'm not the slightest bit interested in what some syndicated fraud invents daily for a gullible public." He stood up, stooped to give her a kiss, and made for the door. "I must be off. Don't expect me for lunch, will you, my dear, because I'm lunching in town today."

"All right, darling . . . have a good day." She saw him to the front door as usual and waved him good-bye as he walked into the street to their white Austin. They had a small house in a quiet tree-lined road barely a mile from the heart of the city, and Benedict had only a short drive to his college. When he had gone, Jane wandered back into the dining room and resumed her search for her horoscope before stacking the dirty dishes.

"Your Fate Today," ran the heading at the top of the column, and then under Jane's zodiac sign were the words: "Think carefully before making any decision today. Now is the time to dream of travel, but be wary of the unexpected invitation."

VIII

"What's his horoscope today?" said Jane's small niece Lucy a day later at Matthew Morrison's home in Surrey. "What does it say?"

" 'Your luck is in,' " read her brother Timothy laborious-

33

ly. " 'Take advantage of an unexpected opportunity. Be bold.' " He looked up in triumph. "That means he'll get a chance to escape from China!"

"Tibet," said Lucy. "Daddy was in Tibet. He crossed the Himalayas with a solitary guide and went down one of those rivers on a raft like that film we saw, and finally he got into a helicopter—"

"Well, well, well," said Lisa Morrison, sweeping into the drawing room where the twins were closeted with the daily horoscopes. "Who's this you're talking about, darlings? The hero of one of those awful comic strips?"

The twins looked guilty and for once seemed at a loss to know what to say. She saw them glance furtively at each other before giving her careful smiles.

"We were just imagining, Mummy," said Lucy. "Just picturing things."

"Just picturing how Daddy would get home if he hadn't been drowned in the boat after all," said Timothy impulsively. "If he'd swum to safety, you see, he would have been on the mainland of China and nobody gets out of China easily so he might have been imprisoned there for some years before he escaped."

"But darling," said Lisa, not knowing what to say but aware that something should be said. "Daddy's dead. He's been dead for a long while now. Do you think I could have married Uncle Matt if I'd thought Daddy was still alive?"

They watched her. Both their faces looked blank. There was a silence.

"Well, of course," said Timothy, "it was only a story. We were only imagining."

"Only imagining," said Lucy.

Lisa felt a wave of relief. "That's all right, then, isn't it?" she said, drawing on her gloves as she spoke. "Now darlings, I'm just off to London with Uncle Matt, so have a lovely day and I'll see you this evening. Where's Costanza?"

Costanza was the Spanish *au pair* girl who was supposed to supervise the twins and leave Lisa free to enjoy an uninterrupted social life. The twins prided themselves on the fact that it was they who supervised Costanza. After three months they had her tightly in control.

"Upstairs," said Lucy.

"All right. Now be good, darlings, won't you?" She kissed both of them, smiled, and swept back toward the door. "I mustn't keep Uncle Matt waiting . . . 'Bye, darlings. Have a lovely time."

They chorused good-bye politely and wandered over to the window to watch her depart. Their stepfather was already striding up and down beside his new Rolls Royce.

"She's kept him waiting," said Timothy.

"As usual," said Lucy. "He looks cross."

"He was awfully cross last night."

"Was he? When?"

"About twelve o'clock. I woke up and heard them. They were being pretty noisy, I thought, considering how late it was."

"What did they say?"

"I couldn't hear properly."

"Didn't you go and listen?"

"Well, I considered it," said Timothy, "but I couldn't be bothered. It didn't sound very interesting anyway."

"Was it actually a row?"

"Oh, definitely."

"Who was crosser, Uncle Matt or Mummy?"

"Uncle Matt. It was all about taxes and money. He wants to live in the Channel Islands or something because he'll save money. Mummy said: 'The Channel Islands?' she said, 'Darling, you have to be crazy,' she said. 'Why would I want to live in a dump like that?' Then Uncle Matt got really angry and said he wasn't going to retire to the Bahamas just to please her. So Mummy said—"

"Timmy, you did listen!"

"Well, just for a minute or two. I was starving hungry and on my way downstairs to the kitchen . . . So Mummy said: 'At least in the Bahamas I might have a bit of fun.' And

35

Uncle Matt said: 'That's all you think about, isn't it?' he said. 'Well, I'll have my fun in the Channel Islands,' he said—he sounded very cross. 'Take it or leave it,' he said."

"What happened then?"

"I had to run because Mummy came out of the room and I only just managed to get away in time."

"Where did she go?"

"Oh, only to the spare room. Nowhere special."

"Married people aren't supposed to spread themselves over two different bedrooms," said Lucy. "I heard Cook say to Mrs. Pierce that that's how you can tell if a marriage is a success or not."

"I expect Mrs. Pierce was grumbling because she had to make two beds instead of one . . . Look, here comes Mummy. Uncle Matt still looks cross."

They watched from the window in silence. Then:

"Timmy, do you suppose—"

"Yes?"

"If Mummy and Uncle Matt got divorced . . . I mean, just supposing—"

"And Daddy came back from China—"

"Tibet."

"—it would be sort of nice . . . although I like Uncle Matt—"

"Yes, he's okay."

"Maybe we could still see him sometimes after the divorce."

"Maybe we could." They smiled at one another. "I'm sure," said Timothy firmly, "that it'll all work out pretty well in the end."

"Yes, but how much longer do we have to wait for Daddy to come home?" said Lucy disconsolately. "Sometimes I feel as if we'll have to wait forever and ever."

Timothy did not answer. They were still standing in silence by the window when the Rolls Royce moved away from the house and purred down the winding drive on its eighteen-mile journey to London.

IX

After a while Matthew Morrison said: "I'm sorry about last night."

It cost him a big effort to say that. Matt was proud enough to hate having to apologize and to hate it even more when he felt that such an initial apology should not have come from him at all.

"Oh?" said Lisa, very cool. She was looking at her best that morning, he noted; the April weather was uncertain but she wore a smart spring dress with a matching coat as if there could be no doubt that winter was over and summer only just around the corner. Her skirt was short; from his position beside her he had a perfect view of her long, elegant legs.

"You're an awful driver, Matt," said Lisa. "You never keep your eyes on the road. I wish you'd hire a chauffeur."

But Matt didn't believe in chauffeurs. He was fifty-five years old and was by now used to the conveniences which money could buy, but he hated the thought of being a passenger in his own car. He also had a secret dread of what he called "giving himself airs and graces" and "trying to be what he wasn't." The result was an inverted snobbism, a desire to maintain the simple habits he had acquired long ago before he had worked his way up from office boy to chairman of the board of an enormous industrial empire. Now he owned a big house in which he always felt faintly uncomfortable, employed a first-class cook who despised the plain English cooking he loved, and possessed a beautiful and well-bred wife whose tastes he could not bring himself to share. Privately he deprecated the house ("that rambling old barn," was how he described it to himself in irritable moments), the cook's prowess ("damned French nonsense"), and even his wife, who he knew was spoiled and willful, but at the same time he was well aware how reluctant he would have been to give any of them up. He might want to believe he was still at heart just a simple fellow whom success had not changed, but he was honest enough to know that he had indeed changed and that, distasteful as it was to have to admit it to himself, he had a sneaking fondness for the glamorous assets his wealth and position had brought him. But this fondness he was careful to keep to himself. He knew what was said about self-made men who openly enjoyed their wealth, and he had a horror of the sneering label "nouveau riche."

"I don't believe in chauffeurs," he said abruptly to his wife. "They're nothing but ostentation nowadays, and you know I don't believe in being ostentatious."

"Oh no," said Lisa, "you just believe in being the 'Simple Man' and hiding yourself away in some deadly corner of the Channel Islands after an early retirement."

"Now Lisa—"

"What's the point of saving money on taxes if there's nothing to spend it on?"

"We needn't be in the Channel Islands all the year round."

"I can't see what you've got against the Bahamas. You could swim and fish and lead your Simple Life just as well there, and the climate's such heaven—"

"It's too far from England."

"Oh Matt, how insular! Anyway nothing's far from anywhere nowadays!"

"Well, if you think I'm about to become a member of the jet set—"

"What's wrong with the jet set if you can afford it? Too 'ostentatious,' I suppose! What a hypocrite you are, Matt!"

"You don't understand," said Matt, and set his mouth in a stubborn line.

"Well, after you retire in June we might at least have a decent holiday before you decide where to settle down! Why don't we go to Spain again?"

"Spain in June's too bloody hot and I can't stand all that silly food they eat. I'd rather stay by the sea somewhere in England."

"My God," said Lisa, "you'll be telling me next you want to join Jane and Benedict at Colwyn."

Matt looked surprised. "Are they down there?"

"Not yet, but Benedict's renting a cottage on the estate for the Long Vacation. Didn't I tell you about the conversation I had with Jane yesterday?"

"You were too busy telling me how you wanted to live in the Bahamas. Maybe we could visit them at the cottage for a couple of weeks in June."

"You're joking, of course."

"How big is the cottage?"

"Oh, it's a horrible little place, very pokey. Matt, you can't be serious!"

"I like that part of the Welsh coast," said Matt. "Walter Colwyn's lucky having an estate in the Gower Peninsula."

"No wonder you were so disappointed when Evan Colwyn jilted Nicola and went off to Africa!"

"He didn't jilt her," said Matt, thinking of his daughter with a painful nostalgia. "There was no engagement."

"Nicola played it too cool," said Lisa. "Of course she has absolutely no idea how to handle men."

"At least she's a decent girl who wouldn't play fast and loose with a man to get him to marry her!"

"How do you know?" said Lisa. "You hardly ever see her."

"Whose fault is that?" yelled Matt, forgetting to watch the road ahead. The car swerved as he swung around on her in a rage and Lisa gave a sharp scream.

"For God's sake, be careful! Matt, if you can't drive properly, I'd rather get out and continue by taxi—my nerves just won't stand it."

Matt said nothing. He gripped the wheel a shade more tightly and stared at the road ahead and after that there was a silence between them until they reached the salon in Knightsbridge where Lisa had a hair appointment.

"Have a good day," was all he said as she got out of the car. "See you this evening."

"Thanks." She was gone. As he watched her walk into the salon he thought of his first wife, Nicola's mother, who had died ten years before, and in a flash of despair he asked himself how after such a successful first marriage he had ever managed to make such a bad mistake with his second.

X

At Colwyn Court, Gwyneth was taking her first exercise since the onset of her mysterious illness by walking with Tristan Poole along the path which wound up to the cliffs where the ruins of Colwyn Castle stood facing the sea. When they reached the castle walls Gwyneth sank down to rest on the grassy turf and listened with interest to the rhythm of her heartbeat.

"I hope the walk wasn't too much for me," she said after a moment.

Poole did not answer. He was standing a few feet from the edge of the cliffs, and his black jacket was flapping in the breeze.

"Tristan."

He turned with a smile. "I'm sorry, what did you say?"

"You don't suppose the walk up here was too much of a strain, do you? My heart seems to be beating awfully fast."

"You'll be all right. Just rest there for a while."

Gwyneth leaned back on the grass, put her hands behind her head and replayed the scene in her imagination. After she had said how fast her heart was beating Tristan would have knelt beside her and felt her heartbeat with his long fingers and then . . .

"You've got a very vivid imagination, Gwyneth," said Tristan Poole.

She sat bolt upright. Her cheeks were burning. For a moment she could not speak.

But he wasn't laughing at her. He was still standing watching the sea, still detached and remote from her.

"Why did you say that?" she demanded unsteadily.

"Why not?" he said, turning to face her. "Isn't it true?"

She was nonplussed. In her confusion she searched around

40

for some way of changing the subject but her ingenuity deserted her.

"Imagination," said Poole, "is seldom so satisfying as reality. Have you ever considered that, Gwyneth?"

Gwyneth's thoughts were whirling in a million jumbled pieces. She opened her mouth to speak but no words came.

"Why are you afraid of reality, Gwyneth?"

"I'm not," said Gwyneth loudly, but she was trembling. She had to fight against an impulse to rush back to the house and imprison herself in the comforting security of her room.

"But you prefer the world of the imagination." Poole sighed. He supposed he had known from the beginning that the girl was too neurotic to be of interest to him. It was such a pity, such a waste. But it was no use working with damaged material. The anxieties in Gwyneth would all work against him with the result that she would be unreceptive to what he had to offer. She could accept him only in the guise of doctor; in any other role her fears would chase her back into the world of her imagination and away from any world he might attempt to present to her.

Gwyneth, gazing around frantically and seeing the chauffeur's cottage far away above the beach, said in a rush: "Daddy's cousin Benedict is definitely going to come here in June—did Daddy tell you?—he's terribly academic and untrendy, not a bit switched on, you know, not a clue Where It's At or anything, he's at least thirty years behind the times, but *she's* rather sweet, his wife, Jane, I mean, although she's old-fashioned too, but she's quite pretty, not as pretty as Lisa though, Lisa's her sister and she's really pretty, gosh, I wish I was Lisa, she's so glamorous and she's even married to a millionaire—have you heard of Matthew Morrison the industrialist?"

Poole was watching the sea crashing on the beach far below. "I believe I have." He glanced sharply back at Gwyneth. "So Mrs. Benedict Shaw has a millionaire for a brother-in-law."

"Yes, because Jane's sister—"

"What did you say her name was?"

"Lisa."

"Lisa," said Poole. "Lisa Morrison. What a charming name."

"Oh, she's as charming as her name," said Gwyneth glibly, relieved to have diverted attention from herself. "She's an awfully attractive person."

"She is?" said Tristan Poole, turning again to watch the sea, and added more to himself than to Gwyneth: "How very interesting . . ."

2

It was June. In Cambridge the river wound limpidly along the "backs" past the colleges, and the lawns of the quadrangles were a weedless green. The students were gone and the city had already begun to shrink in their absence, becoming quieter, more deserted, more overshadowed by the silence of ancient buildings and an even more ancient past. In the little house on the outskirts of the town Jane was packing haphazardly and trying not to panic.

"I'm sure I shan't remember everything," she said to Benedict. "Did I cancel the milk and newspapers? I honestly can't remember what I've done and what I haven't done. If only we were at Colwyn and all this awful packing was over!"

"Since the papers didn't arrive this morning," said Benedict, "and since we seem to have run out of milk, I presume you canceled both orders. What have you done about the cat?"

"Oh, Marble's coming too! I couldn't possibly leave him!"

"My dear Jane, he'll leave *you* if you cart him off to Wales! You know what cats are like! They find their way back to their home by instinct if you try to remove them to a new environment."

"Marble's not like other cats," said Jane.

"Well, if you think I'm going to drive all the way to Wales with that wretched animal caterwauling every mile of the way on the back seat—"

"He'll be in his basket on my lap," said Jane firmly. "He'll be as good as gold."

"I'll believe that when I see it," said Benedict, but he made no effort to argue the point further. He had himself given the cat to Jane a year ago after she had seen the white kitten in the window of the local pet shop, and the cat had been dotingly cared for ever since. It was now fourteen months old, a large elegant creature with thick fluffy white fur, malevolent pink eyes, and pale, destructive claws. Benedict, who though not a cat lover had admired the animal at first, now regarded its presence in the house with mixed feelings. He felt there was an element of sadness about Jane's affection for it; it seemed such a waste to him that Jane, who had such an abundant supply of maternal affection, should have to expend it all on a bad-tempered albino feline.

"Come along, Marble," said Jane, picking the cat up and placing him in his basket. "We're going on a lovely holiday."

Marble looked at her in disgust. Once in the car he started to protest and the air vibrated with angry noises.

"I told you so," said Benedict.

"He'll settle down," said Jane defensively.

"Hm . . . Have we got everything?"

"I think so . . . oh my goodness, I didn't throw out the bread! Just a minute—"

"I'll do it," said Benedict. "You'd better stay with the animal. I'd rather not be responsible for him."

They eventually managed to leave, Benedict driving in his usual erratic fashion out of the city and setting a westward course across the middle of England toward South Wales. The cat settled down, Jane heaved a sigh of relief, and Benedict began to hum a phrase from Beethoven's "Pastoral Symphony."

"I never thought we'd finally get away," said Jane to him. "Why am I always so disorganized? How marvelous it must

44

be to be one of those dynamic, practical, efficient women who never get in a muddle."

"I detest dynamic, practical, efficient women," said Benedict. "If you hadn't been exactly the way you are I wouldn't have dreamed of marrying you."

Jane sighed happily. For a second she could remember overhearing Lisa say to a friend at a party: "I can't think what Jane sees in him!" Lisa had never understood. Neither had their mother, who had died a year ago. Jane, her thoughts drifting further into the past, could hear her mother saying to her with polite exasperation: "Jane, dear, don't you think it's time you changed your hairstyle? . . . not quite up to date, is it, and your hair gets so untidy . . . dear, I don't think that dress really suits you. . . . Jane, you're really quite pretty—if you made a little more effort you could be so attractive . . . just a question of being smart . . . Lisa, for instance—"

"But I'm not Lisa," Jane had said. "I'm me."

She could remember the boys at parties long ago. "You're not Lisa's sister, are you? Are you really? Oh . . ." Then there were the teachers at school. "Jane tries hard, but . . ." Lisa hadn't done well at school either but that, everyone agreed, was because Lisa hadn't tried. And finally there arose the awful problem of being overweight. "It's such bad luck you're not like Lisa, dear—Lisa eats twice as much as you yet never seems to put on an ounce . . ."

Lisa. Always, always Lisa.

"You can't possibly be in love with me," she had blurted out to Benedict. "I'm fat and very stupid and I usually look a mess and I always get in a muddle, and compared to Lisa—"

"I despise women like Lisa," Benedict had said.

"But—"

"I like you exactly the way you are," Benedict had said. "If you ever try to change I shall be extremely cross."

He had repeated this several times during the six years since they had first met, but even now Jane hardly dared to believe he meant what he said. As the car droned steadily west toward Wales on that long day in June, she stroked

Marble's thick fur and found herself thinking that the cat's sleepy purrs echoed her own overwhelming feeling of contentment and peace.

It was evening by the time they reached the big industrial port of Swansea, and the sun had set by the time they had skirted all the man-made ugliness and emerged into the wild country of the Gower Peninsula. Colwyn village lay a mile from the sea on the peninsula's southern side; as they approached the village, the wooded part of the countryside faded behind them until they were surrounded by open country, fields enclosed by stone walls, remote farms with acres reaching up to the heathland on top of the cliffs or stretching toward the rocky shore. It might have been two hundred instead of merely twenty miles from Swansea.

"How anxious Evan must be to get home!" Jane said, gazing dreamily at the darkening sea beyond the fields. "It's not long now till his return, is it? How excited he must be."

They drove through the village and down the lane to the gates of Colwyn Court. The drive wound through borders of flowering shrubs until finally it twisted around to end before the front of the house. It was an old house, Elizabethan in origin, which had been remodeled in the eighteenth century by a Colwyn who had wanted to keep abreast of the latest trends in architecture. The facade was Georgian, white, grave and symmetrical, but behind it, invisible from the drive, stretched the two wings of the Elizabethan E and the formal precision of an Elizabethan garden.

"The place looks as quiet as a morgue," said Benedict. "Perhaps everyone's gone to bed. What time is it, my dear?"

"Nine o'clock."

"It must be more than that!"

"Well . . . yes, my watch has stopped. I must have forgotten to wind it—how silly of me! What shall we do?"

"I'd better just see if Walter's still up—or at least leave a message to say that we've arrived safely—and then we can drive on to the cottage."

"All right." Jane carefully put the lid on Marble's basket and followed Benedict out of the car. Her legs felt stiff after the long journey, and she had a sudden longing to relax in a hot bath.

There was a pause after Benedict had rung the doorbell. Above them the stars shone and a bat swooped blindly through the dusk.

"It looks as if everyone's gone to bed." He rang the doorbell again. "We should have made an earlier start from Cambridge," he added as he turned away, "but never mind—we can walk up from the cottage after breakfast tomorrow. I hope Walter had the presence of mind to leave the place unlocked for us."

A light went on in the hall. As Benedict swung around again and Jane hesitated by the car, the door opened to reveal a plump middle-aged woman with softly waving gray hair and a serene smile.

"Good evening," she said warmly. "Professor and Mrs. Shaw? Allow me to introduce myself: I'm Agnes Miller, secretary of the Colwyn branch of the Society for the Propagation of Nature Foods. Do come in!"

II

Marble peered through the chinks of his basket on the front seat of the car and pawed fretfully at the wickerwork. On hearing Benedict's voice some way off and Jane's murmur from closer at hand he was aware of being abandoned and yet not abandoned. Rage overcame him. He hated his wicker basket. He hated cars. It had been a long hard day.

Taking a deep breath he yowled, arched his back, and flayed out with all four paws.

The lid of his basket burst open. Marble blinked in the bright light from the porch and then sprang triumphantly through the open window of the car to the freedom of the gravel drive below.

"What a lovely cat!" exclaimed an unknown feminine voice, and an alien hand stooped to caress him delicately on the back of his neck.

47

"Careful, Miss Miller," said Benedict nervously. "He's not at all friendly to strangers."

Marble quivered. His spine was tingling so hard that his fur stood out in a huge white ruff around his neck. He felt bemused and overwhelmed and quite unlike himself.

"Here, Marble," said Jane suddenly, and picked him up. The alien caressing stopped. Marble blinked, remembered he was free, and bounded out of Jane's arms and up the steps into the house.

"Marble!" exclaimed Jane.

Marble took no notice. There was an elderly man coming down the stairs and saying: "Benedict, how nice to see you again! I do apologize for being so slow to greet you—I was in my study and . . ."

"Marble!" called Jane, distressed.

Marble felt deliciously wicked. It had been a long hard day and now that it was over he had every intention of celebrating. He found a passage leading off the hall and darted down it. Halfway along he paused, nostrils flaring, but there was no enticing smell, only his unerring instinct that he was heading in the right direction.

"Marble!" cried Jane desperately from a long way off. "You naughty cat! Come here at once."

Marble skipped smartly round a corner and found himself in another corridor. On his left a beam of light streamed into the passage from a door left ajar. Marble shot forward, stood up on his hind legs, and brought both front paws to bear against the door. To his gratification the door swung wide and the next moment he was padding into an enormous kitchen.

A strange smell from the stove assailed his nostrils. He paused. Somebody noticed him.

"What a beautiful cat!" another strange feminine voice said. "Look, Harriet, look at that cat!"

"Here, pussy!"

Marble backed away.

"Give him some milk."

"Where did he come from?"

Someone opened a refrigerator and took out a milk bottle. Someone else stooped to touch him but Marble arched his back and hissed. He wasn't at all sure where he was and he didn't like the strange smell from the stove. Instinctively he looked around for Jane but Jane seemed to have given up the chase. He was alone.

"Here, kitty!" said one of the strange women.

They were all women. Every one of them.

"Isn't he sweet?"

"Put the milk in a saucer for him."

Marble tried to find the door and bumped into a table leg. He began to panic. He was about to make an undignified bolt for the nearest corner where he could ward off anyone who approached him when a soft draft ruffled his fur and he saw a door open nearby, a door leading outside into the freedom of the night.

Marble shot across the room so fast that he did not even see the man's black trousers until he cannoned into them. The collision gave him the shock of his life; yelping, he sprang backward in fright and clawed at the air as he toppled over onto his back.

"I see we have an unexpected guest," said a dark, quiet voice from the doorway.

Marble was breathing very hard. The door was still open and he could see a yard beyond and could feel the fresh sea air from the night outside, but he found it curiously hard to move. And then a man stooped over him and touched the nape of his neck with long delicate fingers, and Marble forgot about the car journey and the smell from the stove and the promise of freedom inches away outside the back door.

"What's your name?" said the stranger in that quiet, dark voice. "Or have you always been nameless, waiting for me?"

Marble put out a weak paw and fastened his claws around a black shoelace.

"I name you Zequiel," said the quiet voice, "and claim you for my own."

And suddenly strong hands were lifting him through the air and there was the smell of a clean white shirt and the soothing silk of a man's tie and a feeling of immeasurable peace.

"Marble!" called Jane's voice from the passage outside the kitchen door. "Marble, where are you?"

But Marble did not hear her. He had closed his eyes and relaxed every limb and was purring in a trance of shivering ecstasy.

III

"Don't worry, Mrs. Shaw," said Agnes Miller, catching Jane just outside the kitchen. "We'll find him. Please don't worry about it. He's bound to turn up soon."

Jane was distraught. She knew her distress was irrational and knew that Miss Miller's advice contained nothing but commonsense, but she was still upset. She tried to tell herself that her uncharacteristic behavior was the result of the long journey but she knew it was not. Her distress seemed to spring from some strange atmosphere in the house; perhaps it even sprang from the presence of this unknown woman who had befriended Marble so easily or from the bat which had flickered through the dusk after Benedict had rung the doorbell. Maybe her distress even had some connection with the alien but fragrant odor which was wafting toward her from the half-open kitchen door. But whatever the source of her anxiety was, Jane was conscious of unreasoning panic. With horror she realized she was on the verge of tears.

"I've got to find him," she said, turning blindly toward the door. "I must."

Miss Miller stepped neatly in front of her and poked her head around the door of the kitchen. "Has anyone seen—" she began brightly, and then exclaimed in delight. "Why, there he is! It's all right, Mrs. Shaw, he's safe and sound! He's among friends and having a lovely time!"

Marble has no friends, thought Jane fiercely, only me and Benedict. Her eyes were blurring with the ridiculous tears again, and then as she stood there, not trusting herself to speak, a shadow fell between her and the light and a man's voice said politely: "Your cat, Mrs. Shaw."

Jane blinked away her tears, but even before she could see properly she could hear Marble's purrs. He was lying limpidly in his captor's arms, his fur very white against the man's black jacket.

"You naughty cat, Marble," said Jane in an unsteady voice, and picking him up crushed him tightly against her breast. "You naughty disobedient cat."

Marble spat and began to struggle.

"Quiet." The stranger laid his index finger on the cat's head. "Behave yourself."

The cat was still.

Jane looked up for the first time at the man facing her.

"Mrs. Shaw," said Agnes Miller, "this is Mr. Poole, the managing director of our society. Perhaps Mr. Colwyn has mentioned him to you."

"I don't think he . . . at least, I'm not sure—I don't remember . . . How do you do, Mr. Poole."

"How do you do, Mrs. Shaw." He smiled at her.

Jane looked away. "Thank you so much for capturing Marble . . . I'm afraid I was rather silly . . . panicky . . . he's not used to strange places, and I was afraid he might run away and get lost."

"Of course," said Poole. "I quite understand."

"Such a lovely cat," said Miss Miller warmly. "Such a very beautiful cat."

Poole said nothing. Jane was suddenly aware of his lack of sentimentality toward Marble. There was no effeminate gushing about how handsome the cat was, no fatuous remarks, forgivable in a woman, about how naughty the animal had been, no uneasy insincerities about how glad he was to have been of service. Instead there had been the competent handling of the cat, the kind of handling a veterinarian might have shown, and the short admonition when the cat had become hostile. Jane had an impression of controlled power, economical movements, and a cool, spare masculinity which seemed incongruous in a man who had a way with cats and who made his living by directing what Benedict had called a crackpot society.

"I wish you a pleasant stay at the cottage, Mrs. Shaw," the man was saying. "I trust we'll be seeing you from time to time during your visit."

"Yes . . . thank you," said Jane, not sure what she was saying. "If you'll excuse me—"

"Of course. Good night, Mrs. Shaw."

"I'll come back to the hall with you," said Agnes Miller, leading the way down the corridor. "Now I do hope you have everything you want at the cottage. I hold myself responsible for the arrangements because Mr. Colwyn's housekeeper gave notice a week or two ago and really, it's so difficult to get staff nowadays, and so the girls and I have been running the house ourselves—"

"The girls?"

"Yes, there are twelve of us," said Miss Miller sociably. "All ages from all walks of life, so stimulating! My sister Harriet and I are 'in charge,' so to speak, and organize the different duties among us. We attend to all the mundane details so that Mr. Poole is free to plan and direct the more important activities."

"I see," said Jane blankly. "So all twelve of you—"

"Thirteen," said Miss Miller, "with Mr. Poole."

"Yes . . . I see, but what do you actually do?"

"We are engaged," said Miss Miller in a brisk, sensible voice, "in a sociological study of the benefits, physical and psychological, of a diet unadulterated by the vagaries of mankind. It is our contention that through eating foods unpolluted by chemicals, foods that spring directly from nature, we may be at one with nature and may move closer to the natural forces which dominate all our destinies."

Heavens, thought Jane. "I see," she said again. It seemed the safest thing to say.

"We are only the newest of several little groups scattered all over the country," said Miss Miller brightly. "We consider ourselves very privileged that Mr. Poole has donated so much of his valuable time to help us get established in our own headquarters. Mr. Poole is—how shall I say?—the Guiding Light. He's in touch with all the groups and directs policy on a national scale. Once we're established on a stable footing he'll move on elsewhere but for the moment we're fortunate enough to have him here directing operations in person."

"Ah," said Jane. "Yes. Of course."

"Dear me, you must be wondering about the cottage and here I am talking nonstop about the society! I *do* apologize. Now, here's the key to the cottage—there's milk in the refrigerator and I put a few things in the larder to tide you over until you can get to the shops . . . The stove is electric; I prefer gas myself, but still, electric cooking is very clean and most efficient once you get used to it. The kitchen is fully stocked with cutlery, pots and pans, dishes, and so on, and all the linen is in the airing cupboard just outside the bathroom. The laundry calls here every Wednesday, so if you bring the dirty linen up to the house on Wednesday morning I'll see that it gets sent away to the wash. I think that's more or less everything, but if you need anything else please don't hesitate to let me know . . . ah, here's your husband and Mr. Colwyn—and Gwyneth in her dressing gown! Gwyneth, dear, I thought Tristan advised you to go to bed early tonight?"

"I've been asleep," said Gwyneth, "but I couldn't help waking up when everyone started shouting for the cat. Hello, Jane! So this is the cat! Is he real? He looks like a toy."

"Unfortunately he's all too real," said Benedict. "Jane, I think we should be on our way."

"Yes," said Jane. "Definitely."

"Come over tomorrow as soon as you're settled in," said Walter. "Meanwhile I hope you sleep well. Jane looks very tired."

"You look tired yourself, Walter," said Benedict crisply. "I think we'd all feel better for a night's rest."

"I'm all right," said Walter vaguely and wandered with them to the door. "You know the way? Just take the lane past the stables toward the sea."

"Fine. How about the key?"

"I've got that somewhere," said Jane. "Good night, Miss

53

Miller. Thank you again. Good night, Gwyneth ... Walter ... see you tomorrow."

They escaped. Marble, too sleepy to protest, was put in his basket again, Benedict switched on the headlights, and the car began to bump forward away from the house down the dark lane which led to the coast.

"Benedict," said Jane, "there's something very peculiar going on in that house. Those people have completely taken it over. Did you notice how awful Gwyneth and Walter looked? What on earth do you think is happening?"

"My dear, don't make a mystery out of it," said Benedict, trying to concentrate on avoiding the potholes in the rough road. "Gwyneth always looks like a Victorian heroine in the last throes of consumption and Walter's aged a bit since we last saw him, that's all. Of course he must be on the verge of bankruptcy to have allowed those people to take over part of his house, but—"

"All his house, Benedict! Miss Miller's running the entire place!"

"Well, if that's so, at least he's saved himself the expense of engaging a housekeeper. But anyway I intend to have a talk with him at the earliest opportunity to see if I can give him any financial advice. I know Walter! He'll muddle into almost anything unless someone takes him firmly by the hand and leads him out of it. The whole trouble probably began when Evan went abroad last year and there was no one to keep an eye on what happened at Colwyn Court. Thank God Evan will be home before the end of the month! Between the two of us we should manage to sort matters out, I should think."

"But Benedict, that society—"

"Just a bunch of harmless middle-aged women, my dear, who like to dabble in herbalism. As a matter of fact, it was a relief to meet Miss Miller and see what a nice woman she is. I'm sure the society poses no threat in itself; they've merely managed to take a legitimate advantage of Walter's unfortunate economic situation."

"You didn't meet Mr. Poole," said Jane.

"Who's Mr. Poole?"

"The 'Guiding Light,' Miss Miller called him."

"That's funny, Walter said they were all women . . . Well, what's wrong with Mr. Poole? I suppose a man who works with a dozen middle-aged women cultivating nature foods is probably some sort of elderly pansy, but—"

"Mr. Poole isn't like that at all," said Jane. "He's about thirty-five, tall, good-looking, well-educated, well-dressed, very polite, and—"

"And?" said Benedict, too astonished to feel even the smallest pang of jealousy.

"—and rather frightening," said Jane, and shivered so violently that Marble's basket nearly slid off her lap onto the floor.

IV

Three days passed. Benedict had begun to settle down to a routine of working all morning, reading in the afternoon, and working again in the evening, a routine which Jane had become accustomed to during the years of her marriage but which still managed to make her feel lonely unless she kept herself fully occupied. The day after they had arrived they had lunched with Walter and Gwyneth, but Colwyn Court had seemed less formidable in daylight and the members of the society had remained out of sight in their own sections of the house so that it had been hard to remember that the Colwyns did not have their home to themselves. Mr. Poole, Walter had announced, had gone to London for some reason and would be away for a day or two. Jane was conscious first of relief when she heard this news and then of regret that Benedict would still not have the chance to meet Miss Miller's Guiding Light.

But perhaps Benedict would have found Mr. Poole as pleasantly ordinary as he had found Miss Miller.

After lunch Jane had suggested to Gwyneth that they leave the men on their own and walk through the grounds to the beach, but Gwyneth had received the suggestion without enthusiasm. It was time for her afternoon rest, she had objected, and anyway it was too hot to consider trekking all the way down to the cove; her health had improved but she had had a small relapse lately and "Tristan" had advised her to be careful for a few days.

"Is Tristan Poole his real name?" Jane had asked suddenly.

Gwyneth had stared at her in astonishment. "Why ever shouldn't it be?"

"Oh . . . I don't know. I suppose it seems rather an unlikely sort of name, that's all."

"I can't imagine why you should say that," Gwyneth had said disapprovingly. "Poole is a very ordinary sort of surname and Tristan . . . well, people *are* called Tristan, aren't they? I don't think it's any more unusual than Benedict."

Jane, not wanting to argue, had abandoned the subject and strolled off to the beach on her own. Colwyn Cove, which was private property and part of Walter's estate, had a small sandy beach sprinkled with rocks and framed by tall cliffs. The cottage where Benedict and Jane were staying was perched above the beach at the point where the cliffs were at their lowest, rising no more than twenty feet above the sands, and was set about two hundred yards from the cliff's edge. It was a perfect position, and from the picture window of the living room it was possible to see not only the surf in the cove but north to the ruined castle and chapel on top of the furthest cliff and south to the windswept bracken and heather of the cliff nearby. The sunsets were superb. After their first dinner at the cottage Jane and Benedict had lingered a long time by the window to watch the sun sink into the darkening sea.

"You were right as usual," Benedict had said, taking her hand and smiling at her. "You knew this would be the best place for me to work." And the very next morning he had unfastened the trunk which contained his books, littered his papers over the table, and begun to hammer away at his elderly typewriter amid a sea of dirty coffee cups and over-

56

flowing ashtrays. Walter's problems were forgotten; Benedict had found out from his cousin that Walter was "a little hard pressed for ready cash," as Walter himself had put it, but by no means insolvent, and the discovery, together with the fact that the society seemed so unobtrusive, had convinced Benedict that he had been worrying unnecessarily.

"Of course if it were me," he had said to Jane, "I wouldn't care to let part of my home to a group of strangers, even if they were as orderly and well behaved as these people seem to be, but if it helps Walter financially and he doesn't mind their presence, I don't see why the arrangement shouldn't work out satisfactorily for all concerned. It'll do Gwyneth good to see a few more people. The life she leads here is much too isolated, in my opinion."

Jane spent some time pondering on the subject of Gwyneth. Despite the fact that she was Gwyneth's senior by more than thirteen years, Jane was always aware of a sense of inferiority on the rare occasions when they met. Gwyneth had received a poor education at home from a governess, but this made no difference to the fact that her intelligence was sharp; she had spent most of her life in indifferent health, but this had not affected her looks, which were striking. Jane had long admired her slender figure, curling red hair, and wide-set blue eyes, and in Gwyneth's presence she inevitably felt large and clumsy and not a little stupid. Moreover, Gwyneth's obsession with the modern subculture, her psychedelic posters of pop artists, her records of the fashionable white American blues, her literature on such nineteen-sixties note-worthies as Che Guevara, Andy Warhol, and Stokely Carmichael all contrived to make Jane feel hopelessly out of touch with such an aggressive and mysterious generation.

So even when Benedict had settled down to his work and Jane found she had too much time to herself, she avoided a routine of daily visits to Colwyn Court. Her excuse to herself was that she did not want to bore Gwyneth by turning up every day for a chat and that if Gwyneth wanted to be sociable she would manage to walk the three-quarters of a mile from the main house to the cottage. But Gwyneth evidently had no wish to be sociable. She paid no visits to the cottage, and although Jane was secretly relieved by this she was regretful as well. Apart from her morning visits to the village stores for food she saw no one but Benedict, and it would have been pleasant to have another woman to talk to now and then.

She contented herself by going for long walks. She walked up to the ruined castle on the cliffs and beyond, around the headland past a dozen deserted rocky coves toward the furthest tip of the Gower Peninsula, the rocky arm of the Worm's Head. She walked the other way too, walked east of Colwyn around a dozen more coves toward Port Eynon, and each time she walked she met no one. In June the holiday season was not yet in full swing and the weather was still too uncertain to attract the day-trippers. After her walks she felt increasingly aware of the cottage's isolation.

On the fourth day after their arrival the weather improved; the last two days had been showery but that morning the sun was shining and Jane decided to take advantage of the better weather by spending the morning sunbathing on the beach. After she had finished washing up the breakfast dishes she left Benedict among his cigarette smoke and intellectual thoughts and went down to the sands with her bathing wrap and the latest issue of her favorite women's magazine.

The cat followed her when she left. She had hardly seen him since they had arrived, for every morning he had disappeared on his own expeditions and not returned till nightfall, but this morning he stayed with her, padding down the path to the beach behind her, and scrambling over the rocks onto the sand. He was restless. Once a gull landed only a few feet away from them and he chased it fretfully toward the sea, but the menace of the incoming tide made him nervous and he could not settle down and sun himself in peace.

After a while his restlessness communicated itself to Jane and she looked up but there was nothing to see, no living thing in sight except for the gulls, and up on the cliff by the ruined castle, the wild horses grazing placidly on the short grass. She returned to her magazine but presently realized she had no memory of what she had been reading. When she looked up again she saw that Marble had gone.

He was pattering across the sand toward the path which led up from the beach, his tail waving gently, his ears very erect, and as Jane watched, wondering what had attracted him, she saw a figure reach the top of the path and pause before making the descent to the beach.

It was Tristan Poole.

V

He raised his hand when he saw her, and after a second she waved back and reached for her wrap. Why she felt the need to put on her wrap she had no idea. Her swimsuit was respectable and even flattering to her figure, and she was certainly not ashamed of her legs which had always, even during the fattest stages of her life, been good. But she put on the wrap all the same. It was not until she tried to fasten it that she realized how nervous she was. Her fingers were trembling and her palms were damp against the rough toweling.

Marble had reached Poole and was trying to attract his attention by rubbing himself around the man's ankles. Poole said something—Jane heard his voice but not what he said—and the cat dropped back a pace obediently.

No man should have such control over a strange cat, thought Jane suddenly. It's unnatural.

And she had to use all her willpower to stop herself shivering again as he came toward her.

"Hello," he said, sounding so normal that in a second she had forgotten her nervousness. "How are you? By the way, your cat seems to have taken a fancy to me, I can't imagine why. What did you say his name was?"

"Marble. You must have a way with cats. He's usually very hostile to strangers."

"Hostility is usually only a manifestation of fear. Your

59

cat, like many people, is afraid of a great many things. Eliminate the fear and you eliminate the hostility—and you have a docile cat." He stooped, patted Marble's head absentmindedly, and glanced down with a smile at Jane. "May I join you for a moment?"

"Yes, of course," said Jane, anxious not to manifest her fear by a display of hostility. "When did you get back to Colwyn?"

"Late last night. I had business in London . . . Do you know London at all?"

"Not really. My family came from Hampshire and since my marriage I've lived in Cambridge. My sister lived in London for some time, but I never followed her example."

"You have a sister?"

"Just the one sister, yes. No brothers. She's younger than me."

"Does she still live in London?"

"No, she and her husband live about twenty miles away in Surrey, but I think Lisa would like a flat in town as well as the house in the country if she had the chance. However, Matt—my brother-in-law—isn't too keen on that idea. He's just about to retire early and he's anxious to get right away from London for a while." Heavens, she thought to herself, amazed, why am I telling him all this? She tried to ask him a question about himself, but he spoke before she could think of anything to say.

"If any man wants to escape from city life for a while," said Poole, "he should come down here. I don't know if your brother-in-law likes the sea, but this stretch of the coast is as good as a hundred light-years from London in my opinion."

"Yes, that's just what Matt says—he came down here after he married Lisa three years ago, and when they were staying at Colwyn Court I know he was very impressed by the countryside. You see, he's really a very straightforward person with very simple tastes . . ." And she found herself telling him all about Matthew Morrison, all about his whirlwind romance with Lisa, all about Lisa's first husband who had been a television producer specializing in documentaries on

60

current affairs. She even told him how Lisa's first husband had met his death when he had been in the Far East filming an essay on the Chinese infiltration of Hong Kong and had drowned at sea during a foolhardy reconnaissance up the coast of Red China. From the subject of Lisa's first husband the conversation veered into a discussion of Lisa's children, and the subject of children led Jane to talk about Nicola who was Matt's only child. She was on the point of launching into the saga of Nicola's ill-fated romance with Evan Colwyn when she suddenly realized how much she was talking. "I'm sorry," she said, embarrassed. "Of course you can't be interested in all that. How silly of me."

He smiled. He had a very attractive smile. His teeth were not quite even, she noticed, but somehow this only made his smile more attractive than ever. Now that she had the chance to observe him more closely she saw that in fact he was not as good-looking as he had seemed at first glance; his mouth was too wide, his cheekbones too broad, his chin a fraction too square. But he was attractive. Not handsome in the classical sense, but very attractive. Too attractive, she thought, and glanced away quickly for fear that her unwilling interest in his face should be misinterpreted.

"You're wrong," he was saying idly. "I was most intrigued by what you were saying. People—especially people like your brother-in-law—always do intrigue me. I admire anyone who starts off in life as an office boy and ends as chairman of the board. I suppose there's no chance of your sister and brother-in-law visiting you while you're at the cottage?"

"Matt would like to, I'm sure," said Jane, "and so would the twins." She began to picture herself taking the twins for walks and playing with them on the sands.

"Why don't you give your sister a call and suggest it?"

"Well, the cottage is a bit small—"

"There are four bedrooms, aren't there? Wouldn't that be sufficient?"

"Yes . . . yes, I suppose so. Yes, it would be nice. But you see, my husband is working—a thesis—it would be a bit difficult—"

"He'd be on his own during the day. Everyone would be out enjoying themselves."

"Yes, that's true."

"When does your brother-in-law retire?"

"It's this month—I'm not sure of the exact date. It's soon, I know."

"Wouldn't it be fun for you to have some visitors? It must be dull for you here on your own."

"Well . . ."

"It must be lonely," said Poole. "Admit it. It's isolated here."

"It's isolated," said Jane.

"There's plenty of room at the cottage."

"Yes, plenty of room."

"I'm sure your husband wouldn't mind."

"No, I'm sure he wouldn't."

"Of course, they may have made other plans, but—"

"I'll phone Lisa," said Jane, "and find out."

"Good!" He smiled at her again and stood up, dusting the sand off his dark slacks. "Well, I must be on my way. No doubt I'll see you again soon, Mrs. Shaw. Give my regards to your husband, won't you? I hope I'll have the chance to meet him before long."

The cat stirred but made no effort to follow him.

"I'm sure you will," said Jane. "Good-bye, Mr. Poole."

He was gone. She watched him walk off up the cliff path, and when he had disappeared from sight she lay back limply on the sand and thought about him.

After a while she thought: I won't do it. I won't phone Lisa. I won't.

This made her feel better. She sat up, tossed back her hair, and flung off her wrap in a gesture of liberation. But then she thought: It would be nice if the twins were here. Perhaps they could come down on their own.

But the twins would be at school. How could she have forgotten that? They were at their separate boarding schools, and their terms would not end until the third week of July.

All desire to phone Lisa vanished. Jane put on her sunglasses again, dragged her magazine toward her and spent the rest of the morning trying not to remember the curious interview with Tristan Poole. But she remembered it just the same. Even when she returned to the house to prepare lunch she found she was still thinking of the odd effect his presence had had on her.

The telephone was ringing as she walked into the living room. Normally there was no phone at the cottage in order to protect Walter from any whim of his summer tenants to make long-distance calls, but a portable phone had originally been installed there for the retired chauffeur and had been reinstated a week ago for the Shaws' benefit.

Jane crossed the living room and picked up the receiver. "Hello?"

"Darling," said Lisa, "it's me. Listen, the twins are in quarantine for mumps, Matt's on the verge of flying to the Channel Islands, and everything's a perfect nightmare. Jane, you *must* help me, I'm desperate. I've got to play for time and stop Matt buying property in Guernsey, and the only way to stop him now, as far as I can see, is for me to wangle an invitation to Colwyn Cottage from you and Benedict. Darling, I hate to ask you, but do you think you could possibly—"

"Did you say the twins were at home?" said Jane.

"Yes, it's such a nuisance for them, poor things. Their half-terms fell on the same weekend so we took them out and went to see a friend of Matt's who has some grandchildren about the same age. Then one of the grandchildren came down with mumps the day afterward, so Matt said: 'Good, that gives us an excuse to take the twins away from school before the end of term and make an early start for Guernsey before the worst of the holiday crowds arrive.' Well, I . . . hello, are you still there?"

"Yes," said Jane.

"You're not saying very much," said Lisa accusingly. "Are you in the middle of lunch or something?"

"No. Lisa—"

"The point is that Matt's dead set on this Channel Islands

63

scheme, and I'm equally dead set against it. But I'm sure I could still talk him out of it if only I had the tiniest bit more time, so if we could come down for a visit—"

"Bendict's working, Lisa."

"Well, we wouldn't interfere! After all, Matt would be out all day leading his wretched Simple-Life-Away-from-It-All, and the twins would be on the beach and—well, I can't imagine what *I'll* do, but I'm sure I won't disturb Benedict. I could leave the *au pair* in Surrey if that would help out with the accommodation. The twins are really quite sensible on their own nowadays and in an isolated spot like Colwyn I'm sure they wouldn't get up to too much mischief."

"I could look after the twins," said Jane.

"Oh darling, you know I wouldn't expect you to be an unpaid *au pair* girl, but you *are* so marvelous with children and the twins so enjoy seeing you—"

"When will you come?" said Jane.

"Perhaps at the end of the week—would that be all right? Oh Jane, you're wonderful! Honestly, I sometimes wonder what I would ever do without you to fall back upon whenever I get into one of these awful jams! Listen, I mustn't hold you up any longer—I expect you're busy cooking, and I want to find Matt straight away to tell him you've invited us all to stay for a couple of weeks. I'll phone you again later and let you know what time we'll be arriving."

"Yes . . . all right, Lisa. Fine."

" 'Bye, darling. Love to Benedict and thanks a million."

" 'Bye," said Jane, and began to wonder how she would ever summon the courage to tell Benedict such unwelcome news.

Benedict was furious.

"That woman!" he yelled, pounding the table so hard with his fist that the typewriter leaped half an inch into the air. "How dare she use us in an effort to stave off her marital troubles! How dare she!"

"Well, it's not quite as bad as that, Benedict. I mean—"

"It's not only as bad as that," cried Benedict, "it's worse.

How on earth am I supposed to have any peace and quiet once the house is bursting at the seams with visitors? How am I supposed to do any serious writing when the Morrisons are airing their incompatability and the children are running around playing games—"

"I'll see the children don't disturb you," said Jane.

"I've no doubt you will! Lisa thought of that! She used those two children as bait!"

"No, she didn't," said Jane.

"Of course she did! And then in addition to everyone else there's that wretched *au pair* girl—"

"She won't be coming. Benedict, it'll only be for two weeks."

"I don't think I could be in the same house as Lisa for two weeks! I don't think I could do so without suffering a nervous breakdown!"

Jane turned without a word, went back to the phone, and started to dial the operator for Lisa's number.

"For God's sake," growled Benedict, ripping the paper out of his typewriter, throwing it on the floor, and stamping on it to relieve his feelings, "what are you up to now?" He stormed over to the phone, grabbed the receiver from Jane's hand, and hurled it back into its cradle. "You weren't phoning her to cancel the visit, were you?"

Jane was on the verge of tears. "What else can I do?"

"There, there," said Benedict guiltily. "There, there. You mustn't take me so seriously. You know I often say things I don't mean in the heat of the moment. Let the invitation stand."

"But—"

"I like Morrison and the only reason I resent Lisa so much is because I think she takes advantage of you most of the time, that's all. I resent her for your sake, not for my own."

"But your work—it was wrong of me to invite them—"

"Well, it's only for two weeks and if they're not tactful enough to leave me alone most of the time I shall have no compunction about asking them to do so."

"I don't know why I agreed to it," said Jane in despair. "I just don't know why I agreed to it."

The children, thought Benedict, and felt a quick stab of pain. Aloud he said, "Well, you'll enjoy entertaining the twins."

"It wasn't just because of the twins," said Jane stubbornly. "It really wasn't, Benedict."

"Oh." He thought: we ought to talk about adoption again. I was too rigid before, saying I couldn't care enough about a child unless it were my own flesh and blood. It was unfair to her. "Well—"

"I mean, perhaps it was partly because of the twins, but . . . Benedict, I met Mr. Poole on the beach this morning. We talked about Lisa and Matt and he—he told me to invite them down, and . . . well, when Lisa suggested the invitation I found I simply couldn't refuse. I hadn't the will to refuse. It was as if . . . oh, I don't know! But it's all Mr. Poole's fault somehow, I know it is. I just know it."

"There, there," said Benedict soothingly again. He took her in his arms and kissed her. "It doesn't matter. I'm sorry I lost my temper like that."

"Benedict, you weren't listening to what I was saying. Mr. Poole—"

"This man Poole obviously has you spellbound," said Benedict. "I can see I shall have to meet him as soon as possible to discover why you find him so irresistible."

"Benedict, I know you're not taking me seriously, but it really was as if I was spellbound—or hypnotized—or something—"

"Fiddlesticks," said Benedict placidly. "You love a mystery, my dear, that's your trouble, and if one doesn't exist you'll invent one. It's your romantic and feminine nature. The truth of the matter is that Poole, seeing you were on your own on the beach, suggested you should invite the rest of your family down for a visit. Then by coincidence Lisa rang up and suggested the same thing. You were tempted by the prospect of seeing the twins and agreed to the visit. I can't think why you should want to blame everything on poor Poole who was probably only doing his best to be friendly and sociable."

"Yes," said Jane. "Yes, you're right. Of course you're right. It's just that—"

"Yes?" said Benedict curiously.

"—I don't like Mr. Poole," said Jane. "I can't help it, I just don't like him at all."

VI

When Poole returned to Colwyn Court after his talk with Jane he found Agnes Miller in the small sitting room which had once belonged to the housekeeper. Agnes was adding up a column of figures in the ledger before her and looking perplexed.

"Don't say anything," she said as Poole entered the room. "I'm at a crucial stage. Four from nine is five, six from thirteen is seven, seven from two . . . seven from two? Oh yes, I see." She wrote down a figure and sat looking at it doubtfully.

"I'll have to buy you an adding machine," said Poole amused.

"My dear, we hardly have enough money left to buy a loaf of bread, let alone an adding machine! What on earth are we going to do?"

"How women enjoy a crisis," said Poole, sitting down on the nearby sofa and putting his feet up on the coffee table. "How women love to worry."

"You're quite wrong," said Agnes. "I absolutely hate it." She closed the ledger with a bang. "How sordid money is!"

"Not at all," said Poole. "It's the lack of money that's sordid. Money itself is highly enjoyable."

"Don't split hairs!" said Agnes crossly.

He laughed. She looked at him and in spite of herself smiled.

"Well, I must say," she said, "it's hard to be depressed when you're always so confident. I only wish I could be as confident as you are."

"Agnes," he said, "you're a woman of very little faith sometimes."

Agnes became unexpectedly serious. "It's not that," she protested. "Of course I have faith! When I think of all you've done for us, getting us settled in this ideal environment, handling the Colwyns, coping with everything—"

"Then don't worry about the money."

"All right," said Agnes. "But how do you plan to—"

"Never ask me my plans. It's a waste of time. If I want you to know them I'll tell them to you."

"Yes . . . well, let me tell you how we're placed at the moment. So far we've been existing well enough on the legacy from our last benefactor, but the way things are going the money will be running out some time in the middle of August, and if we have the usual Lammas expenses . . . Don't look like that, Tristan! After all, one must be practical, mustn't one? These things do cost money! One can't entertain more than fifty people and only expect to spend a shilling."

"Indeed not," said Poole without expression.

"Besides," said Agnes, warming to her subject, "I don't think it's disrespectful to be practical about such matters. Think of the Other Church. They've always been very money-conscious. The Other Church is very good at raising money and being practical in that respect."

He was silent. Agnes saw she had gone too far.

"I'm sorry," she said quickly. "I shouldn't have said that. I meant no disrespect."

There was another pause, and then suddenly he was smiling at her and she was able to relax again.

"There's no harm in being reminded of a rival from time to time," said Poole lightly. "One could almost say it spurs one to greater effort."

"Well, exactly!" said Agnes pleased. She glanced at the

ledger again and wished, despite all he had said, that he would give her one small word of reassurance. "Tristan—"

"You've no faith at all, have you, Agnes!" he said, laughing at her. "None whatsoever!"

"I have," pleaded Agnes, "but . . . Tristan, how long do you plan to stay here?"

"My dear Agnes, you know the answer to that question so well I can't think why you bother to ask it. I shall leave when my work here is done, when you and the others are established here with enough money to live on in comfort. Walter Colwyn's an old man and won't live forever. His son has an urge to emigrate to America. Gwyneth will either get married or end up in a home for the mentally disturbed or possibly, depending on what she wants, both. One day before very long Colwyn Court will be up for sale, everyone will point out what an economic liability large houses are these days, and you'll be able to buy it for a song with the fund I shall provide for the purpose. I'm not worried about your future here—I'm fully convinced that I've provided you with a stable environment. By Lammas you'll have a stable bank balance as well, and after Lammas I shall probably move on. There! Is that what you wanted to hear?"

"I hope you're not relying on the Colwyn family for the money," said Agnes. "I'm absolutely sure Mr. Colwyn has a mortgage on the house, and Harriet's convinced he has. I think he'll die penniless."

"Probably."

"Well," said Agnes, "I just wanted to reassure myself that you weren't relying on any Colwyn inheritance."

Poole did not answer. After a moment he stood up and wandered over to the window. "Where is everyone?"

"Working in the herb garden. We're having trouble with the coriander and henbane—so tiresome . . . Oh, and Margaret and Jackie are in the kitchen preparing lunch. Tristan, I'm a little worried about Jackie—I've a suspicion that the weekly meetings in your room no longer satisfy her, especially now that we're all being so ascetic to prepare for Lammas, and I think she's hankering for a few bright lights and a good time. You know how young she is, and how immature in some ways. Anyway, this morning she said she wanted to borrow the car to go into Swansea next Saturday night, and I couldn't help wondering if—"

"Let her go."

"But supposing—"

"Agnes, sometimes you talk as if you were the Mother Superior of a convent!"

"Well, it's not *that*," said Agnes. "It's just that I suppose it's a little dull for her here at the moment, and if she dissipates her energies before August the first, she won't find the rites nearly such a rewarding experience. I do wish you'd have a word with her about it."

"She'll do as she's been told, don't worry. Since this is her first experience of Lammas she won't want to risk not getting the most out of it. That's basic psychology."

"It's her basic sexuality I worry about," muttered Agnes. "Not her basic psychology." She put the ledger away in the drawer and locked it. "What were you up to this morning?"

"Oh, I went for a walk. To the beach. The cat was there with Mrs. Shaw."

"She seemed a nice woman," said Agnes vaguely. "Intuitive too. She doesn't like us very much because of all your fun and games with the cat."

"Fun and games! Agnes, what an extraordinary word choice you have sometimes!" He fingered the edge of the curtain idly. "Mrs. Shaw could be an attractive woman if she wanted to be," he said after a moment. "The strange part is that for some reason she doesn't want to be. A subconscious opting-out of sibling rivalry, perhaps. Gwyneth tells me Mrs. Shaw's sister, Lisa, is very attractive indeed."

Agnes began to get the drift of the conversation. Her mind, always nimble, began to leap from one possibility to another. "You can't be interested in Mrs. Shaw," she said. "Too much basic hostility."

"But very intuitive," said Poole, "and most susceptible to suggestion."

70

"But—"

"No, I'm not particularly interested in Mrs. Shaw. Since when have professors been millionaires? But Mrs. Shaw has a beautiful sister and the beautiful sister has a husband who even in these overtaxed days has managed to become excessively rich."

Agnes' heart began to flutter excitedly in her breast. "How on earth did you find that out?"

"It didn't need a Sherlock Holmes to discover that one. The man's name is Matthew Morrison."

"The Matthew Morrison?"

"Uh-huh. And Agnes, you want to know something else?"

He's getting excited too, thought Agnes. He's forgetting his English accent. "Tell me," she invited with a smile.

"Professor and Mrs. Shaw are going to have visitors in the very near future. And you want to know who those visitors are going to be?"

"Matthew Morrison, the millionaire industrialist," said Agnes promptly, her faith restored in full, "and his very beautiful, very attractive, very desirable wife, Lisa."

3

I

Four days later in the back of Matt's Rolls Royce the twins were studying the road map. The car was traveling through orchard country on the way west to the Welsh border, and the boughs of the trees near the roadside were drooping with the burden of ripening fruit. It was raining, a steady drizzle, and the grass was lush and thick beneath the hedgerows.

"Wonderful weather for a holiday," said Lisa dryly, flicking a speck of ash off her belted white raincoat. "That's the trouble with England. Unless you're in love with the rain you might just as well spend your holiday abroad."

"Too many people knock England nowadays," said Matt. "Self-criticism can be healthy but constant self-abuse is a mistake."

"Patriotism's out of fashion nowadays, darling," said Lisa. "Everyone says so, even the Americans."

"Mum," said Timothy from the back seat. "Wales isn't England. You said we're going on holiday in England but we're not. We're going to Wales."

"Oh well, it's all the same thing really," said Lisa.

"You'd get lynched if you said that to a crowd of Welshmen," said Matt.

"Uncle Walter says the Gower Peninsula isn't really either Welsh or English," said Lucy, attempting one-upmanship. "He says there are a lot of English names in Gower as well as the Welsh ones and hardly anyone speaks Welsh there as they do in the rest of Wales."

"It's officially Welsh," argued Timothy. "Look at the map."

"I'm bored with the map," said Lucy. She twisted restlessly and pressed her face to the window.

"For heaven's sake, Lucy," said Lisa, "can't you sit still for more than five minutes at a time?"

"Why should I?" said Lucy, tired with the journey and annoyed by what she thought was an unjust criticism. "There's plenty of room in the back here and Timmy doesn't mind."

"Well, I do," said Lisa, "and don't answer back like that. It's rude."

"I'm not the only one in this family that likes to talk back," said Lucy rashly.

"Lucy!"

"That's enough," said Matt shortly in a tone of voice which reduced everyone to silence. "The journey's long enough without everyone trying to make it longer."

"I wish we were there already," said Timothy at last to no one in particular.

So do I, thought Matt.

If only we were on our way to the airport, thought Lisa, en route to Nassau or Bermuda or Jamaica.

"I wish it would stop raining," said Lucy, blowing on the windowpane and drawing a picture on the misted glass. "Surely it'll stop raining soon."

It did. By the time they reached the bleak landscape of the Rhondda Valley the clouds were higher, the rain had stopped, and the sky was clear toward the west. In Swansea the sun was shining, and by the time they reached Colwyn the evening light was already casting a golden glow over the fields which stretched to the sea.

"We can walk up to the castle," said Timothy. It was three

years since they had all visited Colwyn Court after Matt's marriage to Lisa and the twins had only been six at the time, but Timothy remembered the ruined castle on top of the cliffs and the sea pounding against the rocks below.

"And the horses," said Lucy. "Don't forget the wild horses by the castle."

"And the caves on the beach!"

"And the rock pools—"

"—and shells—" "And the silly sheep all along the top of the cliffs—the other cliffs, the cliffs opposite the castle—"

"Maybe Aunt Jane's made some biscuits for us."

"Cakes, I expect."

"Or fudge! Remember Aunt Jane's fudge!"

"Yummy!"

The twins' spirits had revived. They were bouncing around in the back of the Rolls Royce in anticipation.

"I wish we could stay at Colwyn Court," said Lisa, not for the first time. "Can this weird society have taken up *all* the available space? It does seem a shame."

"I'd rather stay with Jane," said Matt. "I'll bet she cooks much better than any housekeeper Walter employs."

"That's Jane's whole problem," said Lisa. "She's too good at cooking. All those calories!"

"Not all men like women who look like lampposts, you know."

"Thanks, darling," said Lisa.

They reached Colwyn Court and Matt took the rough road which led down to the cottage. The Rolls, enormous on the narrow track, purred gently in and out of the potholes with swaying distaste.

"There's Aunt Jane!" squealed Lucy and wound down the window. "Aunt Jane! Hey, have you made fudge for us?"

"Lucy!" exclaimed Lisa. "Haven't you got any manners at all?"

Timothy pushed Lucy out of the way and stuck his own head out of the window. "Have you made a cake?"

Jane was laughing as Matt halted the Rolls behind Benedict's small Austin. "I've made one chocolate cake," she called, "one tray of fudge, and one chocolate trifle."

The twins howled with delight and tumbled out of the car into her arms.

Matt was just opening the door for his wife when Benedict emerged, his scanty hair standing on end, his glasses on the tip of his nose. "God, what a noise!" he said mildly.

"I'm terribly sorry," said Lisa, feeling guilty. "Lucy—Timothy—stop it! That's enough!"

"It's all right," said Jane. "Benedict doesn't really mind . . . How are you all? It's so nice to see you . . ."

There followed several confused moments during which Benedict and Matt coped with the luggage, the twins raced off to sample the chocolate cake, and Lisa sank into an armchair in the living room and requested a drink.

"Yes, of course," said Jane, and hunted around for the bottle of gin which she had bought that morning. It seemed to have disappeared.

"Here it is," said Lisa. "Do you usually keep the drink in the coal scuttle?"

"Oh . . . I must have left it there for some reason . . ." Jane was aware of a growing feeling of helpless disorganization.

"Give it to me," said Lisa competently. "I'll do it. Matt! Do you want a drink?"

"I did buy whiskey as well," said Jane. "It's here somewhere."

Lisa had the drinks mixed in less than three minutes. The men were still upstairs with the luggage, and the twins' voices were receding as they abandoned the cake and wandered out of the back door.

"I can't tell you how awful the journey was," said Lisa. "Thank God it's over. Jane, it's so good to see you—listen, you simply must give me some advice. If your husband decided to go off and live at the North Pole, what on earth would you do?"

"Go with him, I suppose," said Jane, "but I can't see why Benedict would want to go and live at the North Pole."

"Oh Jane, don't be so dim! You see, the point is—"

The two husbands came clattering down the stairs and the conversation was brought to an abrupt end.

"Here's your drink, Matt," said Lisa.

"In a minute," said Matt. "I want to get the case of wine out of the car."

"Case of wine!" ejaculated Benedict, and followed his guest out of the front door to see if he had heard correctly.

"Of course there's always divorce," said Lisa in a low voice. "But . . . well, I don't really want that. I mean, I know I'd get alimony and that sort of thing, but it wouldn't be the same, and you know how it is, Jane, one gets used to all the little luxuries, and besides, the twins . . . I mean, for their sakes I should try to stick it out, shouldn't I? Matt's very good to them, and it's because of him that I can send them to the best schools . . . And I do love Matt. I really do. It's just that lately he hasn't been very understanding—you know how men are sometimes—"

"I suppose so," said Jane. "Well, yes, perhaps. No, I don't think I do. Lisa—"

The men returned with the case of wine between them and set it down on the dining-room table.

"This is very good of you, Matt," said Benedict, examining the label with interest.

"It's very good of you," said Matt, "to have us descend on you like this. Where's that drink, Lisa?"

"Here, darling."

"How's your daughter, Matt?" said Benedict, reaching for his own whiskey and soda.

"Yes, how's Nicola?" said Jane, seizing the chance to avoid thinking about Lisa's marital problems. "I wish she'd come and see us in Cambridge sometimes."

"Well, you know Nicola," said Matt. "She has to be pushed a bit before she does anything. But I'm sure she'd like to visit you."

"Nicola's in such a rut," said Lisa. "Same old job, same old flat in Hampstead. It's such a pity."

"If she's contented I don't see why it's a pity," said Matt sharply. "She's lucky if she's satisfied with the way things are."

"Don't be naive, Matt," said Lisa. "No unmarried unattached girl in her mid-twenties is ever satisfied with the way things are."

"I was," said Jane. "It was one of the happiest times in my life. I was looking after those children in Scotland and having a lovely time. The whole family was so nice."

The conversation drifted into a discussion of Scotland, and Matt, who was a keen fisherman, began to describe the prize salmon he had caught there the previous summer.

Jane suddenly remembered the casserole she had in the oven and set down her glass of sherry. "Heavens, I'd forgotten all about dinner! Excuse me, everyone."

Lisa slipped after her into the kitchen.

"I wonder where the twins are," said Jane, hoping to stave off a further discussion of Lisa's marital situation. "Dinner will be ready in about twenty minutes. Do you think that perhaps you should see if you can find them?"

"Perhaps I should," said Lisa disconsolately. "Can I do anything to help you in here?"

"No, no—it's all right. It looks a muddle, I know, but I think I've got everything under control . . ." She opened the oven door and peered inside.

"Well, maybe we can have a talk later," said Lisa. "Just you and me. I feel I *must* pour out my heart to someone or I'll burst, and you're always so understanding, Jane."

"Hm," said Jane, poking a carrot to see if it was done.

"Maybe tomorrow sometime?"

"All right." To her relief she saw Lisa move over to the back door in search of the twins. "Twenty minutes, Lisa," she called after her.

"Fine, darling. I hope those little monsters haven't gone too far." Lisa wandered away from the house and took the path which led down to the beach. The twins were nowhere in sight. Fortunately she was wearing her new narrow suede walking shoes designed specifically for weekends in the country so she had no difficulty in reaching the beach and setting off toward the caves which she knew the twins had found irresistible on their previous visit to Colwyn.

"Lucy!" called Lisa. "Timothy!" But there was no reply.

She walked on. It had been raining shortly before their arrival, she realized, because the sands were now steaming in the strong light from the sun. The rising steam created a ghostly effect, and Lisa began to have a strange feeling of unreality as if she were moving through the landscape of a fantasy. She could no longer see the caves clearly.

"Lucy!" she called. "Lucy, are you there?"

There was still no answer. Reluctantly she moved forward toward the caves at the foot of the cliff, and as she moved she thought she saw someone drifting toward her through the wraithlike columns of the mist.

Lisa stopped. Like many people at home in a metropolis she had the secret fear of rural isolation and the city nervousness of meeting a stranger when she was alone in a deserted place.

"Who's that?" she called sharply.

It was a man. She still could not see him clearly, but she knew he was tall and wore a dark sweater and dark slacks.

Damn the twins, thought Lisa, bringing me down here like this. She didn't know whether to turn and run or whether to stay and pretend she hadn't a care in the world. Instinct told her to run, but he was too close now and she had a sudden horror of making a fool of herself by bolting for safety like a startled rabbit. She took another look at him and was reassured by what she saw. He looked eminently sane, not in the least like a homicidal maniac on the loose.

"Excuse me," she called, acting on an impulse. "Have you by any chance seen two children, a boy and a girl, about nine years old, fair-haired and blue-eyed?"

"I'm afraid not." He smiled at her. "You must be Mrs. Morrison—am I right?"

Now that he was closer to her and the sinister mist was no longer separating them, she found her fears ebbing and was glad she had not been so foolish as to run away. He looked rather nice. She liked his smile and found herself smiling back.

"How did you know that?" she said, surprised.

"I'm from Colwyn Court and I knew the Shaws were expecting you and your family today."

"Oh," said Lisa, understanding, "you must be one of the Society for—I'm sorry I forget its title, but—"

"Yes, I'm the managing director."

"Oh, I see! Well, how do you do, Mr.—"

"Poole. Tristan Poole. How do you do, Mrs. Morrison." He held out his hand.

Lisa held out her own hand automatically and felt his fingers close on hers. There was a pause. Beyond them the tide was going out and the gulls were wheeling over the wet beach and the steam was still rising from the sands, but Lisa did not notice. All she saw was the line of Poole's jaw and his windblown hair and the bright luminous quality of his eyes.

"Well, well," said Poole. "Things are looking up on the Colwyn estate." And he smiled again.

God, thought Lisa, what an attractive man. "What are you doing down here?" she said, saying the first thing that came into her head. "You look the sort of person who ought to be in London—or Paris or New York."

"And so do you, Mrs. Morrison. Maybe we can help each other adjust to the rigors of country living."

"The Simple Life," said Lisa, thinking of Matt.

"There's no simple life," said Poole. "Just simple people. And some people are more simple than others."

"You can say *that* again," said Lisa, and then checked herself. What was she doing talking to a stranger like this? The unfamiliar country air must be going to her head. "Well," she said, "I really must try to find my children—my sister's going to dish up dinner in ten minutes, and—"

"Let me help you search for them. Are you sure they came down to the beach?"

"No, I—"

"Perhaps they went up to the ruined castle and chapel. That would be the kind of place to appeal to children, I should think."

"Of course!" exclaimed Lisa, remembering that the twins

had mentioned the castle earlier in the car. "How silly of me! Why didn't I think of that?"

"It was natural for you to think of the beach first," he said easily and offered her his hand again. "Be careful of the rocks here," he said. "They're very slippery."

Lisa took his hand without a word. Her heart was beginning to thump against her ribs and she knew it wasn't solely due to the scramble up the rocky path from the beach. When she paused for breath at the top, she found her self-restraint was slipping away and her tongue had a will of its own.

"Are you married?" she heard herself say abruptly.

"Not at the moment."

"You mean you've been married?"

"In a certain sense."

Lisa's mind flickered over her vocabulary of sophisticated euphemisms. "You mean you lived with someone," she said, "without the blessing of the church."

He smiled but said nothing.

"I've been married twice," said Lisa. "My first marriage was just about finished when my husband got himself killed. The second isn't doing much better. Sometimes I feel very anti-marriage and think it's the most idiotic social institution."

"You can always opt out."

"No, I can't. I've got too much to lose. There's no question of me getting a divorce."

"Who said anything about a divorce?"

"But . . . well, because either I stay married all the way or else I finish it off completely. Matt wouldn't let me compromise. There's no question of him letting me have some sort of arrangement—I mean, I couldn't possibly consider being unfaithful to him—"

"Who are you trying to fool? Not me, I hope."

"But—"

"All you've lacked so far is the perfect opportunity. Once that comes you won't even hesitate."

"That's not true!" cried Lisa.

"Liar," said Poole, and she felt his long fingers slipping around her waist.

Afterward Lisa could not remember clearly what happened next. She had the incredulous feeling she had actually turned to him and offered her mouth to be kissed, but this couldn't have been true. She had done some wild things in her time but she had never considered herself promiscuous, and what could be more promiscuous than offering oneself to a strange man one had known for only five minutes? But whether her role had been passive or not there could be no doubt that Poole had kissed her on the mouth and that she had clung to him until he had gently disentangled himself.

"We mustn't let your husband see us," he said with a smile, and glanced over his shoulder at the cottage.

Lisa felt herself incapable of speech. She was trembling in every limb. Even movement was impossible.

"It's all right," said Poole. "We were just out of sight of the cottage windows, thanks to this large and very opportune boulder." He gave the boulder a friendly slap with the palm of his hand and turned away from her. "Why don't you come up to the main house tomorrow?"

"All right," said Lisa. Then: "No, I'd better not."

He shrugged, amused by her ineffectual struggles with her conscience and commonsense.

"I have to go now," said Lisa, not moving. "I must go."

"Well, if you must," said Poole, "I suppose you must."

They stood still, facing each other. Poole suddenly made an odd gesture with his hand. "Go ahead."

Strength and coordination seeped back into Lisa's limbs. She began to run. The path led uphill and her breath was soon sobbing in her throat but she went on running. She ran until she reached the back door of the cottage and stood panting on the threshold of the empty kitchen.

Jane came in a second later. "Lisa! What's the matter? What's happened?"

"Nothing," said Lisa fiercely. "Nothing."

"But—"

"Don't talk to me."

"All right," said Jane. "The twins came back, by the way, and I sent them upstairs to wash their hands. Dinner'll be in about five minutes. The vegetables took a bit longer than I thought they would, so—"

Lisa went into the living room. Matt was telling Benedict about the characteristics of the salmon which were found in the River Wye.

Lisa ran upstairs, and through the open door of the bathroom she saw the twins pause to look at her guiltily as they washed their hands in the basin.

"I'm sorry if you went searching for us, Mum," said Timothy at last. The twins had long since decided that Timothy was the best at apologizing. "We didn't mean to make you upset."

"It's all right, darlings," said Lisa. "I'm not upset." And seeing one of her suitcases in a nearby bedroom she plunged across the threshold, slammed the door behind her, and collapsed in a heap upon the bed.

II

"Maybe we ought to walk up to the main house this morning," Matt said to Lisa as they dressed before breakfast the next day. "We ought to see Walter and Gwyneth."

"I don't think I want to do that," said Lisa in a rush, and as Matt looked at her in astonishment she added, confused: "I mean, I want to see Walter and Gwyneth but I don't want to go up to Colwyn Court just yet. Maybe they'll come down here to visit us instead."

"Why the devil don't you want to go up to Colwyn Court?"

"Oh . . ." Lisa looked listless. "I don't feel like walking anywhere today. I don't feel too well."

It was a weak excuse but to her relief Matt seemed to accept it without an argument.

"All right," he said. "I'll take the twins up there this morning for a few minutes to be polite, and while we're there I'll suggest to Walter that he and Gwyneth come down to the cottage some time this afternoon. I'm sorry you're not feeling good—why don't you stay in bed this morning and rest?"

"Well, I might, I suppose," said Lisa, but she did not. As soon as Matt and the twins had left after breakfast she put on her blue and white pantsuit, applied her makeup to give her a casual country-style complexion, and tied back her thick blond hair with a scarf which matched the blue of her outfit.

"I'm going down to the beach, Jane," she said, finding her sister in the kitchen. "I think the sea air might do me some good . . . can I give you a hand with that washing up?"

"Of course not!" said Jane, fearing a forthcoming discussion of Lisa's problems. "You're on holiday! I'm glad you're feeling better."

"It was just that I felt tired after the journey," said Lisa vaguely. "I feel more rested now." She wandered through the open back door and Jane's cat followed her, his pink tongue licking furtively around the corners of his mouth as if he expected her to give him something delicious to eat.

"Shoo!" said Lisa, afraid of Marble's dirty paws on the pastel shades of her pantsuit. "Scram!"

But he followed her all the way to the top of the beach and only turned back when she began to scramble down over the rocks to the sand. She saw him dart away in the direction of Colwyn Court, his fluffy tail waving behind him, his legs moving so fast that they were a mere white blur against the brown of the path.

Lisa wandered across the beach and watched the incoming tide. The sun shone fitfully; the air was cool but Lisa was warm enough in her jacket and sweater and did not notice. She stood watching the sea for a long time, watching the white foam bite into the sand as the surf thudded on the beach, and when she turned at last and found herself no longer alone she was aware only of a surprise that she should be so unsurprised. The next moment her heart was beating very fast and her mouth was dry and her spine was tingling with anticipation.

"Hello, Lisa," said Tristan Poole as he strolled across the sands toward her. "How very nice to see you again."

III

"Uncle Matt," said Lucy, taking her stepfather's hand. "Let's go up to the castle."

The social politenesses had been exchanged at Colwyn Court. The twins had drunk lemonade and eaten ginger biscuits while Walter had shown them the latest additions to his collection of rare wild flowers and Gwyneth had graciously allowed them to hear the tangled notes of the latest single to reach the top of the hit parade.

"I like Gwyneth," Timothy had said to Lucy. "She's not really like a grown-up at all."

After the interlude with Gwyneth they had met Miss Agnes Miller of the Society for the Propagation of Nature Foods, and had played their "twins" role beautifully for her, gazing at her with wide innocent eyes and smiling sweetly as she had exclaimed what fun it must be to be twins and how they looked just like two little angels.

"Looks can be deceiving, Miss Miller!" Matt had retorted, and all the grown-ups had laughed—very fatuously, the twins had thought. "You're little devils really, aren't you, twins?"

"Fiends incarnate," Lucy had said sedately, and Miss Miller had given her a very odd look indeed.

"I didn't like that Miss Miller," Timothy had said afterward.

"Why not? She was just another silly old woman. You know how stupid they get at that age."

Finally after several glasses of lemonade and innumerable ginger biscuits, the social obligations had been completed and Matt had led the twins through the garden and down the path to the cottage.

"Were we all right, Uncle Matt?" Lucy had demanded, knowing they had been on their best behavior but anxious for a compliment. "Were we good?"

"Perfect!" Matt had smiled broadly at her as she bounced up and down at his side. "You both were."

It had been then that Lucy, flushed with triumph, had suggested that they all walk up to the castle.

"You don't want an old man like me tagging along, do you?" said Matt, thinking he ought to return to the cottage to see how Lisa was.

"Yes, yes, yes!" cried Lucy, and grabbed his hand to imprison him.

"Triple-yes!" yelled Timothy and grabbed the other hand so that the prisoner had no chance to escape.

"Okay!" Matt laughed. "Whoa!" It wouldn't matter about Lisa. She'd probably be still lying in bed and sulking about the Bahamas. "All right, we'll go up to the castle."

The castle had been built some six hundred years ago after Edward I had subjugated the Welsh, but had already been abandoned by the time the Tudors came to power at the end of the fifteenth century, and was now a mere weathered ruin astride the cliffs on the west side of Colwyn Cove. There was part of a keep, the shell of a tower and an assortment of scattered walls, while through the Norman windows one could still look out across the headland to the sea, the surf, and the sands.

"Isn't it a super place?" said Timothy with shining eyes.

Adjoining the castle was a chapel, roofless but better preserved than the castle itself. An archeologist had told Walter the chapel had been built later with bricks from the castle that had already begun to fall into disrepair, but the chapel had not been used since the time of the Reformation and its active life must have been short. Walter had applied for a grant from the Ministry of Works to keep the ruins safe and prevent them from deteriorating further, and in return he was obliged to open the grounds of Colwyn Court to the public once a month so that the taxpayers could see the castle and chapel on which their money had been spent. But few people came. There were no printed guidebooks available for them, no postcards, no snack bars or souvenir shops, and most of the tourists who visited the area could not be bothered to investigate what many would have considered to be "just another heap of old ruins."

Around the castle were about twenty of the wild horses from the family which had existed on the Colwyn estate since time out of mind. They were lean graceful animals with long necks, soft eyes, and tails which streamed in the wind whenever they galloped down the hill to the shore. They began to gallop now as Matt and the twins approached the castle, and a minute later the entire herd was thundering down the path which led into the next cove where a stream flowing into the sea provided the horses with a supply of fresh water.

"I'd like to live here," said Timothy. "Forever. In the castle with my own horse." When he saw that Matt was a few paces away and gazing down into Colwyn Cove he whispered to Lucy: "If Daddy got out of China—"

"Timmy, we'd agreed it was Tibet!"

"Maybe he's in India by now. Is India next to Tibet? But when he finally gets home—"

"With all his riches," said Lucy, "his jewels from the Taj Mahal, he could restore the castle and we could all live in it—"

"—forever," said Timothy, and added suddenly: "What's Uncle Matt looking at?"

"I don't know . . . Uncle Matt! What are you looking at?"

Matt did not answer so the twins wandered over to him to see for themselves.

"Why, it's Mummy!" said Lucy surprised. "On the beach! Who's that m '

'Let's go and find out," said Matt, and set off abruptly down the hill from the castle.

"Hey, wait for us!" cried Lucy.

"Wait, Uncle Matt!" called Timothy, but Matt barely

slackened his pace and they were obliged to run to keep up with him.

"They're leaving the beach," panted Timothy after a minute. "They'll just be at the top of the rocks by the time we get there."

"Let's race them," said Lucy, inspired by Matt's long strides. "Come on, Timmy, let's run!"

They ran, rushing downhill to the top of the beach, and presently arrived gasping for breath at the path which led from the beach to the cottage.

"Ooooh!" panted Lucy, clutching her side. "I've got a stitch!"

"Me too!" Timothy flopped down in the heather.

"Where's Mummy? Oh, here she comes. Gosh, the man with her looks like the man in that TV series."

"Which series?"

"*You* know, stupid . . . oh, he's not so like him after all. But he looks nice anyway. Nicer than the man in the TV series."

Timothy did not answer. He stood up slowly, watching his mother and thinking how pretty she looked. Her cheeks were pink from the sea breeze and her eyes were sparkling and her hair shimmered in the pale sunlight.

"Darlings!" said Lisa. "What a lovely surprise! Have you been to Colwyn Court already?"

"And up to the castle." Lucy looked at Poole. "Who's this?"

"This is Mr. Poole, who's the managing director of the society at Colwyn Court. Tristan, this is—"

"How do you do," said Lucy, jumping at the chance to demonstrate yet again how exquisitely she could behave if the occasion demanded it. She gave her sweetest, most innocent smile, the one that never failed, and said with her best diction: "We met Miss Miller at Colwyn Court just now. She mentioned you and told us all about your wonderful society. We thought she was such a nice lady, didn't we, Timothy?"

For some reason which he did not understand, Timothy was acutely embarrassed. He could feel himself blushing and turned away to hide his confusion.

Poole was smiling. He saw Timothy's discomfort and noted it. He saw Lucy's long, straight, fair hair, her wide, black-lashed, violet eyes and her rose-colored mouth, and noted that she was an exceptionally pretty child. He saw the innocence in her eyes and the angelic expression on her face and noted that she was lying about Agnes Miller. But he went on smiling.

"Hello, Lucy," he said pleasantly.

The child hesitated, but after a second smiled back willingly enough.

"Timothy, say how do you do to Mr. Poole," said Lisa sharply, but Timothy was rescued from having to respond by Matt's arrival on the scene. Lisa was at once diverted. "Matt," she began, "this is Mr. Tristan Poole, the managing director of the society at Colwyn Court . . . Tristan, this is my husband."

The two men looked at one another. There was a small pause before Poole held out his hand and murmured a conventional phrase.

Matt took the hand, shook it once and dropped it without a word. "Do you feel better?" he said without expression to his wife.

"Marvelous!" said Lisa rashly and added, making matters worse: "The sea air cured me completely!"

There was another pause.

"Tristan's invited us up to Colwyn Court for lunch," said Lisa in a rush. "All of us, I mean. I was just on my way up to the cottage to tell Jane not to bother to cook anything for us."

"I've made other plans," said Matt.

"Oh, but—"

Matt looked at her with an expression he had perfected in a thousand board meetings and she was silent.

"Some other time perhaps," said Poole carelessly. "There's no reason why it should have to be today. And now, if you'll excuse me . . ." He moved away, casual and unconcerned, and as he took the path up to Colwyn Court they could hear him whistling to himself before he disappeared from sight.

"Darlings," said Lisa to the twins, "run on ahead to the cottage for me, would you, and tell Aunt Jane I shan't be in for lunch."

The twins looked at Matt but Matt said nothing.

"Run along," said Lisa with a smile.

The twins turned and walked away toward the cottage without a word. After a moment they joined hands and began to walk two abreast on the narrow path, but they made no attempt to look back.

"All right," said Matt in a low voice. "Talk and talk fast. Just what the bloody hell's going on?"

"Matt, I—"

"And don't start lying or you'll be sorry! I saw what you were doing on the beach!"

"But Matt, we weren't doing anything—"

He slapped her across the mouth and she stepped backward with a gasp.

"Why, you—"

"I told you you'd be sorry," he said, "if you started lying."

"How dare you strike me like that! If you were a gentleman instead of someone who'd dragged himself out of a Birmingham backstreet—"

"Don't give me that kind of rubbish. If you were a lady instead of the selfish little bitch you are I wouldn't have laid a finger on you. Now look here, Lisa. I don't know who that man is and I don't know how long you've known him, but I know this: You're not seeing him again. If you're flirting with him to pay me back for not giving in to you about the Bahamas—"

"I wasn't flirting with him! Just because I choose to sit on the beach with an attractive man my own age—"

"You were lying full length on the sand and he was kissing you until he became aware that he was being watched. Don't be a damned fool, Lisa! You can't get out of this by lying, so why waste breath trying to? If the twins hadn't been here I'd have taken that man by the scruff of his neck and thrown him back onto the beach. You're not seeing him again and you're not going up to Colwyn Court for lunch."

"Oh, don't be so absurd, Matt! Walter will be there, and Gwyneth, and Tristan's assistant, Miss Miller—"

"Look," said Matt. "Do I really have to spell it out to you? I may be old-fashioned, but I have certain views and I've no intention of changing them. You're my wife, and as long as you're my wife you don't play around with other men. If I catch you so much as batting an eyelid at that bastard again, I'll—"

"Oh Matt!" Lisa burst into tears. The tears happened to be entirely genuine, but it was the cleverest move she could have made; like most men given to flexing the dominant side of their personalities, Matt was softhearted beneath the steel of his boardroom manner.

"Now Lisa . . ." He could feel himself weakening.

"You just don't understand me!" sobbed Lisa, twisting away from his outstretched arms, and stumbled off, still sobbing wildly, up the path to the shelter of the cottage.

But Matt was afraid he understood all too well.

IV

In the afternoon Jane took the twins down to the beach, Benedict returned to his work and Lisa remained in her bedroom to which she had retired before lunch. Matt was on his own. After considering several ways of passing the afternoon he rejected all of them and drove his car out of the Gower Peninsula toward Swansea. In the suburbs he stopped at a cluster of shops, found a telephone kiosk, and began to count his change for a London call.

"I want a person-to-person call," he told the operator. "To Miss Nicola Morrison. Hampstead 59611."

90

But Nicola was out. It was a Saturday and she had gone off on some expedition of her own.

"Sorry," he heard the roommate's cheerful voice say to the operator, "but I'll tell her who phoned as soon as she gets in." The operator had disclosed Matt's identity at the start of the call.

Matt sighed. He did not know why he had had such a strong urge to talk to his daughter but he felt alone and unhappy and Nicola was all the family he had in the world.

The telephone was ringing just as he walked through the front door of the cottage. Benedict, taking a nap upstairs, had not heard the bell, and no one else seemed to be about.

Matt picked up the receiver. "Hello?"

"Daddy? I've just got in. Judy said you'd phoned but I had an awful job getting through to the cottage—the operator said first of all that it wasn't on the phone. How's everything at Colwyn?"

"Well . . ." He glanced up the stairs to see if the door of Lisa's room was shut, but found he could not see the door from where he was standing. "Not too good. Walter's leased half the place to some crazy health-food group and I think Lisa's about to join."

"Oh Lord! Daddy, you're not serious, are you?"

He ignored that one. "Why don't you come down for a few days? Walter and Gwyneth were both asking after you when I saw them this morning."

"Oh, I couldn't possibly."

"Why not?"

"Well . . . my holiday doesn't crop up till September."

"Take it earlier."

"It would be too much of an inconvenience to my boss."

"Rubbish," said Matt. "No one's indispensable. That boss of yours would appreciate you more if you didn't fall in with his wishes just for once."

"Well . . ."

"Evan isn't here, you know. He's not due back till next week."

"It's got nothing to do with that," said Nicola, knowing perfectly well that her reluctance to visit Colwyn was because it was so full of memories of Evan and the good times they had had there together. "Nothing at all."

"Well, think about it. There's not much room here at the cottage but Gwyneth said there was still one spare room at Colwyn Court in spite of the damned society." He heard the door of Lisa's room open with a small creak. "How's life in Hampstead?"

"Fine. No news really."

"All right, well, look after yourself and try to get down here if you can. I hardly see anything of you nowadays."

Nicola felt guilty. After they had said good-bye and she had replaced the receiver she spent some time wishing that Lisa did not make visits home such a trial. And what had Matt meant about the society and Lisa's interest in it? Nicola frowned and wandered into the kitchen to make herself some coffee. For the first time she began to wonder if her father were as happily married as she had always assumed he was; her brief, uneasy visits home had given her no obvious hints that Matt and Lisa's relationship was not all it should have been.

She was still thinking of them ten minutes later when the phone rang. Judy was out by this time and Nicola was alone in the apartment. Tilting back her chair she reached for the receiver.

"Hello?"

There was a stream of pips from an STD phone before the coin dropped and the line cleared. She heard some assorted background sounds which suggested that the call was being made in a transport terminal; there was the distant drone of a loudspeaker announcement, the dull murmur of footsteps and voices.

"Hello?" repeated Nicola.

"Hello," said the voice she had told herself a thousand times she would never hear again. "So you're still at the same flat. How are you?"

92

The shock was so great that she could not speak. It was a hallucination, she thought. She was going mad.

"Nicki, are you there?"

He sounded just the same, terse and friendly, and suddenly she could see him, his red hair short and tousled, the freckled nose broken long ago at rugger, the blue, humorous eyes.

"It can't be," she said aloud. "You're not here till next week. It's a hoax."

"Some hoax!" He spoke lightly but she knew he was having trouble choosing his words. "I've been worried about my father and I managed to get away early from Africa. My plane arrived half an hour ago, and at the moment you're the only person in the entire country who knows I'm here."

"Is that a cue to swoon with delight?" She could have kicked herself as soon as the words were spoken; she had had no wish to sound so sarcastic.

"No, I don't expect that." She knew he was rebuffed and her heart ached. She wanted to say: "I'm so glad you're back! I'm so glad you phoned! Oh, how I'd love to see you again!" but all she found herself saying was: "When are you going down to Colwyn?"

"Tomorrow. But I thought I'd rest tonight in London to recover from the long journey. Look, Nicki—"

"Yes?" she said, her mouth dry.

"—you won't tell anyone I'm here, will you? I want to take them by surprise at Colwyn."

"All right."

There was a silence. I must say something, thought Nicola desperately, or he'll go away. "How was Africa?" she asked, saying the first thing that came into her head, and her words sounded horribly bright and false to her. "It must have been a wonderful experience."

"Yes."

Oh God, thought Nicola. She was clenching the phone so tightly her fingers hurt. Say something, she prayed silently. Please. Say something. Don't hang up. Please.

"Nicki," said Evan.

"Yes?"

"I had a lot of time to think in Africa."

"Oh."

"I would have written, but—"

"No, I told you not to."

"Yes, I know but . . . well, I almost wrote many times."

"Did you?" Tears filled her eyes. She had to struggle to keep her voice level.

"Yes, I . . . well, it seemed so unnecessary in retrospect. The way things ended . . . you understand? Although maybe you were justified in taking the line you did, but—"

"You were justified too," said Nicola. "I should have realized that going to Africa was something you had to do."

"Yes. Well . . ." She heard him take a deep breath. "I suppose you've got someone else by this time," said Evan, "but perhaps we could meet just for old time's sake. What do you think?"

"Why not?" said Nicola. Her blandness amazed and appalled her. How could she possibly sound so indifferent? She began to panic again. "Yes," she said, trying to sound enthusiastic but only managing to recapture that awful false brightness. "That would be nice."

"How about a drink tonight? As it's Saturday I suppose you'll have already made arrangements for dinner, but—"

"Not this Saturday," said Nicola.

"No? Well, how about dinner as well?"

She realized to her astonishment that she was crying. Huge tears were rolling silently down her cheeks. "Yes," she said. "I'd like that."

"Good. I'll hire a car and pick you up at six-thirty."

"Fine."

"Marvelous! See you soon, Nicki," he said, pleased, and was so excited he even forgot to say good-bye. Bursting out of the phone booth he grabbed his suitcases, collared a taxi, and sang out the address of the hotel in Central London where he had reserved a room for the night. He was home, he was within hours of seeing Nicola again, and as the cab swept him toward the city he forgot all his worries about his family and thought only of the evening to come.

V

After everyone else at the cottage had gone to bed that night Matt stayed up to write to his daughter. It was quiet. A few hundred yards away the sea was breaking on the sands but apart from the murmur of the surf and the tick of the grandfather clock by the stairs the house was silent. The twins were long since asleep; Lisa had gone upstairs complaining of a headache directly after dinner, and Benedict had stubbed out his last cigarette an hour ago to follow Jane upstairs to their room. Matt was alone.

". . . so that's how the land lies at the moment," he was writing to Nicola as he tried to unburden himself of his pain by spelling it out on paper. "By the way, have you ever heard of this man Tristan Poole? He's a youngish bloke about Lisa's age . . ."

That hurt, he thought looking at the words wryly and remembering that he was now nearer sixty than fifty. But it served him right for marrying a girl young enough to be his daughter.

". . . ordinary looking, nothing obviously special about him, casual sort of manner, polite and well spoken—I wondered if you might have bumped into him at one of your London parties, but maybe that would be too much of a long shot. However, I'm sure Lisa's met him before—can't believe she's only met him twice and both times just for a few minutes, though she swears that's the truth. She's been making a real fool of herself so far, but I think I've straightened things out a bit now . . ."

He wished Nicola were with him in the room. Nicola was the only person he could talk to when he was very depressed.

He remembered the hours they had spent together after her mother had died years ago. He had always felt very close to Nicola after that. Until he had married Lisa.

". . . yet I wish there were a hundred miles between Lisa and this so-and-so Poole," he wrote, his pen digging into the white paper so that the words glared boldly back at him. "I wouldn't be surprised if he was something of a crook. Walter Colwyn's one of the most gullible men under the sun and you know how things are with Gwyneth . . ."

The door creaked. He looked up sharply but it was only the cat coming in from the kitchen.

". . . I think Evan will have something to say about affairs at Colwyn Court once he gets back from Africa. I hope he doesn't find that Poole's conned Walter out of his home and fortune . . ."

Marble sat on the hearth and began to wash his paws.

". . . sorry this is all about Poole but the blighter happens to have upset me. I can tell you, if I find Lisa messing around with him again there'll be all hell to pay because I'm too proud to stomach that sort of thing, and that's a fact. I'd rather be divorced than made a fool of—and the truth is I don't think Lisa would mind a divorce if it weren't for the money. Well, she'll get my money when I'm alive but that's it. If there's any more fuss I'll see she doesn't get a penny after I'm dead . . ."

He stopped. He suddenly realized that the cat had sprung onto the dresser behind him and was breathing down his neck.

"Off!" said Matt sternly, and when the cat did not move he gave it a shove onto the floor.

Marble yelped. His pink eyes narrowed to hostile slits.

Matt added a sentence to finish the letter, addressed an envelope, and put the letter inside. It was time to go to bed. Leaving the sealed letter on the table he went slowly upstairs to his room where Lisa was pretending to be asleep, and the living room was plunged into darkness as he switched off the light.

Marble waited for several minutes. Then, when even the light beneath Matt's bedroom door had vanished, he sprang onto the table, picked the letter up between his sharp white teeth, and disappeared silently into the night.

VI

"That's odd," said Matt. "Jane, did you move the letter I left on the table last night?"

"Letter? No, I didn't. I don't think I even noticed it. Benedict, did you see a letter which Matt left on the table in the living room?"

"There wasn't one," said Benedict. "I was downstairs at seven and there was nothing on the living-room table. I particularly noticed because I put my foot on the chair there to retie a shoelace."

"Twins," said Jane, "did you see a letter Uncle Matt left on the living-room table last night?"

"No," said Timothy. "What's for breakfast, Aunt Jane?"

"Sausages and eggs. Lucy, did you—"

"No," said Lucy yawning. "Can I have my egg poached, please?"

"Not today, it's too complicated. I'm scrambling them all," said Jane, and added to Matt. "Are you sure you left it there?"

"It's all right," said Matt. "I think I can guess what happened." And he went swiftly upstairs to his room.

Lisa was dressed and sitting at the dressing table examining her mascara brush. She looked up as he came in.

"Okay," said Matt. "Where is it?"

"Where's what?" said Lisa astonished.

"The letter I wrote to Nicola last night."

"My dear Matt! Why on earth should I take a letter you wrote to Nicola?"

"Because I said a few uncomplimentary things to Nicola about your precious Mr. Poole!"

97

Lisa did not know whether to feel bewildered, angry, or indignant. In the end anger won. "How dare you tell Nicola about what happened between me and Tristan!"

"So you did take it," said Matt.

"I didn't!"

"Then how did you know I'd told Nicola you'd made a fool of yourself with that man!"

"You said—"

"I said I told her about Poole. I didn't tell you what it was I said."

"But I thought—"

"Where is it, Lisa?"

"But I didn't take it!" said Lisa desperately. "I didn't!"

"You got up in the night, went downstairs—"

"I never moved from this room!" Anger blazed through her again. "How dare you tell that daughter of yours about our private and personal troubles!"

"You think everyone doesn't know about them already?" He turned, made sure the door was tightly shut, and swung back to face her. "All right," he said shortly. "Let's sit down and consider this quietly for a moment. I think it's time you and I had a very serious talk together."

VII

An hour later a disheveled and breathless Lisa arrived at Colwyn Court and asked to speak to Tristan Poole.

"I'll fetch him," said Agnes when the message was brought to her in the kitchens. "Show her into the sitting room." She had just finished delegating the morning's chores and was herself helping to dry the breakfast dishes.

Poole was in his room. When she knocked he came to the door.

"Yes?"

"Lisa's here to see you."

"Trouble?"

"I've no idea—I haven't seen her."

He turned back into his room without a word. She saw one of his books was lying open on the bedside table, and in the dressing room beyond the black box was unlocked and the lid thrown back.

"Was there some complication, Tristan?"

"Morrison's hard to control. He's a tough customer." He shut the book with a bang and went into the dressing room to replace it in the black box. When he returned all he said was a casual: "Where is she?"

"Downstairs in the sitting room."

"All right, I'll see her." He gave Agnes a folded sheet of notepaper as he passed her in the doorway. "Read that and burn it."

"Yes, Tristan." She glanced down and began to read Matt's letter to Nicola.

She was still in his room, still looking at the letter, when he rejoined her ten minutes later. He found her sitting on the edge of the bed and looking thoughtful; as he entered the room she looked up with a start.

"Has she gone already?"

"She's still there. I had to have a quick word with you. Listen, Agnes, this marriage is disintegrating much too fast for my liking. I hoped we'd find him the doting husband anxious to shower his young wife with everything he possessed but as you can see from the letter, it isn't like that at all—quite the reverse, in fact. They had a bad quarrel this morning when he blamed her for the lost letter, and one thing led to another until the word divorce was being bandied around like a ping-pong ball. It was a pity about the letter, of course, but it might have had unfortunate repercussions if it had been sent and anyway the marriage is so rocky that if the letter hadn't started the latest quarrel something else would have done. So we've got to act and act fast. She says Morrison took the car and drove off to Swansea in a rage—the situation's highly inflammable, but I reckon we've still got twenty-four hours before he makes any definite move which would be adverse to us. Now this is what I want you to do: drive down to the village, go to the public phone box there, and call me here at Colwyn Court. I'll take the call in the sitting room in Lisa's presence and tell her I've had an urgent summons to Swansea. That'll get her out of the way. Then, when you come back, make sure no one disturbs me. How are we off for sacrifices?"

"We've got four black cocks and six hares at the moment."

"Good. Bring one of the cocks to my room. After the sacrifice I'll give you the bloodstained knife and you can cut the hazel rod for the wand while I take a bath and get into my robes. Oh, and purify my room, please. You'd better do that first. Use juice from laurel leaves, camphor, white resin, and sulfur—and don't omit the salt. I know salt is anathema to us all, but it does represent purity and I want to run no risk of the room not being purified. We're running enough risks as it is by not cutting the hazel rod at dawn and taking all the other routine precautions, but time's running against us so we have no choice."

"Yes, Tristan. And when you're ready—shall I help you draw the circle? Would you like me to be in attendance?"

"Did you eat breakfast this morning?"

Agnes' face fell.

"I'm sorry, Agnes, but I'd better have someone who's at least gone through the motions of fasting. Who's dieting hard enough at present to have skipped breakfast?"

"There's Jackie. But—"

"She'll do. I'll need a clairvoyant anyway."

"Try Sandra," suggested Agnes. "Her powers are so much better developed in that direction, and she never has more than a glass of orange juice for breakfast."

"No, it's time Jackie earned her keep, and besides it'll alleviate her boredom with country life for a few hours. Oh, and Agnes—"

"Yes, Tristan?"

"Summon the cat."

Matt was a man accustomed to summing up evidence and making a quick decision under pressure. He had been conducting his business affairs in that manner for over thirty years and when the opportunity presented itself to him he had no hesitation in handling his private affairs in exactly the same way. The latest bitter quarrel with Lisa had presented him with what he considered was irrefutable evidence: his wife did not love him, had secretly wanted a divorce for some time, and had only hesitated because of his money and material possessions. All right, he thought furiously, all right. Perhaps it was his fault for losing his head in a middle-aged infatuation with a girl such as Lisa. Perhaps he shouldn't have married her in the first place. But they had married and the marriage had failed and now he wanted to recognize the fact by severing his marital ties to Lisa as soon as possible. Matt preferred to be honest. He preferred to face the truth, accept it, and learn to live with it. It was part of the strength on which he had always prided himself. So now he faced the end of his marriage, and in facing it he faced it in his own hardheaded practical way and immediately began to think about his money.

As soon as he reached Swansea that morning he went to one of the largest hotels, used their writing room for ten minutes, and then made a long-distance call from the public phone in the lobby.

A string of rules, learned long ago when he had been making his way in the world, kept flickering back and forth in his mind. Never put off till tomorrow what you can do today. Examine the evidence, make the decision, and stick to it. Indecision and hesitation lost both time and money. Indecision and hesitation were signs of weakness.

Just before he made the phone call he thought: men of my age drop dead with coronaries every day. Leave nothing to chance. Nothing.

His conversation on the phone lasted some time because

the man on the other end of the wire was so doubtful and disapproving, but at last it was over and Matt was able to complete the necessary formalities of the task he had set himself. His next step was to consider what he should do next. After some consideration he decided to return to the cottage to see what had happened in his absence; if Lisa had gone he would stay on to complete his holiday as planned, but if she were still there he would have to forgo the holiday and leave the cottage himself. He found himself wondering what would happen to the twins. Would Lisa take them with her when she left the cottage or would she leave them with Jane while she saw her lawyers and tried to reorganize her private life? He did not know, but his mouth twisted in bitter regret as he thought of them.

The drive out of Swansea was uneventful, but as he entered the Gower Peninsula he increased the speed of the car until he was cutting corners on the empty road and ignoring the signs posting the speed limit. A light rain began to fall as he approached Colwyn; the open landscape looked bleak as it stretched to the gray blur of the sea. By this time he was in farming country, and on either side of the road stood the stone walls which bordered the fields.

He did not see the cat until too late. He swung around a corner and there it was, sitting in the middle of the road and washing its damnable white paws as if it had every right in the world to sit there.

Shouting a curse, Matt slammed on the brakes and wrenched the wheel. The last thing he saw before the car slewed out of control was the cat leaping for safety, its white fur flying and its skin drawn back in a sneer from its sharp malevolent teeth.

4

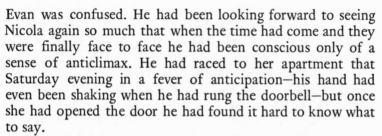

I

Evan was confused. He had been looking forward to seeing Nicola again so much that when the time had come and they were finally face to face he had been conscious only of a sense of anticlimax. He had raced to her apartment that Saturday evening in a fever of anticipation—his hand had even been shaking when he had rung the doorbell—but once she had opened the door he had found it hard to know what to say.

Even now, at the end of the evening, he could not understand what had happened. Why, he asked himself in bewilderment, should he feel so disappointed? It was not that she did not look her best. Her shining dark hair curled softly upward at the ends, just as it always had; her gray eyes were just as wide, just as steady and just as beautiful as he remembered. But the spontaneity he had liked so much had ebbed; she seemed more serious, more withdrawn, and much harder to approach. Finally he decided it was the formality of her manner which grated on him the most.

"Would you like to come in and have a drink before we leave?" she had asked him politely when he had arrived at the apartment at six-thirty, and he had been unable to tell whether she had wanted him to accept the invitation or not.

"Well . . . I don't want to disturb your roommate—"

"She went home for the weekend this afternoon."

"Oh. Well, perhaps later . . ."

But later he wasn't asked.

"Can I come up?" he said at last after that baffling evening during which he had sustained a seemingly endless conversation about Africa. The taxi had halted outside the house where Nicola had her flat, and he had helped her out of the car before paying off the driver.

"Yes, all right," she said without much interest and turned away as he told the driver not to wait.

They went into the house, through the hall and up the stairs to the landing without saying a word. Evan wondered why he had invited himself in. After such a stilted evening his first impulse should have been to escape as soon as possible, but some stubborn instinct made him insist on extending the evening until he had made contact with Nicola on a more intimate level. He felt he had invested so much time thinking about her while he was in Africa that it would be too humiliating now to turn his back on her without a struggle to understand what had happened.

"Coffee?" she said in that polite voice he had come to detest.

"Please." He began to roam around the living room while she went into the kitchen. After a minute he could feel the frustration welling inside him till he could bear it no longer. "Nicki."

"Yes?"

"What happened?"

She looked up with a start. "Nothing! What do you mean?"

"There's someone else, isn't there."

"No." She thrust the kettle onto the stove and turned on the gas. "It's instant coffee—I hope you don't mind."

"Would you rather I left?"

She shook her head violently and began to drag the cups and saucers from the cabinet.

"Who is he?"

No answer. Anger began to mingle with Evan's frustration. "Why didn't you tell me to get lost if you didn't want to see me again? Why lead me on? What was the point?"

"I did want to see you again. I'm sorry the evening was a failure." She had her back to him and was shoveling the coffee jerkily into the cups.

"Oh, for God's sake!" He tried to clamp down on his rage. "Let's stop playing around, shall we? Why don't we get right down to the truth? You've found someone else, you saw me merely as a friendly gesture for old times' sake, and I've made a complete fool of myself. That's the way it is, isn't it?"

No answer.

"Are you sleeping with him?"

That got to her. He saw her back stiffen with pride and her head jerk up.

"No."

"So there *is* someone else!"

"No."

"Then why—"

"No, no, no!" She whirled to face him, her composure gone, her eyes bright with tears. "There's no one else—no one, no one, no one! Now go away and leave me alone!"

"Nicki . . ." When he took her in his arms she made no effort to push him away. He began to kiss her. On the stove the kettle began to boil but neither of them noticed.

"Evan, I—"

He kissed her on the mouth, and suddenly everything was as he remembered and her body was soft and yielding against his own.

"Oh, how I've missed you!" he heard her say when her mouth was free again. "Oh, how I've longed for you to be here . . ."

He was hazily aware of steam from a boiling kettle and the harsh glare from the overhead light, but he had forgotten where he was. The world was reduced to shining dark hair and smooth, silky skin and his own aching longing.

105

"Here . . ." He kept one arm tightly around her waist and groped for the door.

"Evan—"

He picked her up to avoid argument. It was so easy to swing her off her feet and edge out of the kitchen toward the closed door of the bedroom.

"Open the door," he said to her as he held her in his arms, and waited for her to reach out with her free hand, but she did not. "Go on, open it."

"Evan, I—"

He set her down, flung open the door so violently that it shuddered on its hinges, and turned to pull her into the bedroom with him, but she had moved away.

"Nicki," he said. "Nicki."

She stood there looking at him, and there was a silence. At last she said: "You must think I'm an awful fool."

"Look, I love you. I'm crazy about you. I—"

"So you said fifteen months ago. Those were your exact words."

"Things are different now—"

"They'd damned well better be," she said, "or I want no part of it."

"Listen, I—"

"No!" she said, suddenly as spontaneous and honest as he remembered her to be. "No, you listen to me for a change! For three whole years, ever since my father remarried and I happened to meet you and your family through Lisa and Jane, I've been mooning around over you like some teen-ager with a crush on the current teen idol. After the first eighteen months—during which you barely noticed my existence—you finally looked down from your high and mighty cloud and noticed me. Marvelous! No wonder I lost my head and acted like a crazy schoolgirl without an ounce of sense! All right, so you went away. Served me right. It was no more than I deserved. I then had a whole year to recover. Fine! Just what I needed! And yet now—*now* you have the insufferable nerve to wander back from Africa, glance down from your high cloud again, and think you can carry on exactly where you left off! How dare you think that! If you knew what I've been going through all these months while you've been flexing your noble soul in the wilds of Africa—"

"I'm sorry. I didn't mean it to seem that way."

"Well, it did!"

"But Nicki—"

She backed away from him into the kitchen. "Don't ask me to do what you want now," she said, "because I won't. I'm too scared of getting hurt again."

"But Nicki, I promise—"

"Yes?" she said fiercely, turning off the kettle. "What do you promise?"

But Evan wasn't sure. It seemed to be the wrong moment for a proposal, and besides he wasn't at all certain he ought to propose until he had settled down again in England, straightened out his family problems, and decided what to do next. "All right," he said at last, turning away automatically toward the front door. "If that's the way you want it."

"Evan—"

"Yes?" He was aware of swinging around much too quickly, betraying how much he wanted her to change her mind.

"Don't you want your coffee?"

"Oh . . ." He ran his hand impatiently through his hair. "No, perhaps another time . . . Listen, Nicki, I'll phone you next week from Wales when I feel more settled—maybe you could come down to Colwyn for a long weekend—"

"All right," she said. "I'll expect to hear from you." She moved toward him as he opened the front door. "Thanks for the dinner. I'm sorry if you think I'm stupid—it's not that I don't care—"

"I know," he said, and the longing for her swept over him again so violently that he hardly dared risk even the quickest of kisses. "Take care of yourself," he mumbled. "Nice seeing you. 'Bye." And the next moment he was running downstairs two at a time and racing up the road as if he could dissolve the violence of his emotions in a burst of physical energy.

107

There was a train to Swansea at three o'clock the following afternoon. After a morning which he spent walking feverishly around the park and absorbing the sights and sounds of London again he returned to his hotel room to find the telephone ringing by his bedside.

Nicola was the only person who knew he was in England. He grabbed the receiver so fast he nearly dropped it. "Hello?"

"Evan . . ." Her voice was muffled and far away. He hardly recognized it.

"Nicki?" he said doubtfully.

"Oh, Evan, I—" He heard her choke back a sob.

"What's happened?" he demanded at once. "What is it? What's the matter?"

"I've just heard from Wales . . . Jane phoned . . . about my father, he—had an accident—driving . . . oh Evan, he's dead, I can't believe it, it was a car accident—an open road, no other car involved—he skidded into one of those stone walls and was killed instantly—"

"I'm on my way over," said Evan, the words tumbling out of his mouth in his desire to be with her when she needed him. "Give me ten minutes. I'll be with you just as soon as I possibly can."

II

"Millionaire Industrialist Killed in Car Smash," intoned the Monday editions of the popular press, giving Benedict yet another chance to deplore the vulgarity of the word millionaire. "Mystery Death on Lonely Welsh Road."

"Morrison Inquest Rules Accidental Death," said the Thursday editions. "Coroner Cautions Against Fast Driving."

None of the papers mentioned when or where the funeral was to be held for the simple reason that none of them knew. Matt's secretaries and aides had descended on Colwyn after his death, consulted Nicola who had arrived at Colwyn Court with Evan on Sunday night, and, in between issuing statements to the press, had made the arrangements for a quiet funeral at the village in Surrey where Matt had lived since his second marriage. The secretaries and aides had tried to consult Lisa about the funeral arrangements, but Lisa had been too incoherent to do more than advise them to talk to Nicola instead.

"Poor Lisa's quite prostrate with grief," said Walter, worried, to Agnes Miller. "I feel so sorry for her."

"Poor soul," said Agnes sympathetically. "What a terrible tragedy for a young girl."

"That just shows," said Gwyneth, who had always admired Lisa's glamour, "all those people who said cattily that Lisa married Matt for his money were wrong as could be. She really did love him."

If only I had loved him a little more, thought Lisa in an agony of guilt. If only I could feel grief instead of this awful secret relief that it's all over without the sordidness of a divorce. If only I could talk to someone about how I really feel. If only . . .

If only Tristan Poole had not been summoned away to London for a week on one of his mysterious visits.

She had not dared attempt to see him for the first two days after Matt's death, but at the inquest she had spoken to Agnes Miller, who had told her of Poole's absence from Colwyn. Lisa had wanted to ask her for a phone number where he could be reached, but her nerve failed her. She had not even dared ask when Poole would be returning, although Agnes eventually told her that he was expected back within the week. She was trying very hard not to think of Poole, but the more she longed for someone to confide in the more she longed to see him. At last, unable to bear the isolation of her guilt any longer, she turned to her sister.

"I feel so awful, Jane," she said on the evening after the inquest. They were in the kitchen; Jane was preparing dinner in her haphazard way and Lisa was not sure Jane was concentrating on what she was saying; however, so desperate was her longing to confide in someone that she took no notice of Jane's air of abstraction. "If only Matt and I hadn't quarreled so badly just before he died—"

"Yes, I know," said Jane. "It must be awful, darling. But we all know how much you loved each other despite your troubles. Don't think we don't understand."

"But I didn't love him!" said Lisa wildly. "I'm glad he's dead!"

"Oh, Lisa, darling, you're just upset—you don't know what you're saying . . ."

It was hopeless. Lisa gave up. The next morning, Thursday, they all left the cottage and drove to Surrey for the funeral, which was to be held on Friday afternoon.

Matt's battered Rolls Royce was still in the hands of one of the large Swansea garages, so Benedict drove Lisa and Walter to Surrey in his Austin while Evan followed in Walter's more spacious Bentley with Nicola, Jane, and the twins. Nicola had spent a blurred, confused five days at Colwyn Court, vaguely aware of Walter's kindness, Jane's concern, and Evan's grave attentiveness. She had barely noticed the society's existence. Evan had said to her once or twice that he intended to have a heart-to-heart talk with his father when events had returned to normal, but she had not understood what he meant. She had hardly spoken to Lisa. Lisa had burst into tears as soon as they had met and after that Nicola had avoided her for fear that such noisy grief would be so contagious that she would break down and be unable to pull herself together.

"You ought to cry," said Evan. "It's the natural thing to do. Although I do realize," he added quickly, remembering a book he had once read on psychology, "that grief takes people different ways." It would never do to make her feel guilty because for some reason she felt unable to shed any tears.

"I have cried," said Nicola, "but I don't want to follow Lisa's example and be constantly weeping on the nearest available shoulder."

"Lisa can't help herself, I dare say."

"She can't help being a hypocrite. She only married Daddy for his money."

"I don't think Lisa's as bad as all that," said Evan before he could stop himself, and realized too late that he had said the wrong thing.

"All men say that," said Nicola, and went off for a walk without him.

Evan's immediate reaction was to feel exasperated with her, but he managed to summon his patience and check his irritation. He told himself it was no use expecting her to respond to him in a more normal way until the funeral was over and her shock was on the wane, so in an effort to divert his thoughts from her he turned his attentions to the others. But there was little he could do. Jane and Benedict were shocked but calm; Lisa was tearful but recovering; the twins were unexpectedly phlegmatic.

"All people die when they get old," said Lucy plainly. "What was sad was that this was an accident. That was what was sad."

"The accident was the worst part," echoed Timothy.

"Much the worst. Poor Uncle Matt."

"It's too bad for Mum," said Timothy, "but it's good too."

"Why's that?" said Evan.

"Because . . . just because."

"She's free now," said Lucy."

"Yes, she can get married again one day."

Evan saw them exchange private knowing glances.

"It'll all come right in the end," said Lucy mysteriously, "won't it, Timmy?"

"Of course," said Timothy.

Evan wondered what was going on but made no further effort to discover why the twins should be thinking of their mother's possible remarriage. He had already decided that it would be no surprise to him if Lisa had a lover; after talking to her he had had the suspicion that although her distress was sincere the source of her distress was more obscure than anyone had guessed.

But Lisa did not know that of all the people at Colwyn Court Evan came closest to understanding her. She made no effort to confide in him more fully, and on the day of her return to Surrey she was so busy nerving herself for the funeral that even her guilt was pushed to one side. At last when all the guests were settled in their rooms she was about to retire to bed for an early night when the maid told her that someone wished to speak to her on the telephone.

"If it's the press," said Lisa, "I don't want to talk to them."

"He said he wasn't the press, madam," said the maid. "I asked to make sure. He said he was the director of some society about nature foods—"

"I'll speak to him," said Lisa and flew upstairs to her room.

The receiver slipped in her moist palm. Her heart was banging against her ribs. "Hullo?" she said in a low voice. "Tristan?"

"How are you?"

"Oh . . ." She paused to get her breath. Various conventional phrases slithered around in her mind but she could not decide which one to choose.

"My condolences about the accident."

She tried to say "thank you" but he spoke again before she could frame the words with her lips.

"Are you all right?"

"No, I'm not," she said in a rush. "I feel terrible. I must talk to you. Please. It's so urgent."

"When's the funeral?"

"Tomorrow afternoon. Three o'clock."

"At Wickerfield Church?"

"Yes. It's going to be very quiet. Just the family and one or two of Matt's oldest friends."

"All right," he said. "I'll be in touch with you afterward."

"When?" she said. "Where? Is there some number where I can—"

"I'll be in touch with you," he said in a quiet voice which made her close her eyes weakly in relief. "Good night, Lisa."

And before she could say another word she found herself listening to the hum of an empty line.

III

Near the end of the service she glanced up and saw him. The mourners were outside, grouped around the open grave as the clergyman read the last part of the service, and overhead the sky was overcast with dark clouds. Poole was standing by the lych-gate, and for a moment she thought he was going to enter the churchyard to join them but he did not. He wore a black suit and a black tie and stood watching silently from his position outside the boundaries of the consecrated ground.

As soon as the service was over and the clergyman had closed his book Lisa turned, oblivious of the arm Benedict offered her, and walked quickly toward the lych-gate.

"Who the devil's that?" muttered Evan to Benedict.

"God knows," said Benedict.

Lightning flashed far away beyond the hills; thunder rumbled menacingly in the distance.

"Never saw him before in my life," said Benedict, after polishing his glasses to make sure.

"Benedict," whispered Jane, catching his sleeve. "That's Mr. Poole."

"I think it's going to rain," said the clergyman kindly to Nicola. "It's just as well we held the service when we did."

"Yes," said Nicola. She felt numb and lost. She didn't want to talk to anyone.

"Maybe I can come back to the house with you for a few minutes, Nicola," said a familiar voice. "There's something I think I should speak to you about."

She turned. It was one of her father's oldest friends, the solicitor Peter Marshall who was the senior partner of the firm of Tate, Marshall, Marshall and Tate.

"Oh." She tried to collect herself. "Yes, of course." For the first time she noticed that Lisa had gone on ahead and was talking to some unknown man by the lych-gate.

"Are you all right, Nicki?" said Evan's voice at her side.

She nodded, unable to speak and suddenly terrified of breaking down, but to her relief Walter came to her rescue by diverting Evan's attention.

"Evan," he called. "Let me introduce you to Mr. Poole."

Evan tried not to look annoyed and moved reluctantly toward the stranger who stood in the shadow of the lych-gate.

He saw a man of his own age who looked as though he might be a useful tennis player. The stranger had that silky kind of athletic slimness which would look more at home on a tennis court than on a rugger field or a cricket pitch. A bit soft, thought Evan who had always privately considered tennis a woman's game, and then remembered that the man had bulldozed himself and twelve strangers into Colwyn Court. The hackles rose on the back of Evan's neck. Dislike washed through his body in a huge, silent tide.

"How do you do," said Poole, very courteous.

"How do you do," said Evan shortly and was silent.

"And this is Nicola Morrison," said Walter, feeling it necessary to gloss over any further conversation between his son and his guest. "Nicola, my dear, this is Mr. Tristan Poole, the director of our society at Colwyn Court."

"How do you do, Miss Morrison," said Poole. "Please accept my sympathy."

"Thank you . . ." She was hardly aware of him. She had a vague picture of a man who was shorter and narrower than Evan, a man with nondescript features and some brownish hair. She did not even notice the color of his eyes.

". . . my cousin Benedict Shaw," Walter was saying. "I don't think the two of you have ever met."

"No, we haven't," said Poole. "How do you do, Professor Shaw. I've spoken to your wife a couple of times but you were always too elusive for me."

114

"It's a pity we have to meet on such a sad occasion," Benedict murmured. He was wondering why Jane had found the fellow so sinister. He seemed rather a nice young chap, a little like one of his assistant lecturers up at Cambridge.

"Good afternoon, Mrs. Shaw," said Poole to Jane, and smiled at her. "The twins aren't here, I see."

"We thought it would be too upsetting for them," said Jane awkwardly.

"I don't believe in children going to funerals," said Lisa. "Tristan, let's go."

They all looked at her in surprise.

"Go where?" said Benedict sharply, and took a second look at Poole.

"I've offered Lisa a lift back to her house in my car," said Poole. "I hope that doesn't upset any arrangements. All right, Lisa, I'm sure you want to get home—my car's over there under the oak tree."

"Oh dear," murmured Jane in the silence which followed. "Oh dear, oh dear." She knew her sister had done the wrong thing and was embarrassed for her.

"Poole meant well, I'm sure," said Walter innocently.

So that's how the land lies, thought Evan. Aloud he said: "How long has she known him?"

"Does it matter?" said Nicola. She turned blindly toward the waiting cars. "Let's follow their example and go back to the house before it begins to rain."

The thunder rumbled again in the distance as if on cue; large drops of rain spattered from the darkening skies.

"Nicola's right," said Evan. "Let's go."

Nobody said much on the way back to Wickerfield Manor. When they arrived at Matt's home Nicola was about to dash away to the comforting solitude of her room when she remembered that her father's solicitor was probably on the point of arriving to talk to her.

"When Mr. Marshall arrives," she said hastily to the maid, "show him into my father's study. I'll be waiting for him there."

"Can I do anything?" said Evan, appearing suddenly at her elbow.

"What? Oh, no thanks . . . it's all right. Daddy's solicitor is arriving soon to see me. I suppose it's about the will or something horrible like that."

It was. Mr. Marshall arrived two minutes later and suggested to Nicola that Lisa should be present.

"It won't take long," he said. "But now the funeral's over, I feel I really must speak to you both about one or two things."

"Of course," said Nicola mechanically and went in search of Lisa. After hunting for several minutes she braved the rain, which was now falling heavily, and ran across the lawn to the summer house. They were there. They must have watched her run across the lawn, for neither of them looked surprised to see her when she reached them. She noticed Lisa's defensive expression but ignored it.

"Lisa, could I interrupt you for a few minutes, please? Peter Marshall's here and he wants to talk to us both. Excuse us, Mr. Poole."

"Of course," said the man. "Would you like me to go back to the house and bring an umbrella for you both? It seems to be raining much harder now."

"Please don't bother," said Nicola. "It only takes a minute to run across the lawn. But thank you all the same."

Lightning flared unexpectedly. Lisa jumped, covering her ears as the thunder crashed overhead.

"I'm so afraid of storms!"

"I'll come with you to the house," said Poole. He slipped off his jacket and draped it around her shoulders. "That'll save you from getting too wet."

She flashed him a grateful smile.

Nicola stopped, suddenly aware of the potential of their relationship. Could Lisa possibly . . . on the day of her husband's funeral . . . no, surely not even Lisa would have the nerve to do such a thing! She heard herself say sharply: "Are you staying here, Mr. Poole?"

"No," he said. "I leave for London tonight."

So he at least had some decency, even if Lisa had none. She was so angry she did not trust herself to say anything else. Lightning blazed again as she left the summer house and tore across the lawn through the rain to the French windows of the living room. When Lisa and Poole joined her seconds later she still said nothing but merely led the way across the hall to Matt's study where Mr. Marshall was waiting.

Mr. Marshall seemed to find it difficult to know where to begin. He started by saying how shocked he had been by the tragedy and how deeply he sympathized with both Lisa and Nicola. He said he had long considered Matt one of his closest friends and how said it was to be called upon to execute his will. He then said what a difficult and painful task it was for him to tell them what was in the will. He even admitted he was not altogether sure how to put the contents into words.

"Please, Peter," said Nicola, beginning to feel desperate and well aware that Lisa was on the verge of one of her contagious crying bouts, "don't worry about upsetting us. We couldn't be more upset than we are already and I for one don't care much about what was in Daddy's will anyway. I suppose most of it goes in taxes."

"This is true," said Mr. Marshall, secretly relieved by this plain talking. "However, he had to some extent made arrangements to avoid death duties. Eight years ago he disposed of a large portion of his money in your favor, Nicola, and I'm happy to tell you that you are now in possession of a fund of some half a million pounds which is not subject to death duties."

"Oh," said Nicola blankly.

My God, thought Lisa, half a million pounds outright. My God. She had to grip the sides of her chair tightly for self-control.

"Don't tell me all my share goes to support the Welfare State, Peter," she said with a light little laugh. "But I suppose it does since Matt and I hadn't been married long enough to enable him to avoid death duties where I was concerned."

"This is true," said Mr. Marshall again, and opened his mouth to say something else but nothing came out.

"How much did Matt leave?" said Lisa. "I suppose you can't count this previous arrangement for Nicola as that sum wasn't officially part of the estate."

"This is true," said Mr. Marshall. He cleared his throat. "The exact dimensions of the estate are not known at present but it seems likely that it will be in the nature of at least three million pounds . . ."

That means twenty percent of three million for me, thought Lisa. Six hundred thousand pounds. Or are death duties higher than eighty percent? But I'll get at least three hundred thousand and probably more. Perhaps five hundred thousand. Half a million pounds.

"Originally," said Mr. Marshall, clearing his throat again, "the money was left to you outright, Lisa, since Nicola was already well provided for, and there were certain legacies, of course—one thousand pounds to each of your children—"

"How terribly generous of him," said Lisa, tears springing to her eyes. "They were so fond of him."

"—and various other bequests," Mr. Marshall was saying. "However—" He took a deep breath—"shortly before he died Matt did a very . . . well, it was a very strange thing. I tried to talk him out of it—tried to tell him to wait for a while—"

"What do you mean?" said Lisa. "What did he do?"

"He executed a codicil to his will. He actually telephoned me on the morning he died to check that he had the wording right. In the codicil he said—"

"It's not legal, of course," said Lisa.

"Well, actually," said Mr. Marshall, going to bright pink, "I'm very much afraid that it is, Lisa. He wrote that the words 'National Society for the Prevention of Cruelty to Children' should be substituted for your name whenever it appeared in the will."

There was a silence. Lisa had turned a greenish shade of white.

"As a matter of fact," said Mr. Marshall, "you'd probably

find a judge more than sympathetic to your case. Of course the purpose of the law in construing a will is to follow the testator's wishes and decide what he meant by what he said, but . . . well, a wife is usually entitled to something . . . mitigating circumstances . . . if I were you I'd—"

"I'll contest it," said Lisa.

"Well, take counsel's opinion anyway. I can't act for you, naturally, but I can recommend an excellent solicitor, a friend of mine—"

"Thank you," said Lisa. "Please leave his name and address and I'll get in touch with him on Monday. Excuse me." And rising awkwardly to her feet she stumbled across the room, wrenched open the door, and ran sobbing down the corridor in search of Tristan Poole.

IV

When Poole returned to his unobtrusive London hotel that night he immediately placed a call to Colwyn Court.

Agnes' sister Harriet Miller answered the phone.

"Get Agnes," was all Poole said.

"Yes, Tristan." He could hear the shock in her voice and knew his brusqueness had startled her. There was a pause. Then:

"What happened?" said Agnes.

"Agnes, why the hell did you let me use Jackie as an acolyte instead of Sandra?"

"But I thought Jackie did so well! She told you exactly when Morrison was leaving Swansea, exactly when he reached Colwyn—she provided such a complete monitoring service for you, I thought! After all, I know the demon you summoned to the circle to possess the cat was anxious to do your bidding, but the demon had to be guided and if Jackie had been inaccurate with her forecast—" She stopped abruptly, aware of the silence at the other end of the wire.

"Have you quite finished?" said Poole politely.

"Yes, Tristan. I'm sorry. How did Jackie fail?"

"I asked her what he was doing in Swansea and she told me he was having a talk with an old friend."

"And wasn't he?"

"You bet he was! His goddamned lawyer on the goddamned phone! Sandra could have told me that! But Jackie makes it seem as if Morrison's dropping in at a garden party and chatting about the latest fish he'd caught! You can tell Jackie that if she ever wants to achieve any real credibility in that field of work she'd better learn to concentrate on the job instead of letting part of her mind get lost somewhere along the astral line!"

"Oh dear," said Agnes nervously. "I'm so sorry, Tristan. You're right—I shouldn't have let you use her. I must say, I did have my doubts, but—"

"Yes, you did. All right, Agnes, it was really more my fault than yours. I should have taken her limitations more fully into consideration."

"But what did Morrison say to his lawyer? You're not trying to tell me he—"

"He executed a codicil to his will."

"Oh no!"

"Of course I don't have to tell you what was in the codicil."

"He left little Lisa penniless," said Agnes with a sinking heart.

"She may not be penniless in the long run but after the government has taken eighty percent of the estate and after Lisa's paid her lawyers she's not going to have more than peanuts to play around with. Morrison left the money—or what's left of it after taxes—to the N.S.P.C.C., and from what I hear it seems as if most of it's likely to stay with them. If Lisa's lucky some softhearted judge will give her a cut which may keep her in hats for a few years, but that's all. So forget the idea of Lisa as a rich widow. In fact forget Lisa. We're back at square one."

"Oh *dear,*" said Agnes, almost in tears. "After all our hard work! It does seem a shame."

"Cheer up, Agnes," said Poole, and although she could not see him she thought she could sense his smile. "Perhaps we're not quite back at square one after all. Let's say we're at square two instead of square three."

Agnes felt her spirits rise. "You've got another plan?" she said in excitement.

"Well, I suppose you could call it that," said Poole casually. "But for the moment let's just call it an interesting possibility."

5

Ӿ

I

When Nicola awoke the next morning the sky was clear after the thunderstorm and the air felt fresh and cool after a night of rain. It was late. Her exhaustion had caught up with her at last, and by the time she arrived downstairs for breakfast it was ten o'clock and the dining room was empty. She was just drinking her second cup of coffee and trying to eat a slice of toast when Evan entered the room.

"Hello," he said, and stooped to give her a kiss. "How are you this morning?"

"I'm not sure," said Nicola. "Better, I think, thanks. I had a splitting headache yesterday but that's gone now."

"The storm cleared the air." He pulled over a chair and sat down next to her. "What are your plans?"

"I don't know that I have any. I'll probably go back to London this afternoon and try to get back to normal. I don't want to stay here longer because I know without a doubt I'd end up by having a row with Lisa. You heard what happened yesterday, of course."

"Lisa broadcast the news from the rooftops."

"Isn't it awful? I do feel sorry for her being cut off without a shilling when I'm so embarrassingly well provided for, but I know Daddy wouldn't have changed his will like that if he hadn't had a very good reason."

"It's my bet she was fooling around with that fellow Poole."

"Mine too." Nicola recalled the scene in the summer house with distaste. "Although I can't imagine what she sees in him. He seemed so ordinary to me."

"He didn't seem ordinary to me," said Evan. "He looked like a remarkably smooth operator with a crooked streak, and as soon as I get back to Colwyn Court I'm going to see he and his friends are evicted at the earliest opportunity... Talking of Colwyn, Nicki, why don't you take next week off from work and come down to stay with us? It would do you good to get away from all this for a few extra days, and I don't like to think of you going back to London on your own."

"It's ... very kind of you, Evan, but I really can't take a second week off from work at the moment—it's so inconvenient to my boss, and besides ... well, you may not understand but I *want* to go back to work. Work represents continuity for me at the moment, something stable and unchanging ... If I went to Colwyn I'd probably sit around and get introspective, but if I go back to work I won't have time to think about anything ... Will you be coming back to London soon, do you think?"

"I'm not sure. I have to straighten out affairs at home." He leaned forward on an impulse. "Nicki, won't you think over the invitation to Colwyn? I've been thinking about this all last week, and I've come to the conclusion—"

The door opened, interrupting him. Jane peeped anxiously into the room.

"Oh," she said, embarrassed, "I'm so sorry, I was looking for Benedict. You haven't seen him, have you, by any chance?"

"He wandered off somewhere with my father," said Evan. "Knowing my father's hobbies I suggest you try the greenhouses first. How's Lisa, Jane? I haven't seen her this morning."

123

"Well," said Jane, and hesitated uncomfortably. "She's still awfully upset. In fact—" Jane took a deep breath—"I've insisted that she return to stay at the cottage with us until she's feeling better. Well, actually she asked if she could come and I hadn't the heart to refuse. I do hope Benedict will understand. I mean, I know he'll understand but—"

"I'm sure he will," said Evan, "but doesn't the cottage have sad memories for her?"

"Yes, but Matt wasn't actually killed at the cottage . . ." Jane's voice trailed off uncertainly. She blushed in confusion. "I'm sorry, Nicola."

"Well, he wasn't," said Nicola. "That's all right, Jane."

Jane looked relieved. "Well, I really must find Benedict . . . excuse me . . ." She backed awkwardly out of the room and closed the door again.

There was a pause before Nicola said, pouring herself a third cup of coffee: "That settles it. I'm not going to Colwyn if Lisa's going."

"Oh Nicki, for God's sake—"

"I can't help it," said Nicola. "I just can't stand her. I can't be hypocritical about it. Sorry, Evan."

"Nicki, Lisa'll be at the cottage—you'll be with me at Colwyn Court—"

"I think I'm afraid of that too," said Nicola.

"Look," said Evan, "if you want to give me a hard time, no doubt I deserve it, but why give yourself a hard time too? Don't be so damned proud!"

"I can't help being proud," said Nicola. "It's just the way I am."

"But Nicki, I love you! As soon as I've got things straightened out at home—"

"I'm always waiting for you to straighten things out," said Nicola. "You went to Africa to straighten yourself out. Now you're going to Wales to straighten your family out. There's always something which has to be straightened out before you get to me."

"I'm trying to get to you, aren't I? Why do you think I've invited you to Colwyn?"

124

"Because you want to have your cake and eat it," said Nicola.

"Oh Christ!" yelled Evan and stormed out of the room in a rage.

The maid, coming in to clear the table, collided with him and gave him a look of astonished reproof as he strode past her without an apology. When she had collected herself she said to Nicola: "Excuse me, miss, but have you finished?"

"Yes," said Nicola. "Sorry I was so late this morning." She set down her coffee cup and wandered out into the hall. The house seemed oppressively large. On an impulse she pulled open the front door and stepped out into the morning sunlight. It was then, before she had even had time to recall the unfortunate scene with Evan and give way to her regrets and depression, that she saw the black Jaguar purr smoothly up the drive toward the steps where she was standing.

Lisa's lover, thought Nicola, how dare he come back to my father's house like this! Anger choked in her throat but she conquered it and ran lightly down the steps as he emerged from the car.

"Good morning, Miss Morrison," he said pleasantly, and smiled at her.

He looked different. Nicola hesitated, and as she hesitated she forgot what she was going to say. She found herself staring at him. He wore an expensively cut sports shirt of a smoky red, and the material clung to his body so that she could see the muscles in his chest and the strong set of his shoulders. His slacks were black, as perfectly pressed as they were perfectly tailored, and his shoes were as black as his slacks. Nicola thought she had never seen a casually dressed man look so elegant.

"Good morning," she heard herself say as if from a long way away.

He held out his hand politely and after a moment she held out hers and felt his long fingers close upon her skin. She saw for the first time that he was dark. He had dark eyes, deep-set and brilliant, and dark hair, and his skin was tanned from hours in the summer sun of the Gower Peninsula.

"You look different," she said suddenly.

"No," he said. "You're just more observant today, that's all."

He was still holding her hand and she was suddenly very aware of his long fingers next to her flesh. She withdrew her hand and took a pace away from him.

"Won't you come in?" she said abruptly, and led the way into the hall.

"Thank you," he said and followed her out of the sunlight into the shadows of the house.

"I suppose you want to see Lisa. I think she's still in bed, but if you like I'll go and tell her you're here."

"Well, as a matter of fact," he said from just behind her shoulder, "it was you I came to see, not Lisa."

She swung round in surprise. "Me?" she said, astonished, and felt the hot color suffuse her face as if she were a schoolgirl again. "Why me?"

"Is there a room where we can talk in private?"

"Oh . . . yes, of course . . . Come into the living room."

He opened the door for her.

"Can I offer you some coffee?" said Nicola uneasily, still not sure how to react to his presence.

"Only if it's percolated," said Poole, "and made without that appalling hot milk the English love so much."

Nicola found herself laughing. "Cook would have hysterics! She only keeps instant coffee in the kitchen anyway. How about some tea?"

"I don't think I could face it," said Poole. "Don't think I'm unappreciative of your hospitality, Miss Morrison; it's just that in this particular matter I'm very hard to please. Shall we sit down?"

"Oh . . . yes, of course." She sat down awkwardly on one end of the sofa and after she was seated he sank into the armchair opposite her and interlaced his long sinuous fingers.

"I owe you an apology," he said at last.

"Do you?" said Nicola surprised.

"Yes, a large one, unfortunately."

"What on earth for?"

"My intrusion yesterday on a very private family affair."

"Oh." Nicola felt confused.

"I'm surprised you're being so polite to me this morning. I had a most unpleasant suspicion when I saw you watching my arrival just now that you were about to summon every servant in the house to throw me out in the best nineteenth-century tradition. Wasn't that the way they used to deal with rogues, vagabonds, and unwanted suitors?"

"I suppose it was," said Nicola amused, "But which category of undesirable visitor do you fall into?"

"All of them, of course," said Poole with his wide charming smile. "Haven't you heard about me? According to popular rumor I've tricked Walter Colwyn out of his family home, established a nudist camp and worse at Colwyn Court, and played fast and loose with your stepmother. Surely you can't be unaware of my extreme notoriety!"

Nicola laughed. "You make the gossip all sound very foolish!"

"Gossip often is. Nobody thinks of checking to see if Walter Colwyn gave me a lease; nobody wants to believe that the word 'nature' in the society's title refers to food and not to a lack of decent clothing. Everyone always likes to believe the worst because the worst is usually so much more exciting than the best, isn't it? And the human race loves to be excited and titillated. If there's no excitement they invent it. Even foolish gossip is better than no gossip at all in those circumstances."

After a moment Nicola said: "And Lisa?"

"I'm not responsible for Lisa," said Poole. "She was your father's problem, not mine."

"I don't think he believed that Lisa was faithful to him at the end."

"Of course he didn't," said Poole. "Husbands can never believe that their wives are resistible. To believe such a thing would be an insult to their egos."

"Hm," said Nicola, digesting this with a frown.

"Look," said Poole, leaning forward suddenly, "I really must apologize, Miss Morrison. I know you think I intruded yesterday in order to see Lisa, but in fact it was Lisa who demanded to see me. She sounded so close to hysteria that I gave in, much against my better judgment, and spent some time with her here after the funeral in an attempt to calm her down." He paused. "I have some experience in clinical psychology. I thought I could help her."

"I see," said Nicola slowly.

"I knew when I met her a few days ago that she was troubled and on an impulse I made the mistake of trying to help her. She developed a dependence on me very rapidly—much more rapidly than I'd anticipated—and things got out of control. When I tried to extricate myself she became hysterical and . . . well, you can imagine how it was. I won't go into further details. Suffice it to say that yesterday I tried to persuade her to consult a London specialist about her emotional troubles, and I hope I managed to make her see reason."

"I don't think you did," said Nicola. "She's decided to return to Colwyn Cottage to recuperate with Jane and Benedict."

His eyes were suddenly so dark that they seemed black. His mobile mouth was straight and still. "Oh?" he said at last. "That's unfortunate. But I think she'll soon be obliged to realize that whatever tenuous relationship existed between us is now at an end. There's nothing further I can do for her."

"I'm glad about that," said Nicola before she could stop herself.

He smiled at her. His eyes lightened, sparkled, crinkled at the corners. He had the most extraordinarily expressive eyes. "What about you?" he said. "You're not going to stay on alone in this enormous house, are you?"

"No, I . . . have to get back to work on Monday. I don't live here anyway. I have a flat in Hampstead."

"If you'll forgive me saying so," said Poole, "I don't think you should go back to work so soon."

"But I want to," said Nicola, repeating what she had said to Evan. "If I don't I'll get introspective and maudlin. I want to be so busy that I won't have time to think about myself."

"Exactly," said Poole. "Sometimes that sort of sublimation can be most unwise. Far better to let the shock and grief work itself naturally out of your system."

"Oh," said Nicola. She felt confused again. On an impulse she said quickly: "Are you really a psychologist? Or just an amateur one?"

"I have a degree in psychology. I've had clinical experience. I don't think you could call me an amateur."

"What university did you go to?"

"I was at college in California."

"So that explains it!"

"Explains what?"

"Your accent. It's a bit off-key sometimes. Are you an American?"

"No, I'm a British subject. But I spent my formative years in the States. You haven't been to California, have you, by any chance?"

"No. I'd love to go there one day, though."

"You should," said Poole. "It's the most extraordinary place, a latter-day Garden of Eden . . . After the Fall, of course." He smiled at her. "But never mind California for the moment. I was thinking of places nearer home. Colwyn, for instance. If I were advising you—which I realize I have no business to do at all—I'd recommend you take at least another week off from work and come down to Colwyn Court for some rest and sea air. My society has taken over the east and west wings, but there's still one small spare room in the main part of the house and you'd be more than welcome to stay there for a few days. I can say that with authority because I spoke to Walter Colwyn after the funeral yesterday and he suggested more or less the same thing himself."

"Well . . ."

"If you're worried about Lisa, don't be. There's no reason why you should meet."

129

"How did you know I—"

"My dear Miss Morrison, one doesn't have to be a psychologist to guess your attitude toward your stepmother after her recent behavior."

"I—" Nicola felt dazed.

"I'll look after you if you visit Colwyn. If you're afraid of introspection or simply afraid of being afraid I think I might be able to help you."

"I'll be all right," said Nicola at once.

"So you'll come?"

"Well, I—"

"You will come, won't you."

"I . . ."

"You will come."

"Well, why not?" said Nicola unexpectedly. "It's a bit feeble to be afraid of introspection, isn't it? Why shouldn't I spend a few days by the sea?"

"Good!" said Poole. "That's a much healthier attitude to take." He stood up before adding casually: "Perhaps I can give you a lift down to Wales? I'm leaving on Monday morning and it'd be very easy for me to stop here at Wickerfield to pick you up."

"But I'll be in London too," said Nicola. "I planned to go back after everyone leaves for Wales tomorrow morning."

"Better still! Give me your address and I'll stop by at your apartment."

"You mean you'll call in at my flat," said Nicola, and they laughed together.

"When I'm excited I forget which side of the Atlantic I'm on," said Poole disarmingly.

Nicola was aware of the most extraordinary sense of elation. "Would you like to stay to lunch?" she offered on the spur of the moment.

"I would, but unfortunately I have to get back to town. Now before I forget, what's your address in Hampstead?"

She gave him her address and phone number and asked him where he was staying.

130

"The Salisbury Hotel by the British Museum. I'll call for you at nine-thirty on Monday morning—or will that be too early?"

"No, that'll be fine."

They were in the hall. No one was about.

"I wouldn't tell Lisa I called, if I were you," said Poole, opening the front door. "Best to avoid unnecessary complications in that direction. I'm sure you understand."

"Of course," said Nicola.

He held out his hand again, and Nicola reached automatically to touch him.

"Till Monday," said Poole, turning away from her. The strong sunlight gave his dark hair a reddish tinge.

"Till Monday," said Nicola, and stood watching him as he got into his black Jaguar and drove away out of sight of her mesmerized eyes.

II

"I've changed my mind about coming to Colwyn Court," said Nicola to Evan as they met by chance before lunch. "I'm going to drive down on Monday and stay for a week."

"How do you know the invitation still stands?" said Evan, still smarting from their unfortunate conversation at the breakfast table. "Anyway, what made you change your mind? Did you decide to let me have my cake and eat it?"

"What? Oh . . . Evan, I'm sorry! I was just upset and didn't know what I was saying . . . Would you really prefer me not to come?"

"Don't be such a little ass," he said clumsily, and tried to kiss her but she turned her face away from him.

"I suppose I did get het up about nothing," she said vaguely. "You had every right to be cross."

"Let's forget it. Nicki, let me drive you down to Wales on Monday—Benedict and Jane can take Father home tomorrow as planned, and I can stay on here—"

"No, you don't have to do that, Evan. It's nice of you to suggest it but I've made other plans."

"You mean you've decided to go by train?"

"No, by car. It's all arranged."

"But don't be silly, it would be no trouble for me to—"

"Mr. Poole's traveling back to Colwyn on Monday and he offered to give me a lift."

"Poole!" Evan stared at her. "Are you trying to tell me you're going to shut yourself up in a car for God knows how many hours with that—that—"

"Shhh!" said Nicola. "Don't yell it out to all the world! I don't want Lisa to know or she'll kick up some kind of embarrassing scene."

"When did you talk to Poole, for God's sake?"

"This morning. He confirmed your advice and said I'd be better off if I spent next week quietly at Colwyn instead of returning to work, so that made me feel I'd be stupid to ignore the advice of two doctors—"

"He's no doctor!" shouted Evan.

"Well, he's a psychologist—"

"He's a quack! Nicki, don't believe half of what that man says. In fact, don't believe any of it."

"But my dear Evan, he only gave me exactly the same advice as you did!"

"But—"

"Why do you dislike him so much?"

"He's bogus," said Evan. "He's a fraud. He's wormed his way into my home."

"He says he has a lease from your father."

"I don't believe it!"

"And he has a degree in psychology from a college in California—"

"California!" scoffed Evan.

"—and he's had clinical experience—"

"Did he mention the name of the college where he got his degree?"

"No, he didn't say, but—"

"I don't believe a word of it," said Evan. "He's a fake."

"He's not," said Nicola annoyed. "I think you're being most unreasonable, Evan."

"You're the one who's being unreasonable in believing all that nonsense he told you! Look, Nicki, phone Poole, cancel Monday's drive, and come down with us all to Colwyn tomorrow."

"I can't," said Nicola mulishly. "I must go back to the flat first to do some washing and ironing and repacking.

"Then let me drive you down on Monday. Just the two of us."

"It's not necessary, Evan. Mr. Poole—"

"Damn Mr. Poole!" yelled Evan.

"Oh, for heaven's sake, Evan!" said Nicola, exasperated. "What on earth's the matter with you?"

And they parted once more in anger.

III

"Father," said Evan, finding Walter on his own admiring a rare species of orchid in one of Matt's greenhouses. "I want to talk to you."

"Ah," said Walter, trying not to sound nervous and wondering if this was to be the scene he had tried to postpone for so long. "Of course . . . have you seen these orchids in here before, by the way? They're truly exceptional. Such color—texture—"

"Father," said Evan sternly, "I want to know just where we stand with Tristan Poole and his society."

"Ah," said Walter. "Yes. Exactly."

"I suggest we go outside and sit on that seat over on the far side of the lawn. It's too hot in here to conduct a serious conversation."

"It's very hot, isn't it? Marvelous for orchids, of course." He wandered on to the next species.

"Father—"

"You mustn't worry about it, Evan. It's entirely my responsibility."

"That's not true," said Evan. "It's my responsibility to look after you."

"My dear boy, I'm perfectly capable of fending for myself! I appreciate your solicitude, but you're worrying yourself unnecessarily."

"What's all this about Poole having a lease?"

"Just a gentlemen's agreement," said Walter, wishing the orchids would march forward and swallow him up. "I've leased the east and west wings to Poole for a year. We weren't using the rooms anyway and I thought a bit of extra money might come in useful."

"How much is he paying you?"

"Well," said Walter, frantically playing for time. "That's a good question. I'm very glad you asked that. You see—" He stopped.

"Yes?" said Evan.

"Let's go and sit over on the bench as you suggested," said Walter on an inspiration, and earned himself another two minutes to try to think of a satisfactory answer. But when they were both sitting on the wooden seat facing the lawn and the rose garden, he found he still had not invented a plausible reply.

"Yes, Father?" said his inquisitor relentlessly.

"The fact is," said Walter, "there's no money involved at the moment. The society have the accommodation in exchange for Miss Miller acting as housekeeper and for Poole looking after Gwyneth."

There was a pause. Walter, every limb tense, waited in dread for an explosion which never came.

"I was afraid of that," said Evan at last. "Well, perhaps it's a good thing. If there's no money involved your so-called lease to Poole may not be valid."

"Well, actually—"

"Did he give you any money?"

"Just a shilling as a nominal rent—"

134

"Oh, my God," said Evan. "Father, I don't wish to seem disrespectful, but how did you get mixed up with this man? How did you meet him?"

"Well, you know how I have to open Colwyn Court to the public once a month in return for the Ministry of Works maintaining the castle and chapel ruins? Poole came in March. He said he was a tourist with an interest in old buildings, and Gwyneth, who was feeling well that day, showed him around the garden and took him up to the castle. Poole was tremendously interested and asked such intelligent questions that I invited him to lunch. He then offered to lease the entire estate for a year, but of course I couldn't agree to that and he went away again. The next day Gwyneth was ill—one of her attacks—and I was getting rather worried about her and the doctor was considering the hospital when Poole turned up again to ask if I'd had second thoughts about the lease. On hearing Gwyneth was ill he said he was a herbalist and asked if he could prescribe a remedy. Of course I said yes—I didn't see it could do any harm since the doctor wasn't doing much good, and anyway I'm rather a believer in the power of herbs myself. After all, in the old days—"

"So Poole mixed the potion and Gwyneth was instantly cured," said Evan. "That wasn't the herbs, Father. That was the power of suggestion."

"Perhaps," said Walter, not daring to argue. "Anyway, I was grateful to Poole, as you can imagine, and when he suggested a compromise over the lease—just the two wings instead of the whole house—I found myself agreeing—"

"I see."

"He seemed such a nice young man," said Walter defensively, "and after all, I am saving money on a housekeeper, and the society does do all the cleaning, and Gwyneth really has been much better—"

"Who pays the bills?"

"Bills?" said Walter, hoping he had misheard the question.

"Bills," said Evan. "Who shoulders the expense of feeding and maintaining thirteen extra people at Colwyn Court?"

135

"Well, as a matter of fact," said Walter, "I've been paying them, but Poole is going to repay me after August the first. Apparently the society is a little low in funds at the moment, but as soon as August comes—"

"I understand," said Evan in a quiet level voice that frightened Walter much more than an open display of temper would have done. "Now, Father, how are your financial affairs standing up to this? If you considered renting any part of Colwyn Court you must have been in difficult financial straits, and yet from what you tell me you must be leasing at a loss so far. Are you overdrawn at the bank? Have you had to sell some shares?"

"Well, I do have a little money," said Walter. "Your mother's money—which is in trust for you and Gwyneth to inherit when I die—gives me a small but steady income. I've had to sell one or two stocks and shares, but—"

"How much?"

"Well . . . rather a lot, I suppose, but then I took out a small mortgage on the house—"

"I see," said Evan.

"It's not too bad really," said Walter hopefully.

"Father, I don't want to contradict you, but with all due respect I hardly think matters could be much worse. However, one thing at least seems crystal clear. You're in no position financially to afford to keep thirteen people at your own expense at Colwyn Court. The society will have to go."

"But the lease—Gwyneth's health—I told Poole—"

"I'd be surprised if the lease is valid," said Evan, "but if it is maybe I can buy him out. That would probably be cheaper in the long run. As for Gwyneth, what she needs is a damned good psychiatrist. I don't like the thought of my sister being used as a guinea pig by a quack herbalist—in fact I refuse to sanction it once we're back at Colwyn Court. I admit Gwyneth has her troubles, but she needs professional help, not amateur folklore."

"Gwyneth's just a delicate girl," said Walter timidly.

"Father, this is the twentieth century. She doesn't have to be."

"I know you don't really believe that Gwyneth's genuinely ill, but—"

"Yes, I do. The fact that an illness is psychosomatic in origin doesn't make the physical symptoms of that illness any the less real. But the cause of her illness is mental, not physical."

"But she's so intelligent," said Walter doubtfully. "There's nothing wrong with her mind."

"This has nothing to do with intelligence, Father."

"But . . . well, Gwyneth will want Poole to stay. I know she will. Evan, wouldn't it be easier—less trouble all around— if he stayed?"

"You can't afford it, Father. And you can't afford to let Gwyneth use him as a crutch either. He won't cure her and in the long run she may be worse off than she was before she met him."

"I shan't know how to tell him to go," said Walter heavily. "I shan't know what to say to him. He's been such a nice young fellow—so kind—considerate—"

"I'll deal with him," said Evan. "Let me sort it out for you, Father."

"Well, I don't like to impose my troubles on you like this or you'll start to wish you'd never come home and then you'll think about going away again—"

"Not this time, Father," said Evan.

There was a silence. I must have misheard, thought Walter, not daring to believe his ears. He must have said something else.

"Of course there's so much opportunity for doctors in America," he said. "I know that."

"There are different kinds of opportunity," said Evan, "and money isn't everything. I came to realize while I was in Africa that I wasn't prepared to leave Wales—or England—on a permanent basis."

Walter said nothing but took Evan's hand in his and held it. Presently when he could speak again he said: "That rose garden's a lovely sight at the moment. It's been a very good year for roses."

They sat there for a time and watched the roses beyond the smooth lawn. At last Evan stood up and ran a hand absentmindedly through his hair.

"So I have your permission to speak to Poole about this business?"

"Do whatever you think is best," said Walter, conscious only of relief that the long-dreaded scene was over and of gratitude that his dearest wish had been granted. "I leave it entirely up to you."

"I'll speak to him on Monday as soon as I have the chance to see him in person," said Evan, and against his better judgment began to picture Poole inviting Nicola to Wales as if he, not Walter, were the master of Colwyn Court.

IV

It was late on Sunday when Evan and Walter reached Colwyn Court and Benedict, Jane, Lisa and the twins arrived back at Colwyn Cottage. Evan had decided there was nothing more he could do about the society until Poole returned, but on Monday morning he summoned all his patience and went to see his sister. As he glanced into her room he found her designing an enormous poster with a series of felt-tip pens.

"Can I see you for a moment, please, Gwyneth?" he said politely, raising his voice to be heard above the thunderous noises from the record player. He glanced at the poster again. Gwyneth had drawn a series of circles above a bold black pentagram which stood on one point with two of the other points rising toward the top of the paper.

"What's that?" said Evan, trying to remember what he had read about occupational therapy.

"My concept of the fifth dimension," said Gwyneth, and switched off the record player.

"I see," said Evan. Various Rorschach tests flickered hazily across his mind. "Gwyneth, I want to talk to you about Father."

"If it's going to lead on to something nasty about Tristan," said Gwyneth, sharp as a needle, "you can go and talk to someone else."

"I'm mainly concerned with Father at the moment." He sat down on the rug beside her in an attempt to establish some sort of intimacy. "Gwyneth, Father's in a bad way financially. It seems that the society is living off him at the moment, and the expense is certainly much more than he can afford."

"I'm sure Tristan will pay him back eventually," said Gwyneth, unconcerned, and drew a circle around the entire pentagram.

"Possibly," said Evan, "but meanwhile I don't think Father's in a position to support the society at Colwyn Court. In fact he's hardly in a position to support himself, let alone the society."

"Well, what am I supposed to do about it?" said Gwyneth aggressively. "It's no good expecting me to go out and get a job."

"No, I know you're not fit enough for that at the moment. But medicine's so advanced nowadays, and I really think one of the top men in Harley Street might—"

"I'll never be fit enough to earn my living," said Gwyneth.

"Maybe not, but wouldn't you at least like to live without the fear that one of your attacks might be just around the corner?"

"I'm incurable," said Gwyneth. "Daddy understands, even if you don't."

"Supposing I were to tell you that Father's anxious for you to take my advice and see a Harley Street specialist to see what—if anything—can be done to help you?"

"Daddy would do anything you told him," said Gywneth. "That doesn't mean anything."

"But—"

"Oh, why don't you go away to America and leave us alone!" burst our Gwyneth. "It was so peaceful when you were in Africa! Daddy and I are quite happy here without you barging in and messing everything up! Why do you always have to interfere and spoil everything?"

Phrases from a dozen textbooks on Freud flashed through Evan's memory.

"I'm only trying to help," he said at last.

"No, you're not," said Gwyneth. "You're trying to drive a wedge between me and Daddy."

There was a silence.

"And between me and Daddy and Tristan," added Gwyneth as an afterthought.

"Gwyneth, the society isn't going to stay here forever, you know. Poole's going to leave one day."

"I'll be ill if he goes," said Gwyneth, and drew another circle with a violet marker.

"If you're ill perhaps you'll think differently about seeing someone in Harley Street."

"If I'm ill perhaps I'll die."

"Possibly," said Evan, "but I doubt it." And he stood up and walked abruptly out of the room.

The record player started blaring seconds after he had left.

On an impulse he entered the east wing where half the society had their rooms, and after knocking on the doors opened them and looked inside. All the rooms were littered with feminine possessions but none of the occupants responded to his knock for admittance. The rooms were empty. Retracing his steps Evan moved across to the west wing where the other half of the society was quartered and swiftly followed the same procedure.

The last door was locked.

Evan did not hesitate. Two minutes later he was opening the door of the housekeeper's cupboard off the scullery, and when he did not find what he wanted he immediately sought out Agnes Miller.

"Miss Miller, where is the duplicate key of that very large bedroom at the extreme end of the west wing—the bedroom with the dressing room attached to it?"

"Duplicate key?" said Agnes, very plump and benign.

"Yes, it seems to be missing from the housekeeper's cupboard where all the duplicate keys are kept."

"Ah," said Agnes, "that's because the room belongs to Mr. Poole and he keeps both the key and the duplicate key. Mr. Poole has very strong views on privacy, living as he does in the midst of twelve women. I'm sure you understand."

"I think there should always be a duplicate key available," said Evan, "in case of fire."

"How sensible!" exclaimed Agnes admiringly. "I hadn't thought of that. I'll speak to Mr. Poole about it just as soon as he arrives back this afternoon, and I'm sure he'll be able to suggest a suitable compromise."

"Thank you," said Evan abruptly, and turned aside.

"Is there something you want from Mr. Poole's room, Dr. Colwyn?"

"It's not important. I thought I had some things stored in that big cupboard in the dressing room, and to get to the dressing room one has to go through the bedroom."

"Yes, I see. Have you tried the attics? I know that everything in that particular cupboard at the moment belongs to Mr. Poole, so if you had anything stored there it must have been moved to another part of the house."

"In that case I'll try the attics. Thank you, Miss Miller."

But he made no effort to search the attics. Instead he took the car and spent the afternoon savoring the familiar scenery of the Gower Peninsula and planning his coming interview with Poole. He went to the church by the beach at Oxwich, and drove beyond Oxwich to Port Eynon along the twisting country roads. From Port Eynon he headed for Rhossili and sat for a while on the cliffs while the sheep grazed peacefully nearby and the waves broke on the empty beach which stretched to the sand dunes of Llangenith. By the time he arrived back at Colwyn it was after six and Poole and Nicola had still not arrived from London.

At that point Evan had to take a tight grip on himself. He could feel the rage begin to boil within him and knew he was on the verge of losing his temper before he had even seen the

141

man. Why had Nicola accepted the lift from Poole? How had Poole managed to persuade her to come to Colwyn when Evan himself had failed? Poole . . . Who was Poole anyway?

Evan's patience snapped; recklessness overcame him. Slipping into the potting shed near the greenhouses he found a strip of wire and pocketed a screwdriver. Then, making sure that no one saw him, he returned to the west wing and checked each room again to be certain that no one was about.

No one was. The members of th society were either helping in the preparation of the evening meal or else congregated in their sitting room downstairs, and he was alone on the second floor. Evan made up his mind, bent the wire into the most accommodating shape and inserted it carefully in the keyhole of Poole's locked door.

But the lock was so old and stiff that it was hard to spring. Evan tried the cover of his driving license after he had abandoned the wire, but when this too failed he turned to the screwdriver and resorted to the extreme measure of dismantling the panel which surrounded the handle.

Seconds passed. A succession of small sounds kept him glancing repeatedly over his shoulder, but they all came from the sitting room downstairs and the corridor remained deserted. The front of the lock came off; the unmasked mechanism confronted him. Using the screwdriver Evan flicked the lock aside, pressed the catch back, and walked into the room.

The first noticeable characteristic of the room was its neatness. Everything was in place; no knickknacks littered the room, no discarded clothes, no framed photographs. Above the bed was the only picture in the room, a crude modern painting of a black pentagram on a violent red background. The pentagram, which stood on one of its five points with two other points stretching upward, reminded Evan with a jolt of Gwyneth's drawing. Perhaps, he thought, Poole had brought her to this room. Perhaps he had even . . .

Evan had to grab his self-control again as it threatened to slip away from him. With a great effort he managed to pull himself together. Perhaps Gwyneth had painted the picture and given it to Poole as a token of appreciation. In which case it would be perfectly natural for Poole to hang the picture in his room.

The bedroom was large, but the furniture had been arranged in such a way that the center of the room was empty. The slim single bed was pushed against one wall; the chest of drawers hugged the wall opposite, and the table and chair had been placed beneath one of the windows. A gray, black-flecked carpet yawned emptily across the uncluttered floor. Evan was reminded of a room which had been cleared to allow people to dance. Perplexed, he wandered across to the dressing room beyond and opened the door of the large built-in closet which stretched along one wall, but all he found there were ten suits, either black or gray, and an assortment of black shoes. He was about to leave the dressing room when he saw the dark stain on the bedroom floor where the black-flecked carpet did not quite reach the wall.

The stain looked like blood. Evan pulled back the carpet and saw that the wooden floorboards had been marked by chalk pentagrams and, beyond, the curve of an enormous circle. Rolling back the carpet further he became aware of an odd odor, unpleasant and hard to identify. After a moment he replaced the carpet, straightened his back, and strode back into the dressing room to see if any of the suits in the closets were bloodstained, but he found no mark of any kind on the clothes. He was about to turn away from the closet again when he saw the box.

The closet was deep and the box was at the back of it so Evan was not surprised that he had missed it during his first inspection. He tried to drag the box forward into the light and was surprised how heavy it was. Grabbing the handle he tilted the box on its side, and heard a clink and a thud as the contents fell against one another. His fingers worked at the hasps without success. The box was locked and Poole obviously had the key.

Evan stepped back and surveyed his discovery thoughtfully. One locked black wooden box. Several floorboards defaced with childish drawings and covered by a brand-new carpet. One stain which might or might not be blood and which someone had carelessly left only partially concealed by this same brand-new carpet. One very odd smell of uncertain origin, and a remarkable preponderance of pentagrams.

Mr. Poole, thought Evan, without doubt has a most curious taste in interior decoration.

He was still considering Poole's tastes a second later when without any warning there was a small cough behind him and the sound of someone clearing his throat.

"May I help you, Dr. Colwyn?" inquired Tristan Poole from the doorway.

6

☆

I

Poole was wearing yet another of his dark suits, white shirts, and conservative ties. He looked like a city executive accustomed to daily board meetings in the conference room of some massively influential corporation. Apart from the fact that there was faint creases across the front of his trousers there was no hint that he had just spent several hours sitting at the wheel of a car.

"May I help you?" he repeated politely. His dark eyes were watchful, his face expressionless. "Were you looking for something?"

"Yes, I was," said Evan, keeping his voice cool and controlled. "I had some papers stored in this cupboard and I was wondering where they'd gone."

"They're in the attics, the room where the old upright piano is. The boxes containing your papers are on the floor next to a defunct sewing machine."

"Thank you," said Evan.

"You're entirely welcome," said Poole. "I'm only sorry your need for the papers was so great that you had to dismantle the lock on the door and break into my room."

"Wasn't that a pity?" said Evan blandly. "I'll just put the lock back into place again before I leave."

"Thank you so much. Incidentally, may I, as Miss Miller's friend, inquire—purely as a matter of interest, of course—why you chose to regard her as a liar?"

"I beg your pardon?" said Evan.

"I understand Miss Miller told you the papers were in the attic some hours ago."

"She didn't tell me which attic," said Evan. "I couldn't find the papers and thought she was mistaken. Excuse me, please." And he walked past Poole through the bedroom and proceeded to reassemble the mutilated lock.

"I'm sure you're unaware of this," said Poole's voice behind him, "but the lease your father granted me gave you no right to enter either the east or west wing which are now the private property of the society."

"The landlord usually has an implied right to enter his property to make repairs," said Evan, twisting the screws deftly into place.

"But not to break down doors and commit acts of trespass."

Evan said nothing but continued reassembling the lock.

"Maybe you'd like to see the lease," said Poole.

"I'd be delighted," said Evan, fastening the last screw. "As a matter of fact, that was one of the things I was anxious to talk to you about."

"Oh?" Poole was opening the drawer of the table by the window. When he turned Evan could see a legal document in his hands. "Well, you're welcome to inspect the lease," he said, and held out the document to Evan.

Evan straightened his back, tried the door to make sure the catch was working, and pocketed his screwdriver again. Finally he accepted the document and glanced at it casually.

"Does my father have a copy of this?"

"I'm sure his solicitor gave him a copy, yes."

"His solicitor?"

"His solicitor drew up the lease. Didn't your father tell you?"

"I see." Evan stared at the lease, unable to grasp a word of the fine print confronting him, and clung grimly to the calm manner he had adopted.

"I think you'll find it's all perfectly legal," said Poole serenely.

"Thank you." Evan handed the lease back to him.

"Was there something else you wanted to talk to me about?"

"Yes, I understand you owe my father a considerable amount of money."

"I have nothing to do with household expenses," said Poole. "Miss Miller handles those sort of trivial details for me, I'm glad to say. But I can assure you that all debts will be settled in August. If you like I can ask Miss Miller to itemize the expenses your father has had recently in connection with the society, and present you with a copy so that you can see how minimal the debt really is. Your phrase 'a considerable amount' strikes me, if you'll forgive me saying so, as exaggerated. However, if the situation is troubling you I'd be happy to give you an I.O.U. for the amount in question."

"There's no exaggeration," said Evan. "In relation to my father's current financial situation I still say that you owe him too much money. I'm afraid it's not an economic possibility for him to continue to support your society here at Colwyn Court."

"August is less than four weeks away."

"I'm afraid that makes no difference. He can't afford to lease his home rent-free."

"He's saving money on a housekeeper."

"His expenses are greater than his savings. And talking of a housekeeper, that reminds me of something else I wanted to say. I don't like the cooking this society of yours specializes in. Why should we be obliged to eat nature foods if we don't want to?"

"Your meals are ordinary meals prepared especially for you."

"Well, I don't like the cooking. Doesn't your cook ever use salt? The food is bland, tasteless, and almost inedible."

"Too much salt in a diet, Dr. Colwyn," said Poole, "can have an adverse effect on those who suffer from high blood pressure."

"And no salt at all," said Evan, "can cause painful cramps

147

in certain groups of muscles. Are you trying to teach me my profession, Mr. Poole?"

"Are you trying to tell me to get out of Colwyn Court, Dr. Colwyn?"

"I'm sorry, but all things considered, I think it would be best if the society found somewhere else for its headquarters. If the lease is valid I could of course offer you compensation—"

"The lease is valid," said Poole. "I reject your offer of compensation."

There was a pause. They stood looking at each other, Evan big and untidy with his red hair standing up in tousled, angry tufts, Poole slim and controlled, his appearance immaculate, his eyes dark with a polite detached interest.

Damn him, thought Evan furiously, he's getting the better of me.

"Dr. Colwyn," said Poole, "let's be rational about this. There's no sense in losing our tempers. I appreciate the fact that you're worried about the money we owe your father; I'll have Miss Miller work out exactly what we owe him and then I'll write you a promissory note which I shall be able to honor within the next two months. I appreciate the fact that you're dissatisfied with the cooking; I'll pass on your complaints to Miss Miller and no doubt she'll make the necessary alterations when your meals are prepared in future. But don't, please, expect us to move from Colwyn Court before our lease is up. We have every right to be here and, distasteful though it may be to you, we have every intention of staying."

"I see," said Evan. "Well, at least you've made your intentions clear."

"I'm sorry you should feel so much hostility toward us. If you were to accept our presence I see no reason why we shouldn't coexist peacefully enough."

"Since we're being so frank with one another," said Evan, "I may as well tell you that I have every intention of seeking legal advice on that lease. And while you're at Colwyn Court I'd be obliged if you would have nothing further to do with my sister. I'm aware that she's ill, but I think any amateur help could do more harm than good at this stage."

"I'm not an amateur," said Poole.

"I understand you were educated in America. Are you entitled to put the letters M.D. after your name?"

"Dr. Colwyn, if you'll forgive my saying so, I think your judgment is clouded by the conventional Englishman's dislike of America and all things American."

"You couldn't be more wrong," said Evan. "Are you entitled to the letters M.D. or aren't you?"

"Do I call myself Dr. Poole?"

"Is that an answer?"

"It tells you I don't believe in the conventional worship of initials bestowed by an ignorant establishment."

"So you're not a qualified doctor. Thank you. Now would you kindly leave my sister to the attentions of those who are qualified?"

"The attentions of those who are qualified," said Poole, "were hardly helping your sister before I came on the scene."

"Nevertheless—"

"I have a degree in psychology, Dr. Colwyn. In fact I know a hell of a lot more about Gwyneth's trouble than either the inefficient family doctor who was attending her before I came here or, with respect, you yourself with your admirable—and in this case utterly irrelevant—background of tropical medicine."

"I—"

"Tropical illness," said Poole, "is not what Gwyneth is suffering from."

"Why, you—"

"Would you like a clinical diagnosis about what's wrong with your sister?"

"I'm not interested in a few psychological terms flung together by some fradulent quack!" yelled Evan. "You stay away from my sister or I'll—"

"My dear Dr. Colwyn, anyone would think I was sleeping with her, judging from all the fuss you're making about the relationship!"

"I wouldn't be surprised if you were!" shouted Evan, beside himself with rage. "I wouldn't be surprised if you were sleeping with all twelve of those women you've got here! I wouldn't be surprised if—"

"What a tribute to my sexual capacity," said Poole. "Thank you very much."

"And another thing I want to talk to you about is Nicola Morrison!" Evan burst out, hardly hearing what the other man said. "You stay away from her, do you understand? You keep your hands off my girl! If you think you can—"

"Your girl?" said Poole. "Congratulations! I didn't know you were engaged."

"We weren't engaged!" growled Evan. "But we're engaged now so just you stay away from her."

"All right," said Poole. "But I'd check with Nicola first, if I were you. I had the distinct impression on the journey down here today that she didn't consider herself engaged to anyone. Now if you'll excuse me, I really must have a bath and change my clothes before dinner. Good night, Dr. Colwyn, and—" He paused for a smile—"try to feel more confidence in your self-image. Then you won't feel so threatened by any unfamiliar element in your surroundings."

And before Evan could begin to swing his fist the bedroom door was shut in his face and Poole was deftly turning the key in the lock.

II

"Nicki?" said Evan, knocking on the door of the tiny spare room in the main part of the building. "Nicki, can I talk to you for a minute?"

"Wait." There was a pause before she opened the door an inch. She was wearing a white bathrobe, which he guessed she had dragged on in a hurry, and was barefoot. "Hello," she said. "I'm just changing. Can it wait for half an hour?"

"No, I don't think it can." He wondered if she was

wearing anything beneath the bathrobe. A stream of muddled thoughts began to clamor in his mind and seep deliciously through his body. "Can I come in?"

"Well, I suppose so," said Nicola warily, and hugged her bathrobe closer to her as if it were a life belt. "What's the matter?"

"Nicki—" He stepped into the room and closed the door. "—Nicki, I've been an absolute fool, thinking I didn't know my own mind about all this, putting off any major involvement, wallowing in my indecisiveness the whole damned time. Nicki, I'm sorry about all the mess in the past. I love you and I want to marry you and let's go into Swansea first thing tomorrow morning to see if they've got a decent ring for me to give you to celebrate the engagement."

There was a pause. He was breathing unevenly but felt as if a huge burden had been lifted from his back, and the blood was starting to sing through his veins.

"Engagement?" said Nicola blankly.

"Engagement!" He smiled at her and moved to take her in his arms but she stepped away from him before he could reach her.

All she said was: "Isn't this rather sudden?"

"Sudden! After all these months?" He burst out laughing. "Darling, I've been as slow as a caterpillar and you know it! How can you call it sudden?"

The bathrobe slipped a little; he felt himself moving forward again before he could stop himself. "We can get married as soon as possible," he heard himself say. "This month, next month—any month you like." By this time she had her back to the dressing table and could retreat no further, so he took her in his arms and started to kiss her. So exhilarated was he that it took him a full minute to realize she was making no effort to respond to him.

He stopped. "Nicki?"

Her gray eyes were dark with some expression, he did not understand. At last she said, "I've got to think about this. I can't give you an answer straight away. I'm sorry, Evan, but you've got to give me time to think about it."

151

He heard her words but his mind refused to accept them. "But you've had months and months to think about it!"

"Please," was all she said. "Please, Evan."

"All right," he said, baffled. "If you want to play it that way, what does it matter? Every girl's entitled to time to consider a proposal, no matter how obvious the outcome is! But meanwhile . . . Nicki, I want you so much! Can I—let me—"

"Please don't touch me," she said sharply.

He stopped. A chill began to inch through the heat in his body. He looked at her uncertainly.

"I want to marry you," he said at last. "I'm going to marry you. Surely you're not going to tell me that you—"

"I don't want that at the moment. I don't want to go to bed with you now."

"Isn't that a bit hypocritical? It's not as if nothing's ever happened between us. And since we love each other and we're going to be married—"

"Are we?" said Nicola. "I'm not sure. I've got to think about it. Let's leave it for now, Evan. Please."

Every muscle in his body went taut. He could feel the hurt and anger lock together in his throat so that it was hard for him to breathe.

"Is it Poole?" he said suddenly. "It's Poole, isn't it."

"Don't be ridiculous," said Nicola. "I hardly know the man. Please, Evan, please leave me alone. I don't want to talk about it any more tonight."

He hesitated, then moved awkwardly toward the door. She saw his fingers slip unsteadily on the handle as he wrenched the door open and stumbled into the passage.

She was alone.

For ten long bewildered minutes she sat on the edge of the bed and tried to make sense of her thoughts. What she was most conscious of was that she felt nothing at all. No relief, no joy, no sadness, no anxiety. She felt as if she were in a state of limbo where all emotions were suspended.

"But I'm crazy about Evan," she said aloud. "Crazy about him."

The words echoed hollowly around the empty room. She got up, walked over to the window, leaned her arms upon the sill.

"I've spent fifteen months aching to marry him," she reminded herself incredulously. "Fifteen months of crying at odd moments, fighting off depressions, and turning down dates because no man ever measured up to Evan."

She waited. Nothing happened. She felt surprised but nothing else. Perhaps it was good to feel surprised. To feel something was better than to feel nothing at all.

"Perhaps I've gone mad," she said to herself and sat down on the edge of the bed again to consider the idea with interest. "Or perhaps I'm drunk. Or perhaps I'm dead and don't know it."

She was still considering this intriguing possibility when there was another knock on her door.

"Come in!" called Nicola, too fascinated by her emotional numbness to care who it was.

The door opened. She looked up.

And suddenly her emotions blazed into life. It was as if they were switches on a huge board and someone was flicking them all into action with a gigantic sweep of his hand. She felt lights streaming down on her, the warmth of a thousand flames, the whirl of brilliant colors cascading through her mind.

"Tristan!" she exclaimed. She jumped up and ran over to him. "Tristan, I feel so peculiar I can't even begin to explain it to you!"

He smiled at her. His clothes were black and white but all she could see was color, and color was something she could touch and taste and drink until the well ran dry.

"I'm going to faint," said Nicola.

"No, you're not."

Time was displaced. She could see him grasping it in his hands and turning back the clock. One month. Two months. Three . . . four . . . And time was something one could twist and bend, a slave in the hands of eternity. One year. Two. Three—

And suddenly she was back in the days when she had never known Evan Colwyn and she was free and young and it was good to be alive.

"I'm drugged," said Nicola.

"No, you're just seeing things as they really are."

"I'm going crazy."

"You're sane for the first time in three years."

"Oh my God," whispered Nicola, "I really believe I am."

He touched her and everything seemed to steady down. When she clung to him instinctively the tiny room looked the same again and Poole's suit was black and his shirt was white and his dark eyes were inches from her own.

He kissed her. At first it was just like any other kiss a man might have given her but then it changed and it was like nothing she had ever experienced before. Senses which she had not even known existed flared to life until she saw the world expanding into an unknown and mystical dimension which existed without beginning and without end in a wilderness of time.

He stopped kissing her. The world tilted back to normality and the room spun around to meet her. The evening light was streaming through the window to slant across the panels of the closed door.

"Take me back," said Nicola. "Where we were before. Take me back." And she reached up and pulled his face down to hers so that she could touch his mouth again with her own.

She felt his fingers sliding over her skin and realized for the first time that her bathrobe was on the floor and she was naked. But then his mouth closed on hers and all the conventions of a petty decaying world were lost amid the velvet darkness of a hundred solar systems and the heat was blazing down upon her from a vast and invisible powerhouse.

"Oh God," said Nicola, "I'm in heaven."

He laughed. Opening her eyes she saw him above her, his face so close to her own that she could glimpse only the wide curve of his mouth and the whiteness of his uneven teeth.

"Why are you laughing?" she whispered.

"Because you've just said something which amused me," he said, and his voice was the voice of darkness welcoming her to the brilliance of a fierce and fiery night.

III

The sun had set by the time Poole left Nicola's room and padded downstairs in search of Agnes. He found her in the society's dining room where a place was still set for him at the table, and as soon as he walked in she jumped to her feet with an exclamation of relief.

"At last!" she said as if she had given up all hope of seeing him again that night. "I knew I couldn't interrupt you so I spent the last half hour willing you to make yourself accessible as soon as possible! Listen, Tristan, Lisa's here. She's been waiting in the sitting room and she absolutely refuses to go without seeing you. What on earth are we going to do about her?"

"Agnes," said Poole. "You're an incurable worrier. Where's my dinner?"

"But what about—"

"I'm damned hungry, Agnes. If there's any dinner left I'd like some at once, please."

Agnes sighed. "Yes, Tristan. Just a minute—I'll get it. for you."

"Thanks." He sank down in the high-backed chair at the head of the table and traced a pentagram on the tablecloth with his fork as he thought of Nicola.

When Agnes returned with a plate of steaming food all she said was: "Satisfactory?"

Poole took a mouthful of stuffed aubergine. "Delicious."

"I didn't mean the food," said Agnes.

"Neither did I," said Poole.

They were still smiling at each other when Agnes' sister popped her head around the door of the dining room.

"Lisa's back again, Agnes—bothering us in the kitchen, I mean. She says she refuses to wait in the sitting room any

155

longer and that she absolutely insists on seeing Tristan without delay. What shall I do?"

"Oh, bother the woman!" said Agnes irritably. "I'll go and fend her off again."

"Don't waste your time," said Poole. "Show her in, Harriet."

"Oh, by the way," said Agnes as her sister vanished obediently, "before I forget—Evan's talking of going to London again tomorrow, something about finding a doctor for Gwyneth and consulting some private detectives. You've made an enemy there, Tristan."

"Agnes," said Poole tolerantly, "will you kindly stop worrying? You'll give yourself an ulcer and it's really quite unnecessary."

"All right," said Agnes. "Well, I'll leave you alone with your ladyfriend and try to think about something else."

"You can make an itemized list of how much we owe Walter Colwyn. I promised Evan an I.O.U."

"You brute," said Agnes. "If anything's going to give me an ulcer it's those wretched accounts. Very well, I'll do my best. Good luck with Lisa."

"Good luck with the adding and subtraction." He took another mouthful of aubergine and was still chewing it thoughtfully when Lisa swept into the room. "Hello," he said. "How are you?" He made no effort to stand up but merely motioned her to sit down next to him at the table. "Have a seat."

"Thanks for the five-star welcome," said Lisa. "Where the hell have you been?"

"In London."

"You said you'd phone on Saturday! I waited all day—"

"I'm sorry about that," said Poole.

"Well . . ." She hesitated. She was nervous, he noticed, and there was a stubborn look in her eyes. "I think you might have kept your promise," she said unevenly.

"I'm sorry," said Poole.

There was a pause. Poole kept on eating.

"What's the matter?" demanded Lisa, mystified. "What is it?"

156

"Nothing."

Another pause.

"Tristan, I must talk to you!"

"Go ahead."

"Well, I . . . I'm in an awful mess, and—well, it's not entirely my fault, is it? I mean, if Matt hadn't seen us together on the beach—"

"My dear, you can't blame me just because your husband changed his will in a fit of temper and drove into a wall before he could calm down enough to change the will back again!"

"Of course I can blame you!" stormed Lisa. "If I hadn't met you Matt wouldn't have changed his will like that!"

"If it hadn't been me it would have been someone else."

"How dare you!" She sprang to her feet in a rage.

"Oh, let's be honest, Lisa! You were bored to tears with that husband of yours and were more than ready to offer yourself to the first man that was willing!"

She tried to hit him but he dropped his knife quickly enough to lunge forward and catch her wrist. There was a silence. Lisa tried to back away but he only tightened the grip of his fingers so that her effort to escape was useless. She began to panic.

"Tristan, I'm sorry—I—I didn't mean it, I—"

"Lisa," said Poole in a quiet, level voice, "you didn't love me. You don't love me. You never will love me. I apologize if I seem undeservedly brutal, but at this stage I think it's important that we both face this basic truth. We met, there were unfortunate repercussions that left a nasty taste in my mouth—and in yours too, I've no doubt—and I think it would be best for both of us now if we decided to go our separate ways. I say that for your sake, just as much as for my own. If word gets around about what we were doing before your husband died I think you might find even a sympathetic judge unfriendly when you start to contest the will."

"Well . . ."

He waited.

"Yes," said Lisa at last, "I suppose that's so. But—"

"Yes?"

"I do love you, Tristan. I can't help it—"

"You don't love me, Lisa."

"But—"

"You don't love me."

She was silent.

"I'm right, you know. It's much better to part now before any further harm's done."

"I . . . suppose so."

"It is."

"Yes." She turned away, but he still held her wrist.

"Lisa."

"Yes?"

"One last kiss for old times' sake?"

She smiled shakily and raised her mouth to his but he kissed her on the forehead. His hands stroked her hair softly and began to untie the scarf that tied her hair back from her face. "Will you give me a keepsake?" he said softly. "Something to remember you by?"

She nodded and her gesture shook her hair loose as he pulled the scarf away. He noticed again with a vague pang of regret how pretty she was.

"Good luck, Lisa. I'm sorry, but I know this is for the best."

"Yes." She was groping for the door. "You're right. But it seems pretty damn hard." And then she was gone, her shoes echoing dully in the corridor, and as he listened he thought he heard her crying.

Agnes slipped into the dining room thirty seconds later. "I can't help it," she said, "I couldn't resist coming to find out—what happened?"

Poole had returned to his dinner. "This meal's very good, Agnes. First-class."

"But what about Lisa? Is everything all right?"

"I'm not sure. Sit down, Agnes." He waited until she was seated in Lisa's chair before adding casually: "I want you to do something for me. Do you think you could reverse an induced infatuation?"

"I don't see why not," said Agnes, glancing at Lisa's scarf

158

which lay limply on the table. "Does the scarf have any of her hairs on it?"

"Possibly. But it's her scarf. That's all that matters."

"I'd rather have the hairs. More personal."

"True. Are you sure of the precise preparations needed?"

"I could look them up," said Agnes, "just to make sure."

"Would you? Agnes, I do appreciate the way you take all these trivial matters off my shoulders . . . Use my room first thing tomorrow morning and choose whichever acolyte you feel would be most suitable. I'd do the job myself but I don't want to spend all tomorrow morning playing the magician when Nicola will expect me to spend it playing a very different role . . . I'm sure you understand."

"Of course," said Agnes sympathetically. "Don't worry about Lisa—I'll take care of her for you. But can't you simply hypnotize her? Wouldn't that be equally effective?"

"Perhaps. And perhaps not. Hypnosis is an uncertain tool in some ways, and in Lisa's case I don't want to rely on hypnosis when I have a more reliable way of dealing with her. I'm using some hypnosis at present but I'd prefer you to summon a more permanent force to solve the problem for us."

"Yes, Tristan."

"Oh, and Agnes—"

"Yes, Tristan?"

"Try not to kill her, please. It might cause unfortunate comment so soon after her husband's death."

"Yes, Tristan," said Agnes obediently, and began to dwell with pleasurable anticipation on the powers she would summon to subjugate Lisa's unruly passion . . .

IV

A week passed.

In London, Evan, still smarting from the lack of enthusiasm which had greeted his long-delayed proposal of mar-

159

riage, had talked to a well-known psychiatrist about his sister, taken counsel's opinion on the ill-fated lease, and had hired a firm of private detectives to make inquiries into Poole's past. After four days of brooding the counsel had reported that the lease was legal; the psychiatrist had told Evan he would be willing to see Gwyneth if she could be coaxed to London for treatment; and the detectives had announced that if there was anything unsavory about Mr. Tristan Poole it would certainly be revealed by their unflagging efforts to excavate the details of his background. For the time being Evan had done all that he could, and he decided to return to Colwyn Court to see if Nicola were in a more reasonable frame of mind.

He felt most annoyed with Nicola. As each day passed he became more convinced than ever that she was treating him badly, and he found it hard to restrain himself from phoning Colwyn Court to talk to her. But he did not phone. He had decided to give her exactly what she wanted—time to think over his proposal—so that when he saw her again she could not accuse him of pestering her into a rushed decision.

Meanwhile at Colwyn Cottage Benedict was making good progress with his thesis and Jane was enjoying every minute of her time with the twins. After a while she realized she was seeing more of the twins than Lisa was. Lisa was silent and withdrawn and spent most of the time in her room. After worrying about her Jane decided Lisa was still suffering from the shock of Matt's death, and resolved to make an even greater effort to be kind and sympathetic toward her.

Lisa herself felt indifferent to everything; she had never suffered from such lassitude before but when Jane suggested it was the aftermath of shock Lisa accepted the explanation and ceased to worry about it. She would have liked to have seen Poole again, but she was too tired even to walk up to Colwyn Court. Lying in bed she would think of Poole for hours on end, but gradually her memory of him became dulled and the violent excitement his presence had roused in her was replaced by that same baffling indifference which

Jane had attributed to shock. But after a week of lassitude she began to feel better, and on the day Evan left London again for Colwyn she decided to get up after lunch and take a stroll on the beach.

It was a fine afternoon. As Lisa dressed slowly in her room Jane was mixing a batch of scones in the kitchen and the twins were sprawled full-length on the turf inside the walls of Colwyn Castle. The mythical saga of their long-lost father had reached a crucial and absorbing stage.

"So there he was," said Timothy. "Face to face with the Bengal tiger."

"And the Star of India glittering evilly in his hip pocket."

"Do rubies glitter?"

"The Star of India's not a ruby, stupid! It's a—" Lucy stopped.

"Yes?" said Timothy.

"I hear something." Lucy was listening intently. "Voices."

"Just like Joan of Arc!"

"Shhh! Can't you hear them?"

Timothy could. "Let's hide."

"Okay."

They jumped up, flattened themselves against the castle walls, and peered through one of the slits which served as windows.

"It's that Miss Miller," said Timothy.

"It's both the Miss Millers. The other one's her sister. I wonder if they're coming into the castle."

"No, they're going to the chapel."

"When they're inside let's—"

"—sneak up on them and see what they're doing. Yes, let's," said Timothy, annoyed that Lucy had thought of the idea before he had.

Agnes and her sister Harriet disappeared slowly behind the walls of the chapel and the sound of their voices abruptly vanished.

"Let's go," said Timothy.

"Okay."

They sped along, bent double across the yards of turf which separated the castle from the chapel. Two of the wild horses grazing nearby lifted their heads in astonishment and further down the hillside one of the flock of grazing sheep lifted his head and bleated disapprovingly at the sky.

"Silly sheep," muttered Lucy.

"Shhh!"

They crawled to a gap in the weather-beaten masonry and peered through into the chapel ruins. The voices reached them clearly now; they could hear every word that was said.

"Such a lovely place," said Agnes. "Tristan was so right about it. It's got the most wonderful nuances."

"What a treat for Lammas! I shall feel so proud to be one of the hostesses in a setting like this!"

"Won't we all," said Agnes comfortably. She was examining the stone slab which was all that remained of the altar.

"I suppose there's no doubt about the chapel being deconsecrated?" said Harriet.

"None at all. That was the first thing Tristan confirmed with Walter Colwyn."

"Lovely!" said Harriet. After a pause she asked: "Have you any idea yet what form the rites will take?"

"I haven't discussed it thoroughly with Tristan yet, but there'll be a ceremony of homage as usual, of course, followed by the mass—"

"What's Tristan going to do about the problem of getting a virgin?"

"He's thought of a way out of that one. There's going to be a christening. The virginity will be offered to the powers in the form of a christening instead of in the form of the mass."

"How nice! I don't think I've ever been present at a christening before. Will the mass take a nuptial form?"

"Yes, we must start thinking about making the dress. Black satin, I thought, with lots of black lace . . . Perhaps we can go to Swansea next week and pick out a pattern."

"Lovely!" said Harriet. Then: "What will the sacrifice be?"

"Oh, a lamb, of course. The heroic symbol of the Other Church."

"What about the heroic symbol of *Our* Church? Will there be a goat?"

"You mean for the self-indulgence after the mass and the christening? I don't think so. Not since Tristan will be there in person. Why bother with a substitute in those circumstances?"

"Why indeed?" agreed Harriet as they left the chapel and wandered away leisurely together down the hillside, their black skirts flapping in the breeze.

Far below the surf crashed against the cliffs and flung spray high into the air. A sheep bleated again in the distance and the horses browsed quietly among the short grass.

The twins looked at one another.

"Did you understand any of that?" said Lucy frankly at last. "I thought they were talking English but after a while I wasn't so sure."

" 'Course I understood," said Timothy loftily, making the most of one of Lucy's rare confessions of inadequacy. "The society have their own special religion which is sort of like Roman Catholics but a bit different and there's going to be a wedding and a christening."

"Maybe they *are* Catholics."

"They can't be because of the chapel not being consecrated. Consecrated means holy, and if the chapel's not holy any more, Catholics can't use it. Protestants couldn't either probably."

"Well, if they're not Catholics and not Protestants, what are they? And what was all that about a lamb and a goat?"

"That must be part of the religion. Like the Romans. The Romans were always sacrificing goats and lambs and things."

"They weren't going to sacrifice the goat," said Lucy. "The goat was for self-indulgence. What did that mean, do you think?"

"It must be like the Catholics. They have things called indulgences."

"What are they?"

"Just part of the religion," said Timothy, who had no idea.

"Well, if you ask me," said Lucy dissatisfied, "it's all very peculiar."

"The society *is* peculiar," said Timothy with a yawn. "Everyone knows that."

"Do we tell anyone?"

"Well . . . maybe we could tell Aunt Jane. She's the only person I can think of who might be interested."

"That's a good idea," said Lucy. "Let's tell Aunt Jane."

"Okay."

They set off down the hill and quarter of an hour later were at the back door of the cottage.

"Hello, twins," said Jane. "You're just in time for some scones fresh from the oven! That was good timing."

"Aunt Jane," said Lucy, "guess what. There's going to be a wedding at the chapel on the cliffs. The society is organizing it and—"

"—people are coming from miles around to be there," said Timothy, "because the society is going to be the hosts, just like a party. And there's going to be a christening too."

"But they're not going to have a goat," said Lucy, who somehow felt the goat was important, "only a lamb."

"And they're going to sacrifice the lamb," added Timothy. "Just like the Romans."

"Well!" said Jane, laughing. "Whatever will you two think of next? By the way, did your father manage to escape from the sultan with the saber at the Taj Mahal?"

"Yes, thank you," said Timothy politely. "May I have jam on my scone, please?"

"All right, but run along and wash your hands first."

In the privacy of the bathroom the twins exchanged long looks.

"Aunt Jane's one of the nicest people in the world," said Lucy slowly at last, "but sometimes even the nicest people fall short of what one expects of them. It's not her fault. She can't help it."

"What does it matter," muttered Timothy. "I might have

known not even Aunt Jane would believe us this time. Let's forget all about it."

"Okay," said Lucy willingly enough, and reached for the cake of soap as if to wash her hands of the incident.

V

Lisa left the cottage ten minutes before the twins arrived at the back door and walked briskly to the beach. It was most remarkable, she thought, how her lethargy had vanished. Her apathy had been transformed into a sharp interest in her surroundings; as she scrambled over the rocks to the sands she felt exceptionally full of vitality.

She saw them five minutes later. They were sunning themselves beneath the cliffs on a patch of sand enclosed by a semicircle of rocks. Nicola was lying face downward, her bikini top discarded so that her back would tan evenly, and Poole was lying on his back, his hands behind his head and his long limbs stretched leisurely toward the sea. As Lisa watched he rolled over on his side and ran a finger down Nicola's bare spine.

"Well, well!" drawled Lisa in contempt. "What an intimate little picture!"

Poole spun around. She saw all expression die from his dark eyes and suddenly the floodgates of her self-control burst apart and the rage swept through her in a fierce noisy tide.

"You bastard!" she said, trembling. "You rotten, treacherous, lying, deceitful—"

He was on his feet in a flash. "Lisa," he said in a steady soothing voice. "Lisa, be quiet."

"No, I won't!" cried Lisa passionately. "Not until I've told you how much I hate you! Not until I've told Nicola what a fool she is to get mixed up with a man like you!"

"Nicki, darling," said Poole to Nicola, who was still fumbling, confused, with the top half of her bikini, "there's no need for you to hear this. Wait for me up at the house."

"All right, Tristan." She struggled into her wrap and stooped to pick up the straw bag which contained her possessions.

"You wait!" screamed Lisa to her. "You'll see! I could tell you things about this man which you wouldn't believe! I could tell you—"

Nicola began to run away across the sands.

"Be quiet, Lisa," said Poole, and gripped her shoulders with his strong fingers. "Be quiet, do you hear? Be quiet."

"I hate you!" cried Lisa, unable to control herself, oblivious to everything, even the power in Poole's eyes. She was delirious with the ecstasy of venting such a strong passion. "I hate you, I hate you, I hate you—"

Poole tried an incantation. It was a traditional French method of bringing a woman into submission. "Lisa—" He caught her wrist so that his power could merge with the words more effectively—"Lisa, Bestarbeto corrumpit viscera ejus mulieris."

No use. She was beyond the power of a simple incantation. He made another effort to project his mind around hers and strangle it into submission, but Lisa was making so much noise that he couldn't concentrate. At last in desperation he slapped her.

She slapped him right back.

"Murderer!" she shouted at him. "Do you think I'm so stupid I can't see what's happened? You seduced me to get at Matt's money and when Matt left all his money to Nicola—"

Poole resorted to an invocation. It was humiliating to have to call on the lesser powers for help but the virulence in Lisa had to be controlled at once; the circumstances were too dangerous for him to afford the luxury of pride.

In the name of Baal, he thought, bending his entire will to the signal for assistance, in the name of Astaroth, in the name of Lucifer, help me control this woman and make her obedient to whatever I may suggest.

"—you dropped me and turned to Nicola without a second thought!" sobbed Lisa, and sat down abruptly on a nearby rock.

"Lisa," said Poole, seizing his chance, "you're much too upset to discuss this properly now. Why don't we meet here early tomorrow morning and talk about it in a more level-headed way?"

"And have you kill me as you killed Matt?" scoffed Lisa, not so loud now but still very far from placid. "No, thank you!"

"My dear Lisa, when Matt was killed I was at Colwyn Court among the members of the society! Talk sense, please. However, if you're really afraid for your safety I'll meet you at the point where the beach path reaches the rocks—then you'll be in full view of the cottage and you can tell your sister to watch from the window. Satisfied? Good, I'll see you there at eight o'clock tomorrow morning."

"I'll be there!" said Lisa dangerously. "And don't think it'll be a friendly discussion because it won't be."

"Do I have your word not to discuss this with anyone till after we've met tomorrow?"

"All right, but—"

"Thank you. Eight o'clock tomorrow, Lisa," said Poole and escaped.

He ran all the way back to the house. The kitchens were empty but four members of the society were playing a friendly game of bridge on the terrace outside the sitting room.

"Where's Agnes?" he yelled at them.

"In her room," someone called. "Resting." They were all staring at him with open mouths.

Poole raced upstairs and burst into Agnes' room without even the formality of a knock. Agnes, who was painting her nails and listening to "Woman's Hour" on her transistor radio, was so startled that she knocked over her bottle of nail polish.

"Tristan! What's the matter?"

"What the hell happened to that spell?"

"Spell?" said Agnes, very nervous.

"Spell! I know I told you to stop Lisa being in love with me, but—"

"Oh dear!" said Agnes, flustered. "You mean it didn't work? I was so sure I'd been successful—"

"You've been successful all right! You've been so damned successful that now she hates my guts! Agnes, listen to me, we're in deep water and we've got to act and act fast . . ."

VI

Evan had arrived back at Colwyn after an early start from London ten minutes before Lisa had embarked on her stormy scene on the beach, and on hearing that Nicola and Poole had gone sunbathing he left the house and headed swiftly down the path to the cove.

He was on the sands by the time he saw Nicola. She was running toward him, her wrap flying back from her shoulders, her bikini two strips of pale yellow against the tan of her skin.

"Nicki!" he called.

Perhaps Poole had upset her. She looked upset about something. If Poole had done anything to upset her, Evan thought grimly, he'd soon live to regret it.

"Nicki!" he called again.

It was as if she didn't see him. She kept running toward him until presently she was near enough for him to see her parted lips and windswept hair and the dark abstracted look in her eyes.

"Nicki," he said, reaching out to her, "what's the matter?"

But Nicola was in the landscape of her dream, a silent world where she was running across the sands of a deserted shore. She didn't hear him. As he watched, hardly able to believe his eyes, she ran past him without a word and scrambled up the rocks to the path without looking back.

"Nicki!" shouted Evan in a haze of anger and bewilderment. "Nicki, where are you going?"

But Nicola was fulfilling Maris' prophecy. At that moment, as far as she was concerned, Evan had ceased to exist.

VII

The night passed. Nicola ate dinner in the society's dining room and Evan did not see her; when he knocked on the door of her room later there was no reply and when he tried the door he found it was locked. Evan went to bed in a fever of painful confusion and injured pride, and tossed and turned continually throughout a sleepless night.

Poole also spent a sleepless night. Agnes had slipped a mild drug into Nicola's coffee to make sure that Poole would be unhampered by her presence, and as soon as Nicola was in bed asleep Poole locked the door of her bedroom and returned to the west wing to begin his preparations. He consulted his books, meditated, and made his plans, but shortly before dawn he prepared himself for action. He had eaten no dinner in order to fulfill the need for fasting, and now he took a bath to meet the requirement of cleanliness before dressing in the black linen robe which Agnes brought him. The third requirement, continence, could not be observed, but since it was useless to regret the time he had recently spent with Nicola he merely shrugged his shoulders and asked Agnes if everything else was ready. It was. As soon as the sun had risen they walked up to the castle together and Agnes lit the small brazier amid the castle ruins in order to burn the laurel juice, camphor, white resin, sulfur, and salt and purify the area in preparation for the circle. Poole drew the circle as soon as the purification was complete. He drew it while he moved in counterclockwise direction, and used vermilion paint which contained mercury and sulfur. After it was finished he drew a second circle eight feet in diameter inside the first, and as with the first circle he was careful to leave a gap in the line so that he and Agnes could enter and leave both circles freely until everything was ready. Then, leaving Agnes tracing the appropriate names and symbols in the space between the two circles, he took his fresh hazel rod which served as a wand and walked out of the castle toward the wild horses grazing nearby.

Poole was not unfamiliar with horses but it was some years since he had handled one and he found it hard to suppress a flicker of uneasiness when he approached the large black stallion on the edge of the herd. He had to pause to eliminate the human weakness, but once that was done everything proved to be absurdly easy. He raised his wand; the horse pricked up its ears. Even when the other horses edged away the stallion stayed motionless, waiting for him, and presently he touched the animal with the wand, murmured some words beneath his breath, and slipped the noose of a rope over the horse's head. When he returned to the castle ruins the horse was walking docilely behind him.

"Are we ready, Agnes?"

"Yes, I think so."

"Good." Keeping the animal outside the circle, Poole tied the rope to a corner of fallen masonry in case the horse should try to bolt for freedom, but the horse itself made no protest and only gazed at him trustingly with dark intelligent eyes.

"Light the fire again, Agnes," said Poole.

Agnes lit the charcoal in the brazier. After a moment Poole joined her in the middle of the inner circle and stood watching her.

"Feed the fire," he said at last.

Agnes added camphor and brandy to the inky smoke.

"All right," said Poole quietly. "Close the circle."

Agnes picked up the paintbrush and the can of vermilion paint and quickly completed both the inner and the outer circles.

"Very well, Agnes. Now for the fragrance beloved of the powers of darkness. When I call the name of the herb, feed it to the flames. Ready?"

"Yes, Master."

"Coriander," said Poole, and paused. Then: "Hemlock . . . parsley . . . black poppy liquor . . . fennel . . . sandalwood . . . henbane."

Agnes flung the last ingredient into the flames and for a while they stood watching the fire. A rich dark odor began to envelop them. Poole stooped to the covered basket which Agnes had brought with them into the circle and dragged out the black cock inside.

"To my comrades," called Poole in a loud voice, "to my subjects, to my cohorts, to my legions I offer this sacrifice."

The fumes from the brazier were growing stronger; his voice had thickened and his hand as Agnes gave him the knife was unsteady.

The cock died a bloody death.

Agnes fell to her knees to bow before the unleashed force, but Poole stood his ground and let the force take possession of him. After three seconds of rigid immobility his frame shook with violence; as Agnes watched with worshiping eyes, he stretched his bloodstained hands to the dark morning sky and in a hoarse and vibrant voice summoned his demons to meet him at the circle's edge.

VIII

When her alarm clock went off at seven o'clock that morning Lisa was still sound asleep, exhausted by the exhilaration of her hatred for Poole. She had a hard time dragging herself out of bed, but presently the thought of the rendezvous with him was too tempting to be resisted and she was wide awake when she went downstairs.

Jane was already in the kitchen brewing Benedict's early morning tea. "My goodness!" she said in surprise when she saw her sister. "You're up early!"

"I'm meeting Tristan."

"Oh, Lisa!"

"No, it's not what you think. That's all finished. I'm just going to drive home to him how much I despise him . . . Jane, watch what happens, will you? I'm meeting him above the beach and if he knows someone's watching he won't dare harm me."

"Lisa, wouldn't it be more sensible to—"

"I must go," said Lisa, "or I'll be late." And she slipped out of the back door.

Jane made the tea, took it up to Benedict, and then returned downstairs with a worried frown to the living room windows which faced the sea.

171

Lisa was waiting at the point where the path reached the rocks about twenty feet above the sands. It was a pale, clear morning and the sea was a dark, calm blue beyond the cliffs. Kneeling on the window seat Jane glanced at her watch. Five minutes past eight. Lisa was pacing up and down in a fever of impatience. Ten minutes past eight. No sign of Poole.

He's not going to come, thought Jane. She went to the front door and opened it.

"Lisa!" she called at the top of her voice. "Come back! Please!"

She saw Lisa turn her head at the same time as she saw the horse out of the corner of her eye. She glanced up sharply toward the castle. The largest of the black wild horses seemed to be in the midst of a lone stampede. She saw him gallop down from the castle cliffs, and the flock of sheep in his path took fright and fled before the thunder of his flying hooves.

Jane stared mesmerized. The sheep, bunched together in fright, were pounding blindly across the hillside toward the cottage, but as she watched she saw the horse veer and drive them toward the place where Lisa was standing above the cliffs.

"Lisa!" shouted Jane in terror. "Lisa, look out!"

But Lisa moved too late. The sheep swept down upon her before she could escape them, and the next moment she was jostled over the jagged rocks by their close-packed bodies to meet her death on the beach below.

7

"I'm going to marry Tristan," said Nicola to Evan. "We're getting married on August the second."

They were in Matt's house in Surrey on the evening after Lisa's funeral. A week had passed since Lisa's death, a week filled with newspaper reporters, police, another inquest, and yet another verdict of accidental death. Everything had been disrupted. Benedict was thinking of abandoning the cottage and returning to Cambridge; Jane was suppressing a hundred doubts and a thousand nameless fears by devoting herself to the twins; and the twins were waiting with more dogged patience than ever for their father to return from his travels and make everything right again. Poole had driven Nicola to Surrey for the funeral but had not been present at the service. Afterward, while Poole was still absent, Evan had his first chance for several days to speak to Nicola alone and demand to know what her feelings for Poole were.

"I love him," said Nicola, her gray eyes defiant. "He's proposed and I've accepted. We're going to be married just as soon as possible."

"You're crazy," said Evan. "You must be crazy. You're out of your mind."

"Oh, for God's sake, leave me alone and go away!" cried Nicola and tried to escape, but he wouldn't let her go.

"How can I go away when you're planning to return to Colwyn Court?"

"I'll stay in the west wing with Tristan! You can't stop me staying there!"

And Evan knew he could not. He felt so sick at heart that he wanted to walk onto the next plane to America, but that too was out of the question. Not only was it impossible for him to abandon his family but he found it impossible to abandon Nicola. As the hours passed he became more convinced than ever that she was somehow not responsible for her actions.

"It's wonderful news about Nicola's engagement," said Jane to him doubtfully on the morning after Lisa's funeral. "But I do hope she knows what she's doing. She hardly knows Tristan at all, and . . . oh, Evan, I can't help feeling it's all wrong! I'm sorry—perhaps I shouldn't be saying this, but—"

An ally. In spite of his despair Evan felt his spirits lift a little. He began to talk, pouring out all his doubts and fears to her, and Jane in turn confessed her uneasiness and her intuitive conviction that Poole was the cause of all the recent troubles at Colwyn Court.

They talked for over an hour together.

"Have your private detectives found out anything worthwhile yet?" asked Jane at last.

"Not so far. I'm going up to London this afternoon to see how far they've got with the investigations."

"I'm sure they won't find anything incriminating," said Jane. "Tristan's much too clever—inhumanly clever, Evan, you'll laugh at me I know, but sometimes I've even wondered if Tristan is human at all. The way he attracted Lisa—and now Nicola . . . it's as if he bewitched them. I know it sounds ridiculous to talk about bewitching and black magic nowadays, but—"

"Poole's human all right," said Evan. His mind flickered

174

quickly over the memory of the strangeness of Poole's room before he dismissed the strangeness as eccentricity. "He's just a slick operator with a fair degree of psychological know-how and a sizable gift for hypnosis. I agree with you that Nicola's bewitched, but I don't think anyone's been weaving spells. Poole's simply managed to subject her mind to his so completely that she's a different person."

"That must be witchcraft," said Jane.

"No," said Evan, "just a form of hypnotic control inspired by a very human desire to get his hands on half a million pounds. No, he's human and he's crooked and I'm going to do my damndest to expose him before he marries Nicola, ruins her life, and makes off with her money . . . Jane, I'm going to ask you a big favor. I know you don't want to go back to the cottage after what happened to Lisa, but it would be a great relief to me if I knew you were there—if I knew there was someone at hand who understood the situation and whom I could turn to for help if the need arose. You've no idea what a help it's been to have found someone who can sympathize with me about all this."

"It's been a help to me, too," confessed Jane. "I was beginning to feel neurotic about Tristan. I thought I was the only one who disliked him."

"So will you come back to Colwyn?"

"Well . . . I don't want to go back, but on the other hand I couldn't possibly return to Cambridge now and abandon Nicola—and you—without lifting a finger to help. If I can help you by being at Colwyn, and if you can help Nicola—"

"I'm going to get Nicola away from that man if it's the last thing I ever do!"

"Oh Evan, don't say things like that!" exclaimed Jane, touching wood in superstitious panic. "Not after all these sudden deaths!"

"They were accidents."

"I wonder," said Jane.

"You're not seriously suggesting—"

"No," said Jane, "just wondering . . . Evan, if you're going up to London today to see the detectives, would you do something for me there?"

"Of course. What is it?"

"Go to Foyles and buy me a really good book on witch-craft."

II

On returning to Matt's house the next morning to collect Nicola and drive her back to Wales, Poole met the twins. They had just said good-bye to their *au pair* girl who had departed for her home in Spain to escape from the atmosphere of sudden death which was apparently hovering over the household, and were relaxing in their newfound freedom; although they had liked Costanza they had become tired of looking after her and teaching her English. As Poole drove up to the house in his black Jaguar he found them sitting on the front doorstep and watching his arrival with interest.

"Good morning," said Lucy with impressive formality as he stepped out of the car. "We would like to congratulate you on your engagement."

"Thanks!" He smiled at her and glanced at the boy, but Timothy was looking at his toes.

"Where's the wedding going to be?" said Lucy brightly, abandoning the gravity of the formal welcome. "In the chapel?"

Poole looked at her. Lucy felt a thrill of pleasure tiptoe down her spine. Poole made her feel important and clever when he looked at her like that.

"We heard Agnes talking about it," she said, explaining. "But we didn't tell anyone because we thought it was a secret."

Poole smiled at her. "It was a secret," he said. "In a way it still is. The society is giving a party in the chapel on the evening of August the first, and we're going to stage a pageant in the chapel to fulfill a tradition of the society's history. Since Nicola and I are getting married the pageant will take the form of a wedding this time, but it won't be a proper wedding because the chapel isn't consecrated. The legal wedding is to take place the next morning at the registry office in Swansea."

"Can we come to the pageant?" said Lucy promptly.

"I thought you were both going to Cambridge to stay with your Aunt Jane."

"Oh, Aunt Jane's changed her mind," said Lucy. "We're all going back to the cottage. We're glad, aren't we, Timmy? It's nicer by the sea than in the middle of a big town."

"I wish we were going to Cambridge," said Timothy. "I wouldn't think of Mum so much there."

"Yes, you would," said Lucy roughly, and to divert herself as well as Timothy she turned to Poole. "Can we come to the pageant?"

Poole was giving her that special look again. She jumped up, ran over to him, and slipped her hand in his. "Please!" she begged, opening her blue eyes very wide and assuming her most appealing expression. "Please, Tristan! Can I call you Tristan now that you're going to be my step-brother-in-law?"

"Why not?" said Poole, and thought again what an exceptionally pretty child she was. A perfect offering . . . He began to picture the christening robes. "Would you like to be a bridesmaid in the pageant?" he suggested with a smile.

"Ooooh!" Lucy squealed. "May I?"

"Of course you can, but keep it a secret, will you, Lucy? The pageant is a private affair held by the society for their friends and we don't want a crowd of outsiders standing by and gaping at us."

"I won't tell a soul," promised Lucy fervently. "Can Timmy be a page?"

This was awkward. Poole looked at Timothy, at his straw-colored hair and downcast eyes and hostile mouth, and decided that the boy was totally unsuitable for his purposes. "You don't want to be a page, do you, Tim?" he said lightly. "You're too old for that sort of stuff, aren't you? I know how boys of your age feel about that kind of thing."

Timothy was smitten with an irresistible urge to be difficult. He was not at ease with Poole and privately thought Lucy was making a fool of herself. "If Lucy's going to be a bridesmaid," he said, staring at the ground by Poole's black shoes, "I want to be a page."

Poole knew when a subject left him no room to maneuver. "All right," he said, well aware that he had no intention of admitting Timothy to the rites. "We'll talk about it later when we're all back at Colwyn, and remember—not a word to anyone meanwhile. Okay?"

"Our lips are sealed," said Lucy grandly.

Timothy said nothing.

"Tim?" said Poole.

"Okay," said Timothy, "if you like. And my name's Timothy, not Tim. Lucy's the only person who doesn't have to call me by my full name."

"Honestly, Timmy!" exclaimed Lucy, annoyed after Poole had disappeared into the house. "How could you be so rude when he was so nice to you?"

"I didn't like the way you jumped all over him as if you were a puppy who wanted to be taken for a walk."

"I've never been so insulted in all my life!" said Lucy furiously and walked off in a huff to leave Timothy still sitting unhappily on the front doorstep.

A quarrel was rare for the twins; Timothy was aware of his distrust of Poole turning to an active dislike . . .

III

When Evan arrived at Colwyn Court a day later, he left the house at the first available opportunity and hurried down to the cottage above the beach. He found Jane alone in the kitchen; the twins were exploring the caves and Benedict had gone into Swansea for more stationery supplies.

"Oh, good!" said Jane, abandoning the cream she was whipping and leading the way into the living room. "I was just thinking about you. Is there any news?"

"Yes, there is." Evan looked better. His eyes were less

178

bloodshot and his face had lost its drawn, tired look. "By the way, here's your book on witchcraft—it seemed both readable and comprehensive, so I hope you'll find I chose the right one."

"Did you read it?"

"I read the parts about witchcraft in Africa and they seemed reliable enough. I didn't bother with all the mumbo jumbo about witches and black cats and the orgies on Halloween." He flung himself down in an armchair and pulled some folded sheets of paper out of the inside pocket of his jacket. "Jane, I've got some data on Poole and the detectives are still working on the investigation so I hope they'll discover even more than they've discovered already. Meanwhile, listen to this. Poole's thirty-five years old, born Tristan Robert Poole in Cheltenham, Gloucestershire—"

"How respectable," said Jane.

"—only child, father an engineer, attended kindergarten in Cheltenham and later Wyndham Hall prep school near Salisbury—"

"More respectable than ever."

"—emigrated to America with parents at age twelve and attended high school in San Francisco, graduated high school and attended courses in psychology and anthropology at Berkeley—"

"There must be a catch somewhere," said Jane. "I don't believe it."

"'—dropped out of Berkeley after one year, and went to a smaller college at Las Corridas, a town near Sacramento, where he majored in psychology. After getting his degree he went on to study for his master's, and the subject of his master's thesis was—" Evan took a deep breath: " 'The Role of Psychology in the Modern Practice of the Occult.' "

"What did I tell you!" exclaimed Jane in triumph.

"Wait! Listen to this. At this stage 'subject', as the detectives' report calls him, became involved with several groups loosely classifiable as eccentric religious sects. Subject has no police record, but he was present at a witchcraft ceremony held twelve years ago on August the first, in an orange grove some miles northwest of Los Angeles. Apparently the first of August is one of the four big days of the year for those who practice witchcraft—they still call it Lammas, the name given by the early English church to the harvest festival which was celebrated on that date, and it seems to be on a par with the more famous date of Halloween. On this particular occasion the ceremony was interrupted by the police who made several arrests for disorderly conduct, lewd behavior, and so on, but Poole wasn't one of the ones arrested. He was found unconscious and taken to the hospital. For ten days he remained unconscious while the doctors tried to decide what was wrong with him, but eventually he recovered and settled down to an elusive but legal life, traveling all over America and establishing chapter houses of this damned society. So great was his success that he decided to expand his operations to England, and during the past three years he's set up various other groups, of which this Colwyn Court bunch happen to be the latest. He seems to have a private income, although the detectives are still trying to find out where it comes from—I would suspect a Swiss bank. The various chapter houses of the society seem to be financed by a mixture of subscriptions and bequests, but everything appears to be legal and above suspicion." Evan paused. " 'Subject's parents are now dead, he has no known relatives, and he's unmarried.' " He looked up at her. "What do you make of all that?"

"I don't think he's the real Tristan Poole at all," said Jane promptly. "I think they succeeded in summoning the devil in that orange grove twelve years ago during the Lammas rites, and the devil took possession of one of his most promising followers."

"Seriously, Jane!"

"I *am* serious!"

"Well . . ." Evan gave an awkward laugh. "I agree that you were right when you suspected Poole of witchcraft. I think myself that this society of his is a cover for a phony religion—for dabbling in the occult—and if this is true it should give me some sort of lever to use against him. If they're practicing witchcraft in between harvesting their nature foods, they'll be tempted to celebrate Lammas, and if the celebration they have in mind is the one I suspect they have in mind, I can call the police and catch them all redhanded in the middle of the orgy. As soon as I leave you now I'm going to confront Poole, warn him that I know what kind of game he's playing, and advise him that unless he wants trouble on his hands he'd better give up Nicola pretty damn quickly. Thanks to the detectives I believe I have enough evidence to shake him out of his complacency and prise him away from Colwyn Court—and from Nicola too."

"Oh Evan, do be careful!"

"Poole's the one who's going to have to be careful! Don't worry, Jane, 'subject' is going to have second thoughts about marrying Nicola and staying at Colwyn Court! I think I've got him exactly where I want him . . ."

IV

Poole was working out some astral positions from his charts and scanning the forces to be at his disposal on the first of August. He was so absorbed in his work that when Evan knocked on the door of his room he did not even bother to inquire who it was.

"Come in!" he called.

The door opened. "I'd like to talk to you, Poole," said Evan's voice abruptly from behind him.

Poole swung around. His left hand moved automatically to close his book and when he stood up his body blocked Evan's view of his calculations. "Shall we go downstairs?" he suggested evenly.

"No, we can talk here. I merely wanted to tell you that the game's up as far as Colwyn Court's concerned. I know exactly what your society does in its spare time, and unless all of you clear out of here as soon as possible you'll regret it. Oh, and when you go you can leave Nicola behind because she's not going to marry you. I'll see that the police make this part of Wales too hot to hold you before I'll see you hypnotize her to the nearest registry office. I trust I make myself quite clear."

There was a pause. Poole put his hands in his pockets so that his clenched fists would be out of sight.

"Dr. Colwyn, I think there must be some mistake. I've done nothing legally wrong. I have no criminal record. The behavior of the society has been exemplary, as I'm sure the police would be the first to admit. And please let's not talk about my fiancée because I can't believe you and I could ever have a profitable discussion on the subject."

"Profitable must be a very favorite word of yours," said Evan. "Especially in relation to Nicola."

"I refuse to discuss Nicola with you."

"How about discussing the occult?"

"A fascinating subject," said Poole, "but not one which I would have thought appealed to you."

"Look, Poole, you're walking on thin ice. I've only got to catch you using your hobby as an excuse for sexual aberration—"

Poole made up his mind. "Dr. Colwyn, why is it that you're always dragging up the subject of my sexuality? As a psychologist I must say I find your obsession with my relationships with women unhealthy, to say the least. Are you so unsure of your own sexuality that you have to be constantly jeering at a man who's sexually confident?"

He achieved the exact result he wanted.

"Why you—" spluttered Evan, and swung his fist wildly in Poole's direction.

Sidestepping the expected blow, Poole moved so deliberately that he might have been parodying a slow-motion film. As Evan lunged off balance Poole hit him on the jaw, flung him back against the wall, and watched as the other man sank unconscious to the floor.

"Agnes!" called Poole sharply, but Agnes did not fail him. She was in the doorway.

"Scissors."

"Here." She handed them to him as if she were a nurse in an operating theater.

Poole knelt, snipped off a lock of Evan's hair and said without looking up: "Envelope."

Agnes held the envelope open for him. He slipped the red hairs inside and gave the scissors back to her.

"Do we act straight away?" said Agnes.

"No, he can't do a damn thing before Lammas unless he wants to make a fool of himself."

"And on Lammas Evening?"

"Agnes," said Poole, "how you love to worry!"

She smiled at him. On the floor Evan stirred and groaned.

"He's coming around. Get a glass of water." He knelt down by Evan's body as Evan shook his head and raised himself gingerly on one elbow. "Dr. Colwyn, are you all right?"

"Leave me alone, you bastard," growled Evan, and tried without success to stand up.

"Here, Dr. Colwyn," said Agnes, offering him a glass of water. "Drink this."

"I must warn you, Dr. Colwyn," said Poole politely, "that Miss Miller witnessed the entire incident and should you wish to charge me with assault she won't hesitate to tell the police that you struck the first blow."

Evan did not answer. He drank the water, levered himself to his feet, and turned to the door. "I'll get you in the end," he said between his teeth. "You'll see. You'll regret this."

"Dr. Colwyn, your hostility does you no credit, if you'll forgive me saying so. In fact it may even rebound with unfortunate results on those you love. If you try to make trouble for me you can rest assured that I'll have no hesitation whatsoever about making trouble for you."

Evan whirled around. "What do you mean?"

Poole was very still. Agnes stood silent and grave behind him. "Dr. Colwyn," said Poole at last, "you have a very delicate sister. Perhaps you may have underestimated how delicate she is."

Evan groped for words. "Are you trying to—"

"I'm merely making statements, Dr. Colwyn. That's all. Just statements."

"You're not qualified to make statements like that about my sister," said Evan.

Poole said nothing.

"If you threaten me like that again—"

"I'm not threatening you, Dr. Colwyn, just making statements. By the way, when you were in Africa did you hear how the witch doctors there have been known to put a man to death simply by use of the power of suggestion? A most macabre achievement, I've always thought." He paused. "Some people are very susceptible to the power of suggestion, Dr. Colwyn."

Evan swallowed. Words deserted him. For the first time in his meetings with Poole he felt totally unnerved.

"I ask just one thing," said Poole at last. "Leave us alone. Make trouble for us and we'll make trouble for you, but if you leave us alone no one will get hurt. Do you understand what I'm saying?"

Evan nodded. There was another pause. Then:

"You can go now," said Poole.

Evan went without a word. His head ached. His eyes smarted with childish tears. He felt as if every nerve in his body had been battered by an unseen force until all his defenses were in ruins. Automatically, without stopping to think, he left the house and stumbled blindly down the path which led to the cottage and to Jane.

V

Jane made him feel better at once. There was something very comforting about her soft, untidy femininity with its sympathy, warmth, and responsiveness. He even recovered himself sufficiently to feel envious of Benedict having such a woman to look after him; after the way he had been treated by first Nicola and then Poole, Evan decided he was much in need of some feminine attention and that Jane's society might in its own platonic way do much to restore his flagging self-esteem.

"I'm not at all surprised Tristan threatened you like that," she said frankly. "It was frightfully brave of you to face him. I should have fainted instantly in sheer terror."

It had not occurred to Evan that he might have acted bravely, but it was nevertheless very pleasant to have a woman regard his foolhardy behavior with such admiration. He smiled at her. "You talk as if he's the devil incarnate!"

"I think he is," said Jane seriously, and reached for her book on witchcraft.

"You don't really believe that, Jane!"

"Yes, I do. Honestly. Listen to this: 'Witches and warlocks form groups called covens, consisting of thirteen people or, according to one authority, twelve people plus a person representing the devil or even the devil himself—' "

"Oh, I don't doubt they're dabbling in witchcraft," said Evan, "but you can't take it seriously, Jane!"

"You took it seriously when Tristan threatened Gwyneth, didn't you? And just listen to this! 'One of the well-known characteristics of a witch or warlock is the presence of the animal familiar, an attendant demon taking the form of a cat, dog, mole, hare, toad . . .' " Jane skipped several species of animals before continuing: " 'The black cat is a famous symbol of witchcraft, but in fact cats of all kinds were used by witches as a physical home for their attendant demons, and a white cat was not unknown—' "

"They haven't got any cats at Colwyn Court at the moment," said Evan, and added as a fascinated after-thought: "But they do keep several hares in hutches."

"Never mind the hares!" exclaimed Jane, too agitated to allow him to finish. "What about my poor Marble? He's lost weight and hardly seems to know who I am and every morning he pads away up to Colwyn Court and stays there all day—"

Evan, who privately thought Jane tended to be somewhat foolish where her cat was concerned, decided that it would

185

be wiser to turn the conversation into other channels. "The tradition of the animal familiar is probably little more than folklore," he said shortly. "I wouldn't worry about Marble if I were you, Jane—take him to the vet if he keeps on losing weight. Now, what does the book say about Lammas—or haven't you got that far yet?"

"Lammas," muttered Jane, turning her distracted gaze back to the book and flicking over several pages. "Oh yes, here we are. 'Each coven holds a sabbath at regular intervals throughout the year, but on the four great days of the occult calendar, namely February 2nd (Candlemas), the eve of May 1st (Walpurgisnacht), August 1st (Lammas), and October 31st, the eve of All Hallows (Halloween), several covens may join together to celebrate the full rites of the Devil's Church—' "

"They're going to celebrate Lammas," said Evan. "I'm sure of it. If I didn't feel so hamstrung by Poole's threats to Gwyneth I'd go this very minute to Swansea and tip off the police."

" 'The Devil's Church is in many ways a direct parallel to God's Church,' " Jane read, barely listening to him. " 'But everything in the Devil's Church is the exact opposite of everything in God's Church. Thus virtue becomes sin and sin becomes virtue—' "

"I'll summon the police somehow," muttered Evan. "I'll catch them all redhanded."

" 'The Christian act of communion is paralleled by the black mass, the christening is paralleled by an act of bestowing the Devil's Mark to welcome the child into the Devil's flock, the marriage with the bride wearing white is reflected by a contrary service in which the bride wears black—' Evan, I've been thinking of this all morning and I'm sure I'm right—before Lisa died the twins told me that the society was going to have a wedding in the ruined chapel on the cliffs, and I took no notice because I thought they were making it up. But now I'm sure they weren't. I think they overheard something Miss Miller or even Tristan himself said. Before

Tristan marries Nicola at the registry office on August the second, I'm sure they're going to be married according to the rites of the Devil's Church when the Lammas ceremonies begin after sundown on August the first."

"I won't let them!" shouted Evan. "My God, if Poole tries something like that—"

But Jane had returned to her book again. " 'The nature of the sabbaths vary and there seems to be no set form,' " she read. " 'However, one or two features appear constantly. Among them is the act of homage wherein each member of the coven pays individual homage to the devil or his representative by the obscene kiss . . .' —Perhaps I'd better skip that bit before I start to blush—'. . . After the religious observances the witches rub themselves with aconite, a drug used in the old days to give the illusion of flying through the air—hence the time-honored picture of the witches flying on the phallic symbol of the broomstick—' "

"Damned perverts!" growled Evan. "Jane, we've got to think up a plan. We've got to stop them."

" '—and this is followed by dancing and mass copulation,' " Jane continued, unable to stop herself by this time. She looked puzzled. "But how can that be if the coven consists entirely of women?"

"No doubt they take the precaution," said Evan dryly, "of inviting a coven of men to share their celebrations. Jane, surely the best plan is to catch the group in the middle of their orgies and have the whole lot of them rounded up on some sort of indecency charge. We've somehow got to see the police and arrange some sort of trap without anyone in the society knowing about it."

"I'm sure Tristan would know," said Jane with a shiver. "He'd find out. I know he would."

"I could leave it until the very last minute—until the morning of the first of August."

"But what would you do then? If you rushed to Swansea and told the police you wanted them to break up some occult rites they simply wouldn't believe you!"

"Oh yes, they would! I'd tell them a bunch of hippies planned to hold an orgy! But perhaps I've got a better idea. My father knows the retired Chief Constable, and as you know, the Chief Constable controls the police in his particular district. I'm sure any Chief Constable, even if he does happen to be retired, would still be able to pull some influential strings. I'll drive over to Milford Haven to see him on Lammas morning and bulldoze him into taking the necessary action. Even if Poole has me followed he won't see anything objectionable about my visiting an old friend of my father's."

"That sounds like a splendid idea. I—Marble! Marble, don't scratch the paint, naughty cat!" She jumped up. The cat was standing by the closed front door and pawing fretfully at the woodwork as he mewed for attention. "I wish Marble would get better," said Jane anxiously as she let him out. "I didn't like leaving him here when we were in Surrey for the funerals, but I was afraid he might run away if I took him to yet another strange environment and when Miss Miller volunteered to look after him . . . oh, Evan, do you think Miss Miller changed him into a familiar when we were away? He's been so odd lately, so tired and unlike himself—"

"My dear Jane," said Evan kindly, "I'm sure the very last thing Marble is suffering from is an attendant demon. Perhaps he has a slight chill on the stomach and feels a bit liverish. Why don't you take him around to the local vet tomorrow and set your mind at rest?"

Outside the front door Marble stood listening. Then, receiving a summons from a different direction he summoned his failing energy and wandered slowly away from the cottage toward the kitchens of Colwyn Court.

VI

The rest of July passed lazily, the days trickling away into the past as effortlessly as leaves floating downstream on an unhurried river. But time meant little to Nicola now. Sometimes she felt she was in a dream and that her one contact with reality lay through Poole. He had helped her write letters to give notice of her intention to leave both her job and her apartment, and he had gone to London to collect her possessions and ensure her roommate had not been inconvenienced financially by Nicola's decision to leave at such short notice. At Poole's suggestion too she had written to several friends and relations to tell them she was planning to marry quietly in the near future, but she felt no distress at the thought that none of them would be at the wedding.

"I think a wedding should be small and private," Poole had said. "It should be a personal, intimate affair."

"But what about the pageant?" Nicola had asked after agreeing wholeheartedly with him. "Surely that will hardly be small and private."

"I think you'll be pleasantly surprised by the pageant," Poole had told her with a smile. "You'll be surprised how personal and intimate it'll turn out to be."

Nicola had spent some time pondering dreamily about the pageant. The idea fascinated her but her knowledge about the ceremony involved remained bewilderingly vague.

"Tristan," she said on the morning of the thirty-first of July, "tell me some more about the pageant. The more I think of it the more exciting it seems—it's such a romantic idea to have a wedding service in that chapel at sunset! You were so clever to think of it."

"You're sure you don't feel it's in bad taste?"

"No, as I told you when you first suggested the idea, I like the tradition of the wedding service but since I don't believe in anything much as far as religion goes I couldn't care less if the chapel is consecrated or not. And we'll be married properly in the registry office the next day, so what does it matter if the service in the pageant isn't strictly valid?" They were sunbathing on the beach again; Poole was drawing mysterious patterns in the sand as she spoke, and she propped herself up on one elbow to watch him. "I hope it doesn't rain," she said as an afterthought.

"It won't." He looked up at her seriously. "You really should believe in something, you know."

"I can't help it if I don't," said Nicola languidly, "and I'm not hypocritical enough to pretend to be religious when I'm not." She rolled over onto her back and reached for her sunglasses. "Tell me more about the order of ceremonies for tomorrow—you still haven't told me what actually happens. Oughtn't we to have a rehearsal or something?"

"There's no need for you to worry about that."

"Well, just tell me one thing," Nicola said with sleepy curiosity. "Why can't Timothy be a page? Lucy really means it, you know, when she says she won't be a bridesmaid unless Timothy takes part in the pageant too. The twins are very loyal to one another."

"Lucy will be a bridesmaid," said Poole. "You don't have to worry about that either . . . Nicki darling, I think we really should discuss your spiritual beliefs. I don't think I approve of my wife being an atheist."

"It's a bit late for disapproval now!" murmured Nicola, amused, thinking he was joking.

"I'm serious, Nicki. How can you visualize the world except as a continuous war between the forces of good and evil?"

"Oh Tristan!" She yawned indolently. "Isn't that sort of talk all rather old-fashioned?"

"You doubt that evil exists?"

"Well, I suppose in an abstract sense—"

"But you doubt the presence of evil as an all-powerful metaphysical force."

"I don't believe in the devil, if that's what you mean," said Nicola placidly.

The last thing she heard him say before her memory deserted her was:

"I want none of your pitiful ignorance in tomorrow's ceremony, my dear, and none of your pathetic skepticism either. Give me your disbelief and your will to disbelieve and your memory of disbelief, and let me cleanse your soul of all taint of heresy . . ."

190

And suddenly the sun was snuffed out and the stars faded one by one and she began her journey along the edge of a black and never-ending night.

VII

Lammas dawned.

The cloudless sky was reflected in the brilliant blue of the sea. The earth glistened after a night of rain, but now that the sun was rising the world was bathed in shimmering light.

"March-hares-and-rabbits," said Lucy to herself as she woke up. Someone had once told her that this was a lucky thing to say when one awoke on the first day of a new month. She looked at the clock by her bedside. Only six! Lucy felt annoyed. She was so wide awake that the idea of returning to sleep was impossible. Slipping out of bed she padded to the window and peered out at the new day.

Nicola's wedding day, she thought, the secret wedding day. If only I could have been in the pageant! She found herself wondering for the hundredth time why Timothy was not allowed to be a page. Nobody had suggested that she should give up her cherished ambition to be a bridesmaid, but after an agony of indecision she knew she had no choice. It wouldn't have been fair to abandon Timothy, and Timothy had to come first.

"Bother Timmy," said Lucy aloud, leaning over the windowsill.

It was then that she heard the cat.

He was mewing outside the back door below her, and sounded lost and forlorn.

"Just a moment, Marble," called Lucy and turned back into the room. It took less than a minute for her to pull on her shorts and slip a sweater over her head; after pushing her feet into her gym shoes she left her room and pattered downstairs to the back door.

But Marble did not want to come in. He mewed, looked at

191

her, ran a little way down the path, stopped to look back, and mewed again.

"Silly cat," said Lucy. "What are you up to? Here!"

Marble edged away.

He's playing a game, thought Lucy with interest. He wants me to follow him. Perhaps he's got something to show me.

"Here, Marble!" she said, following him, and saw him dance out of her reach again as he bounded down the path.

Clever cat, thought Lucy, intrigued, and walked down the path after him.

He kept at a safe distance from her while he led her slowly uphill to the castle. When she saw his white fur vanish amid the gray stone of the castle walls she felt satisfied. Now she'd catch him. She could edge him into a corner and—

Lucy stopped.

Marble was not alone in the castle. He was nestling in the arms of the one who owned him body and soul, and his purrs were so loud that Lucy could hear them as she stood twelve feet away in the gap in the castle walls. Later when she tried to look back at what had happened, the last thing she remembered with any degree of clarity was Tristan Poole giving her that special look and saying in his dark, quiet voice: "Hello, Lucy! I wonder if you realize what an important day this is going to be for you."

VIII

When Evan arrived at the cottage after breakfast he found a distracted Jane telling Timothy to search the beach.

"Hello," he said. "What's the matter?"

"Lucy seems to have disappeared," said Jane anxiously. "Benedict says she's probably gone off on some private expedition and that I shouldn't worry unless she misses lunch, but I can't help worrying a little. She didn't turn up for breakfast and that's so unlike her."

"She can't have gone far," said Evan soothingly. "Timothy will probably find her on the beach."

"That's what Benedict said . . . How are things at Colwyn Court?"

"Everything's fine. Father's well and in good spirits. Gwyneth's playing a new record which arrived in this morning's post. No problems on that score."

"Thank goodness for that! Are you off to see your Chief Constable?"

"Yes, here's his name, address, and phone number in case anything happens. If all goes well—and I don't see why it shouldn't—we'll have the chapel surrounded by police as soon as dusk falls tonight and the ceremonies begin."

"Wonderful," said Jane in relief. "Evan, if you get the chance, do phone me during the day and tell me how things are going. I'll be keeping my fingers crossed for you."

"Will that protect me from evil spells?" said Evan with a laugh, and suddenly winced in pain.

"What's the matter?" said Jane, alarmed.

He put a hand to his head. "I felt as if someone had hit me with a hammer." He swayed unsteadily on his feet. "I feel . . . God, what a headache! That came on suddenly! I feel as if . . . as if . . ."

"Evan!" said Jane, frightened. "Evan!"

". . . as if I'm going to faint," said Evan in a disbelieving voice, and Jane was just in time to break his fall as he slumped unconscious upon the carpet.

8

⋊⋉

I

At Colwyn Court Agnes was in conference with Poole in the dressing room next to his bedroom. The cupboard door was open; Poole's black box was unlocked and its contents set out on a long table.

"All right," said Poole. "Let's make a check. Vestments?"

"They're being pressed downstairs."

"Incense?"

"Rue, myrtle, dried nightshade, henbane, and thorn-apple. Yes, they're all assembled and ready for burning."

"Good. Now, we have the altar cloth here, and the crucifix—is the chalice being polished?"

"Yes, Tristan, and I've set aside the candles. We've made the bread, so as far as the mass goes I think I can safely say that everything's ready."

"What about Lucy's dress?"

"Harriet's finishing that off. Nicola's dress is ready. By the way, Nicola and Lucy are asleep in my room—I locked the door as a precaution, but they won't wake up for hours yet."

"Excellent. What about the food and wine for the festivities after the service?"

"The wine's in the cellar, and the food will be ready by two o'clock. We're going to carry the food up to the cliffs at the last minute in two hampers and leave them in the castle ruins. The wine we plan to take up on two golf-trolleys at about seven. That's all under control. Tristan, is the sacrifice arranged? Did you manage to get hold of a lamb?"

"Ray's bringing one. I spoke to him on the phone."

"Ray? Oh, the farmer from Stockwood. How nice it'll be to see that coven again! Are you paying him by check for the lamb or should I send someone out to the bank?"

"I'll give him a check." He turned to the table and fingered the altar cloth. "We'll go up to the chapel this afternoon and set up the altar. I'll need a small dais too which we can place in front of the altar for the act of homage; perhaps we can use the black box here—it's about the right size . . . oh, and remind me to take the tape recorder to the chapel and check that the tapes are all in order and that the machine's working properly. You did buy the new batteries for it, didn't you?"

"Yes, Tristan. Is there anything else?"

Poole fingered his books, his amulets, and finally the sharp knife with the shining handle. The blade glittered as he caressed it with his fingers. "Bring one or two towels. There'll be a lot of blood."

"Yes, Tristan."

"Incidentally, there's still a bloodstain on the floorboards here from the time Jackie and I were working on the Morrison affair. I want it eliminated."

"Very well, Tristan. I'll arrange for it to be removed first thing tomorrow."

Poole put the knife back on the table. "Did you deal with Evan Colwyn?"

"Yes. Sandra finished the job about ten minutes ago."

"Where is it?"

"Where's—oh, I see. In her room, I suppose. That was where she went to work."

"Bring it here. And I want the door of this room locked. There must be no risk of any accidental meddling. What are you doing about Walter Colwyn and Gwyneth?"

"Walter's in his study and Gwyneth's in her room—both absorbed in their respective hobbies. Harriet has full instructions about drugging the afternoon tea."

"Good," said Poole. "Then we're all set."

There was a pause.

"Tristan," said Agnes tentatively at last, "I know you don't like me to question you about your future plans, but—"

"Aha!" said Poole with a smile. "I thought you wouldn't be able to resist asking me about them!"

"What happens after the registry office wedding tomorrow when you go away on your honeymoon?"

"We go to London for five days, long enough to make mutual wills in each other's favor and long enough for Nicola to write me a check for five hundred pounds which I shall immediately endorse in your favor so that you can settle all debts and pay running expenses until I return."

"And after that?" said Agnes, trying not to sound too excited.

"Nicola will make over her money to me and then have a most tragic nervous collapse which will necessitate her being placed in one of those tasteful nursing homes for wealthy psychiatric cases. She will remain there for just long enough to ensure I won't have to pay death duties on the money she handed over to me, and then she'll suffer a seizure and leave me a grieving widower. Meanwhile, of course, I shall have seen that you're well provided for and firmly established here at Colwyn Court."

"Delightful!" sighed Agnes and added with admiration: "You've been more than good to us, Tristan."

"I always like to take care of those who depend upon me," said Poole, and ran his long index finger lightly along the shining blade of the butcher's knife.

II

"Benedict!" said Jane desperately as the ambulance containing an unconscious Evan bumped away up the track from the cottage on its journey to the hospital at Swansea.

"Benedict, please! You've got to believe me! Evan had discovered that the society practices witchcraft and that they're going to have an orgy tonight and Nicola's going to be in it and Evan was going to talk to the retired Chief Constable to call in the police but it all has to be done secretly because Tristan Poole might harm Gwyneth and now they've struck down Evan and we've just got to *do* something, Benedict, and you can't sit here and wonder how on earth you're going to tell Walter about Evan losing consciousness like that because Walter wouldn't believe you if you told him it was witchcraft—"

"And I wouldn't blame him in the least for not believing such a thing," said Benedict firmly. "My dearest, it's that wretched book that Evan brought you from London the other day. Ever since it came you've been seeing a witch behind every harmless broomstick in the kitchen cupboard."

"But it must be witchcraft! There's no other explanation. Tristan must have made a wax image of Evan and stuck a pin through its head—"

"Absolute nonsense," said Benedict severely. "Witchcraft was evolved by ignorant and superstitious minds to explain any deviation from the norm of recognized social behavior. Nowadays we call the deviates emotionally disturbed and send them to psychiatrists instead of burning them at the stake."

"Benedict," begged Jane, trying another approach, "You know you've always said the society is odd. Well, you were right. It's odd. It's so odd that they're using witchcraft as an excuse to hold an orgy tonight and practice all kinds of sexual—sexual—" Her vocabulary failed her.

"Personally I don't believe in censorship," said Benedict. "I take a very liberal view of all that sort of thing."

"But . . . but Nicola's involved—she's hypnotized—she's . . . Benedict, for my sake, please—please—" She groped for words and to her distress felt her eyes fill with tears. "Benedict, it's not an innocent undergraduate romp where no one gets hurt and everyone laughs afterward and says: 'What a lot of good clean fun!' This is different. This is—this is—"

"There, there!" said Benedict hurriedly. "There's no need to be upset! Don't cry. I had no idea you were taking all this so seriously! What do you want me to do?"

"Oh!" cried Jane, and burst into tears in sheer relief. After he had helped her to mop herself up she managed to say: "Please go to see this retired Chief Constable—here's his name and address which Evan gave me before he fainted—and tell him there's going to be an orgy up on the cliffs directly after sundown. Get him to arrange for the police to surround the chapel and catch everyone redhanded."

"Very well," said Benedict, beginning to be intrigued by the situation. "But perhaps I should see Walter first about Evan."

"I'll see Walter," said Jane, who knew exactly what she was going to do as soon as Benedict was on his way. "Just go, Benedict. You've got a forty-mile drive ahead of you so please, darling, please check the gauge to make sure you don't run out of gas in the middle of nowhere."

"Naturally," said Benedict dryly. As he opened the front door he stopped short on the threshold. "Talk of the devil!" he muttered. "Look who's just arrived."

"Oh my God," said Jane.

"Now my dear, don't panic. Don't worry. I'll—Jane, what on earth are you doing? What's all this?"

Jane was pulling off the gold cross she wore as a necklace and slipping it around Benedict's neck. "Wear this," was all she said, "and go. Quickly."

"But—"

"A cross protects you against—oh, never mind, Benedict! Just go! Please! Go!"

Benedict gave up. With a shrug of his shoulders he walked out to his Austin just as Poole came up the path toward the cottage.

"Good morning, Professor Shaw!" he called. "Off for a drive?"

"Yes," said Benedict, suddenly intoxicated by the cloak-

and-dagger role to which he had so unexpectedly been assigned. "Just off to Milford Haven to see an old friend of Walter's who used to be Chief Constable of this area." That'll put the fear of God into him, he thought, satisfied, if he really is planning any monkey-business.

Jane felt the color drain from her face so fast that she thought she was going to faint.

"How nice," said Poole. "Have a good time." He stood watching as Benedict drove off. When the car was out of sight he turned with a smile to Jane. "Mrs. Shaw," he began pleasantly, "I wonder if you've seen Dr. Colwyn? I'm trying to find him but haven't had any success so far."

Checking up, thought Jane. Every muscle in her body ached with tension. Her throat was dry. "He was taken to the hospital at Swansea quarter of an hour ago," she managed to say. "He lost consciousness here at the cottage and I couldn't bring him around."

"Lost consciousness! But what a shock for you, Mrs. Shaw! Does Mr. Colwyn know about this yet?"

"No, I'm waiting for definite news from the hospital."

"Much the best idea. We don't want to worry Mr. Colwyn unnecessarily about his son . . . I wonder what the trouble is. I hope it's not serious."

"I don't think it is," said Jane. She was amazed by the calmness of her voice. "Evan's been missing sleep and meals lately and worrying too much about—well, about certain things, and I think this morning all the strain came to a head and caused a physical collapse. At least, that was what the local doctor thought when he summoned the ambulance."

"Ah," said Poole and looked rueful. "Yes, I knew he took the news of Nicola's engagement hard." He hesitated before adding: "Mrs. Shaw, may I trouble you for a glass of water? It's a hot day and I'm very thirsty."

"Yes, of course," said Jane, fleeing to the kitchen. "Come in."

"Thanks." He walked swiftly into the living room as Jane disappeared at the back of the house. A discarded sports

199

jacket of Benedict's lay tossed over an armchair. In a lightning search of the pockets Poole found a handkerchief and concealed it as Jane reentered the room with his glass of water.

"Thanks," repeated Poole, accepting the glass and taking a long drink. Then: "That feels better. Well, if you'll excuse me, Mrs. Shaw—"

"Of course," said Jane thankfully and held her breath as he moved down the path away from the cottage. As soon as he had gone she grabbed her book on witchcraft and collapsed weakly into the nearest chair.

"A waxen image of the victim is made," she read from the passage on imitative magic, "usually incorporating either hairs or nail clippings from the victim's body. The image of the face should be as good a likeness as possible, and across the breast of the image the victim's name should be inscribed. A pin or wooden splinter is then inserted into that part of the anatomy where pain is desired; a black candle should be burned if possible and the one who casts the spell must focus all his hatred upon the intended victim. The effect of the insertion of the pin or splinter can range from sudden death (a clean piercing of the pectoral area around the heart) to a mild headache (a slight prick in the skull). Slow death may be achieved by dissolving the image over a flame. When reversing a spell by removing the splinter, great care must be taken or the spell may rebound on the one who cast it and fell him in exactly the same manner as the victim. One authority recommends that in these circumstances the magician should wear an iron cross and chant the Sator formula as he removes the splinter . . ."

Jane closed the book and stood up. She was certain now that somewhere at Colwyn Court was an image of Evan with a splinter embedded in its skull, and if Evan were to recover consciousness someone would first have to find the splinter and remove it. Taking a deep breath she left the cottage and began to walk as quickly as she could along the path to Colwyn Court.

200

III

In Colwyn village Benedict stopped the car and firmly removed the gold cross which Jane had draped around his neck. Superstition was all very well for gullible women, he thought crossly, but he had no intention of turning up at Milford Haven looking like a Christmas tree.

Before he started the engine again he paused and frowned. There was something Jane had told him to do before he embarked on his journey but he could not remember what it was. He stared in annoyance at the dashboard. What was it? He had a feeling it was something very obvious, but the memory still eluded him. When he turned the ignition key the needle of the gas gauge hovered near the "E" to indicate the tank was almost empty, but although Benedict noted this, some unseen force stopped the knowledge from reaching that part of his brain which enabled him to draw a conclusion from the fact and take appropriate action. Still feeling annoyed that his memory had so unaccountably failed him, he put the car into gear, raised his foot from the clutch, and drove off down the country road towards the west.

IV

Timothy was still looking for Lucy. He had tried the beach, the castle and the chapel but there had been no sign of her. Finally he decided to try Colwyn Court. Perhaps Lucy had been unable to resist the lure of the pageant and was hiding at the house because she felt too guilty to face him.

Timothy's mouth turned down at the corners. It had been a bad summer. First Uncle Matt having the accident, then—Timothy's thoughts slid off the word "Mum" before his eyes could fill with tears—and now Lucy abandoning him in favor of Mr. Poole. Timothy knew Mr. Poole was no good. He was like the villains in the old-fashioned westerns that were shown on television. One knew they were villains because

201

they always wore black. Black meant evil and Timothy knew, no matter what Lucy might think, that Mr. Poole was just as evil as any villain in a television western.

"I wish Daddy was here," said Timothy aloud to himself as he padded up the path to Colwyn Court. "Please, God, send Daddy home soon. Even if he did get drowned all those years ago, please raise him from the dead like in the Bible and send him home soon. Lucy and I are relying on You. Thank You. Amen."

He waited, listening in case God answered, but the only voice he heard was a voice from the darkest corner of his mind, the corner he always tried not to listen to, saying he would never see his father again.

It had been a bad summer.

When he reached Colwyn Court he slipped into the house through one of the side doors and pattered up to Gwyneth's room, but Gwyneth hadn't seen Lucy either. "Try the society," she suggested. "Maybe they've seen her."

But Timothy didn't trust the society. The society was the Enemy, the Tool of the Villain. Leaving Gwyneth he crept into the west wing and began peeping into each bedroom until a locked door brought him to an excited halt.

"Lucy!" he hissed into the keyhole, but there was no answer.

They've kidnapped her, thought Timothy, enraged, and turning the key which Agnes had left in the lock, he burst into the room.

She was there. She was lying on one half of a double bed and Nicola was lying beside her. They were both so sound asleep that neither of them stirred when he rushed into the room.

"Lucy!" cried Timothy, and shook her shoulder.

But Lucy, breathing evenly, did not move.

"Lucy, Lucy, wake up, you stupid, silly twit!" Timothy felt frantic. He shook her again. "Lucy, what's the matter with you?"

A hand fell on his shoulder. Strong fingers bit into his flesh and made him yelp with shock as he was swung around to face his captor.

"I had a feeling you were going to make trouble, Tim my friend," said Tristan Poole leisurely. "I can see you and I are going to have to have a little talk together."

V

Jane was also at Colwyn Court. She was pausing in the drawing room in the main part of the house as she tried to decide where Poole would conduct an experiment in black magic. The kitchen? Too public, surely. One of the bedrooms, perhaps. Or the cellar. Jane hesitated. The cellar would be an ideal place. Plenty of space and darkness and privacy . . .

She slipped off toward the kitchens, and after making sure that there was no one about she darted past the sinks in the scullery and opened the cellar door. Her hands scrabbled for the light switch without success; there was no electric light in the old-fashioned cellar of Colwyn Court. Turning back to the stove, Jane grabbed a box of matches and tiptoed hurriedly down the cellar steps, but although she lit a match as soon as she reached the bottom all she saw on the floor was a row of tall bottles containing homemade wine. She was just surveying them in disappointment when the door clicked shut behind her and the draft blew out the match.

Jane jumped. The darkness was suddenly intense. Fumbling with the box she struck another match, ran back up the steps to the door, and reached for the handle.

It took her a full ten seconds to realize what had happened. There was no handle on her side of the door. She was trapped.

VI

"Agnes," said Poole, "if you saw Mrs. Shaw giving her husband a gold cross on a chain, what conclusions would you draw?"

"The worst," said Agnes. "Mrs. Shaw has a lot of feminine intuition."

"She also has a book on witchcraft lying around in her living room. Agnes, I think something should be done about Mrs. Shaw. I'm not worried about the professor. He's not the kind of man who would wear a gold cross to please his wife once he was out of her sight, so I hardly think he constitutes a serious problem. But Mrs. Shaw bothers me. I find myself wondering what she'll be up to next."

"How do you think we should cope with her?"

Poole thought for a moment. "Nothing active," he said at last. "There's been too much of that already. But I think she should be watched. Send someone down to the cottage to keep an eye on her, would you?"

"Very well, Tristan."

They were up at the chapel when the message reached them two hours later. It was afternoon by that time, and they were setting up the long narrow table which was to serve as an altar.

"I watched the cottage for ages," gasped the messenger, "but when there was no sign of life I went inside and—well, she wasn't there. There was no sign of her."

"That's odd," said Agnes. "Where can she have gone?"

"She's probably looking for the twins." Poole decided he did not want to bother himself with the triviality of Jane's whereabouts when there were other more important matters to attend to. "Never mind, forget her. She's basically harmless anyway and I don't think she'll cause us any trouble."

"True," agreed Agnes, "but I rather wish she was under observation . . . By the way, Tristan, what did you do with the boy? Did you hypnotize him?"

"No, he was a bad subject." Poole shrugged. "You find that happens sometimes with children. Their hostility is uncomplicated by adult guilt feelings and raises a powerful barrier against any attempt to control the mind . . . But you needn't worry about the boy. I'll deal with him later. At the moment he's under lock and key and not in a position to give us any trouble."

"But supposing Mrs. Shaw searches the west wing? If the boy's wide awake and waiting to be rescued they'll easily make contact with one another, and then there'd be trouble! Let me put someone on duty in the west wing, Tristan, just to keep an eye out for Mrs. Shaw."

"Whatever you think best," said Poole abruptly, and returned to the absorbing task of erecting the inverted crucifix behind the black altar.

VII

They came down to the cellar to fetch the wine at seven o'clock that evening.

Jane hid behind a packing case in one corner of the huge underground room and watched. Presently she realized that the two women who had been assigned to move the wine were working to a pattern; they would take four bottles at a time up the steps and would disappear for two minutes before returning. After they had disappeared for the third time, Jane dashed up the steps, raced through the wedged-open cellar door, and just had time to squeeze behind the door of the scullery to hide from the two women as they returned for the last of the wine.

Once they were back in the cellar Jane slipped outside and took refuge in the nearby woodshed. She felt dirty and sticky and close to tears. It took her some minutes to reestablish her self-control, but at last she glanced at her watch and tried to decide what she should do. It was evening. Sunset was less than two hours away, and with luck Benedict should have seen the Chief Constable and organized the police raid. Jane's first instinct was to rush home to the cottage to rejoin the twins who she felt sure were anxiously awaiting her, but then she thought of Nicola. Supposing Benedict had by some terrible chance been unsuccessful. Evan was no doubt still unconscious in the hospital, so if Benedict's expedition had gone awry there was no one but Jane herself to help Nicola once darkness fell.

She glanced at her watch again. She could dash back to the cottage to see the twins, but time was short and she knew she had to find a good hiding place in the ruins before everyone arrived for the start of the ceremonies. She reassured herself anxiously that the twins were sensible; when they found that both she and Benedict were missing they would walk up to the main house and Walter would look after them.

Stumbling out of the woodshed Jane began to hurry uphill to the chapel on the cliffs.

VIII

Timothy was watching from the window of Poole's bedroom where he was locked up. The sun was setting and the party on the lawn seemed to be drifting toward an expectant silence, a mass tension Timothy found hard to understand. He had glimpsed parties given by his mother and stepfather, but these parties had usually become noisier, not quieter, as the evening progressed. This was an odd party, he could tell that just by looking at the guests. They all wore black. The younger women wore cocktail dresses, the older women were more conventionally dressed in less sophisticated outfits, and the men wore dark suits. Counting heads to pass the time Timothy decided there were fifty-two people present in addition to the members of the society and that the majority of them by a narrow margin were women.

As he watched he saw the members of the society detach themselves from their friends and file back through the French windows into the house. It was then that he realized that Poole was nowhere to be seen. Timothy was just wondering where his archenemy was when Agnes emerged again onto the terrace and walked across the lawn to make an announcement.

All conversation instantly stopped.

As Agnes turned aside the guests formed four groups of thirteen and waited in silence, their gaze riveted hungrily on the house. Timothy craned his neck to see what they were staring at but could see nothing. He was just wondering if he could open the window and lean out for a better view when the members of the society walked out of the house two by two to join their friends on the lawn.

Poole was behind them.

He wore a long red robe with a red-horned miter and did not look like the Poole Timothy remembered at all but like some presence from another age when men lived in daily fear of heaven and hell and the world was racked by plague, famine, and war. By Poole's side walked Nicola, very erect, very beautiful in a flowing black gown. She was smiling radiantly. And behind Nicola walked Lucy, an angel in scarlet, her fair hair streaming down her back and her eyes wide with innocence.

"Lucy!" yelled Timothy, and beat his fists on the pane. No one heard him. Using all his strength he heaved up the window and leaned over the sill.

"Lucy!" he shouted at the top of his voice.

But no one heard him, least of all Lucy. He shouted again and again but it was as if there were a soundproofed screen between him and the group on the lawn for no one even glanced in his direction. At last when they had all disappeared from sight behind the rose garden he leaped onto the window seat in frustration and wondered if he could jump to the ground below.

But it was too far. He looked down, quailed, and withdrew. However, he noticed that the ledge outside the window was broad, broad enough for him to sit on, and he could see that the window of the locked dressing room next door was open an inch.

Maybe there's a way out into the corridor through the room next door, thought Timothy.

Ten seconds later he was sitting outside the ledge, his legs dangling over the long drop, and trying not to feel sick. It was surprising how rapidly the broad ledge had dwindled into a narrow parapet.

Timothy shivered, squeezed his eyes shut and began to

edge sideways toward the dressing room window. But when he arrived safely he was faced by the problem of heaving up the window far enough to enable him to crawl into the room, and it took him a long time to work himself into a position where he could tug at the window frame without fear of overbalancing. The window was stiff. He was just despairing of ever being able to move it when it shot upward and he was scrambling thankfully onto safer ground—only to discover with a sinking heart that there was no door offering him an easy escape into the corridor.

Timothy shed several tears of acute disappointment and even allowed himself the infantile gesture of stamping his foot. But presently he felt ashamed of this lapse of courage, wiped his eyes with the back of his hand, and began to survey his new surroundings.

The first thing he saw was the cardboard box on the table by the locked door.

Inside he found plasticine, a substance he had played with for hours as a toddler. He had made cars with it, he remembered, and Lucy had made dolls. Occasionally she had stamped on his cars and he had revenged himself by twisting the dolls out of shape until they looked like freaks.

Fancy Mr. Poole playing with plasticine at his age, thought Timothy.

He poked around inside the box again and picked up a small object wrapped in tissue paper. Once the paper was discarded he found himself holding a cleverly made doll about nine inches long, a doll with red hair and a loin cloth which might once have been part of a man's handkerchief, a doll with EVAN COLWYN inscribed across the chest and a slim splinter of wood inserted into the skull at an odd angle.

Timothy stared. Stories began to flicker across his memory, folklore handed down from one generation of schoolboys to another since time out of mind. This was how you won a fight with the school bully even though he was much bigger than you were. You stole a candle from the school pantry, melted it, molded it into the bully's image, pricked it in the groin with a pin, muttered "I hate you" three times, prayed for victory, and then buried the image in the kitchen garden after lights-out. The bully would lose all his strength and flunk the fight. Timothy had never tried the experiment himself but everyone at school was positive that it worked. His own best friend had had no doubts at all on the subject.

Timothy stared down at the little red-haired doll in his hands, and then using his thumb and forefinger he removed the splinter, set it down on the table and rewrapped the doll carefully in its tissue paper.

IX

Jane was hiding in the chapel ruins and watching in mounting horror as the groups assembled for the rites. As soon as she had seen Lucy behind Nicola she had almost fainted; the world had tilted dizzily and she had been gripped by the urge to scream, but she had neither fainted nor cried out. She knew too well that if she interrupted the group before the rites had begun the police would fail to catch the participants in the midst of their obscenities and all Evan's plans would be ruined.

Jane tightened her grip on her self-control, fought her panic, and began to pray for help without even realizing that she was praying.

The next moment she felt better. Harriet Miller was leading Nicola and Lucy away to wait in the castle ruins until the appropriate part of the ceremony arrived, so for the time being at least they were both safe. Abandoning her frightened prayers Jane peered through the gap in the wall in front of her and watched as Poole walked to the altar and motioned Agnes to bring him a brand from the brazier which was already burning in the center of the chapel.

The six black candles surrounding the altar were lit; Jane had a clearer view of the inverted crucifix behind the altar and of the tapestry which had been hung on the wall behind the cross. The tapestry was woven in black and scarlet and showed a goat trampling on a crucifix. In front of the altar was a square black box eighteen inches high, and as Jane watched, Poole stepped in front of it and turned to face the assembled men and women awaiting him.

"Dearly beloved brethren," she heard him say in his dark, quiet voice. "You are gathered together today in Our Presence to celebrate the great festival of Lammas, to worship, to honor, and to obey those Powers of Darkness which have existed since the beginning of time and which will exist until the end of time, through the Grace of Beelzebuth, Astaroth, Adramelek, Baal, Lucifer, Chamos, Melchom, Behemoth, Dagon, Asmodeus, and all other Lords of Darkness in the Hierarchy of Hell—"

The sun had sunk into an opaque sea. The sky was a deep darkening blue shot with the aftermath of sunset, and far away the surf crashed in a burst of boiling foam at the foot of the black cliffs. It was eerily quiet.

"—and lastly," said the figure in the red robes in his measured voice, "through My Grace, which will be bestowed always among my Chosen, World Without End—"

"Hail Satan!" said sixty-four voices in unison. The expressions on the faces of the congregation were as united as their voices. The worshipers had an intense, yearning look, their lips parted as if they were waiting for some magic drink which would slake an unbearable thirst.

"My friends," said Poole, "I come to you as the One God, the administrator of great sins and greater vices, cordial of the vanquished, suzerain of resentment, treasurer of old hatreds, king of the disinherited—"

"Hail Satan!"

"—and I offer each one of you now the chance to demonstrate your loyalty by participating in the act of homage . . . My friends, let us begin our sacred rites in celebration of this sacred day."

The congregation forsook their enrapt immobility and began to strip off their clothes. They moved with quiet speed, the men leaving their clothes on one side of the chapel, the women leaving their clothes on the other, and when they were naked they mingled again and re-formed in front of the altar.

Jane, who was not prudish but thought that human beings usually looked better with clothes than without them, found herself riveted to the spot with an appalled fascination. But even before she could ask herself incredulously how the elderly, the obese, and the ugly could reveal themselves in such a way without a qualm, her attention was caught by Poole. He was tearing off his red robes, hurling them aside, and she saw that around his waist was a thin belt from which a plaited tail of animal hair swung toward the ground.

"Let the ceremony of homage begin!" he shouted, and as Jane watched he sprang onto the black box before the altar and turned his tanned back to the congregation.

Jane began to feel dizzy again. The most horrifying part of all, she realized, was that in spite of her revulsion she found herself unwillingly excited by Poole's strong supple body.

Agnes was the first to pay homage. Phrases from the book on witchcraft tumbled through Jane's mind and she felt the color rush to her face as she recalled her own voice reading about the obscene kiss of a millennium of witches' sabbaths.

"Master," said Agnes in a clear passionate voice, "I promise to love, worship, honor, and obey you, now and forever more."

The rest of the Colwyn Court coven followed her one by one. After that came the turn of each member of the four other covens.

The ceremony lasted some time.

At last when the final act of homage had been paid, Poole turned to face the congregation again and raised his hands toward the stars.

"My blessing be upon you all."

"Hail Satan!"

"May you all prosper."

"Hail Satan!"

"May you work tirelessly in my name."

"Hail Satan!"

"May all power be upon you now and forevermore."

"Hail Satan!"

Poole let his hands fall slowly to his sides. "My friends, let us prepare ourselves for one of our most sublime moments of spiritual communication. I call upon my chief acolyte here tonight to give a brief introduction to the ceremonies."

A light wind blew in from the sea and cooled the sweat on Jane's forehead. As she shivered from head to toe she saw Agnes Miller step forward to the altar to make an announcement to her colleagues.

"Beloved friends," Jane heard her say in a voice which vibrated with emotion, "in a moment the bride will be brought into the chapel for the wedding, and after the wedding will come the traditional offering to the Powers, a young virgin who will receive the Master's Mark and be admitted to Our Church and grow up, we trust, to become one of the Master's most devoted followers. You may wonder why the bride herself is ineligible for this role. There are three reasons: first she is not a virgin, second her intellect is spiritually barren, and third she can be of no use to the Master in this world since her time in it is to be short. She was chosen for the bridal ceremony for her looks—I think you will agree that she is beautiful—and for the size of her dowry . . . After the Wedding and the Marking will come the Festivities." She paused. "Are we all ready?"

There was a murmur of assent. Everyone's eyes turned toward Poole again.

"My friends," said Poole, "prepare yourselves for the Black Mass."

The congregation sucked in their breath greedily. At a sign from Poole two of the Colwyn Court coven began to feed the brazier with bunches of herbs, and when the smoke was rising from the crackling flames Poole shouted: "Let the bride be brought to the altar!"

The first fumes from the brazier reached Jane. She couldn't make up her mind whether it was the fumes which made her feel so sick or the knowledge that as far as she knew there was no policeman within miles of the chapel. She could feel the panic rise inside her as she tried to decide what she should do.

Nicola was brought into the chapel by Harriet Miller and led slowly to the altar where Poole was waiting. Jane noticed with relief that Lucy was still being kept out of sight.

"Let the sacrifice be brought to me!" cried Poole.

One of the men dragged forward a coal-black lamb and Agnes handed Poole the butcher's knife.

Poole began to speak. So unnerved was Jane by the pervasive fumes from the brazier, Nicola's presence at the altar and the prospect of a bloody slaughter, that it took her several seconds to realize that Poole was speaking in a language she did not understand.

He reached the end of his incantation and leaned forward to grab the lamb's halter. The knife flickered wickedly in the candlelight as the animal made a strangled noise and slumped to the ground in a heap. When Jane had finished being sick she saw that Poole had filled a chalice with the lamb's blood while two members of Agnes' coven were piling pieces of a substance which looked like black bread onto two large platters.

The congregation, stimulated by the fumes from the brazier, were beginning to sway on their feet; their voices were droning a hypnotic chant which grew louder as the minutes passed and their excitement grew.

Poole did something unprintable to both the contents of the chalice and the plates of black bread. Several females in the congregation screamed in ecstasy.

I've got to act, thought Jane, I've got to stop this.

Agnes was helping Nicola out of her wedding dress and guiding her into her position on the altar. Nicola had a dreamy expression on her face and looked blissfully happy. The chant of the congregation grew louder as they saw Nicola's bare skin gleaming against the black altar cloth.

Jane stood up. Or tried to. To her horror she found that the fumes had affected her sense of balance and that something had gone wrong with her legs. When she tried to walk she fell to her knees, and it was then, as she made vain efforts to struggle to her feet again, that she realized what had happened. She had failed. Benedict had failed. Evan had failed.

213

And no one was going to come to Nicola's aid.

Poole was saying something, placing the chalice on Nicola's body, moving toward one end of the altar.

God help us, thought Jane, God help us all. Prayers tumbled through her mind, silent pleas to a God to succeed where ordinary men had failed. Please God, stop them. Our Father which art in heaven . . .

At one end of the altar Poole looked down at Nicola and then stooped to run his hands over her thighs.

Several women in the audience screamed again. Black smoke from the brazier was making the light uncertain and the black candles were flickering in the draft.

Hallowed be thy name, prayed Jane, thy kingdom come . . .

Poole stopped.

"Master?" whispered Agnes nervously, seeing the expression in his eyes.

He swung around on her. "There's a heretic among us!" He whirled to face the congregation and flung up his arms for silence. "There's heresy here!"

The chanting died abruptly. A sea of faces stared at him in shocked disbelief.

And then Poole turned his back on them. He turned very slowly until he was facing the place where Jane was hidden.

"She's there," was all he said.

The congregation howled like a pack of wolves and raced to drag Jane from her hiding place but Poole held them in check.

"Let her come to me of her own free will."

Jane found herself able to walk again. She walked to the altar to meet him because she had no power to do anything else, and when she reached him she knelt at his feet.

"Agnes, take this woman to the other side of the castle. Mrs. Shaw, look at me."

Jane looked at him.

"Go where Agnes takes you. Stay there until you're told you can leave."

Jane nodded.

"You'll remember nothing of what you have seen since sunset."

Jane nodded again. Agnes led her away.

The congregation began to chant and sway again, building up the tension afresh as Poole stood by Nicola's inert body and waited for Agnes to return.

She slipped back into the chapel a minute later and rejoined Poole at the altar.

"All's well, Master."

Poole smiled. As Agnes watched he returned to the end of the altar and stooped over Nicola's body.

"In the name of Satan and all the Lords of Darkness—"

A torch blazed from the doorway of the chapel. As everyone shouted in alarm and moved to close the ranks against the intruder, Evan's voice shouted: "In the name of God, STOP!" and the next moment there was an icy draft which blew out all the candles, an enormous thunderclap which shattered the torch in Evan's hand, and finally, a second later, the acrid reek of brimstone.

9

When Evan recovered consciousness some time later he could
not at first remember where he was or what had happened.
And then it all came back to him in a rush, how he had
awoken earlier to find himself in the hospital, how he had
discharged himself amid the protests of the staff and dashed
outside to hitch a lift from Swansea to Colwyn; he could
remember tearing up to the cliffs, bursting into the chapel,
staring at the naked bodies illuminated by black candles, the
glint of the chalice, Poole moving to possess Nicola's body on
the black altar . . .

"In the name of God, STOP!" yelled Evan, reenacting the
scene in confusion, and sat up with a start.

He was alone. It was pitch dark and a soft sea wind was
moaning through the ruined walls of the deserted chapel.

After a moment he hauled himself shakily to his feet and
stumbled through the chapel to the altar. His foot knocked
against a small rattling object. Stooping he found an
abandoned box of matches, and after striking a light he was
able to see that the altar cloth, the desecrated crucifix, and
the tapestry were all gone and that the only signs left to hint
at what had taken place that evening were the table which

had served as an altar and the pool of lamb's blood on the floor. But the lamb's corpse was gone and so was Nicola's inert body. Shaking out the match, Evan left the chapel and stumbled down the hillside to Colwyn Court.

Agnes was waiting for him. As he opened the back door he saw her sitting at the kitchen table, her face expressionless, her hands clasped in front of her as if in prayer.

She was alone.

"Where's Nicola?" demanded Evan roughly, and his voice was unsteady. "Where is she?"

"In her room asleep. You don't have to worry about her any more. She'll wake up tomorrow with no memory of the last thirty-six hours and an imperfect memory of the last month. I think you'll find her condition satisfactory." Agnes stood up. "Dr. Colwyn, I want to negotiate with you about what happened this evening and I'd be grateful if you would spare a few minutes to talk to me."

Evan stared at her blankly. "There's nothing to negotiate, Miss Miller, Where's Poole?"

There was a silence. He was just noticing that her eyes were red-rimmed from crying when she said in a flat voice, "He's dead."

"I don't believe it," said Evan. "Show me his body."

Agnes stood up without a word and led the way upstairs to Poole's room. "You won't recognize him," was all she said.

"Why not?"

"You'll see."

Poole was laid out on his bed, his body clad in pajamas. Evan walked up to him and looked down at the face he had hated so violently.

He saw a mild, easy-going man with a mouth capable of a cheerful smile and features which in life might have reflected a good-natured intelligence. The eyes were closed so that their secret was hidden forever, but Evan thought he could glimpse the recklessness in them which had led the man to the Lammas rites in the California orange grove where he had offered his body for his Master's use.

217

"You're right," said Evan to Agnes. "I don't recognize him."

"He will rise again," said Agnes, and with a shock he realized she was speaking not of Poole, but of her Master. "He will be reborn in someone else. The history of Tristan Poole is at an end. But the history of some other unknown man is just beginning." She turned to face Evan again. "I must talk to you, Dr. Colwyn."

"I'll see Nicola first," said Evan, checking Poole's pulse as a matter of routine before he left the room.

Nicola was sound asleep in her tiny bedroom in the main part of the house. He took her pulse, felt her forehead, and lifted an eyelid.

"She's drugged."

"She'll be all right tomorrow," said Agnes. "That's a promise, Dr. Colwyn. Unless you make trouble for us with the police, of course."

There was a pause.

"All right," said Evan abruptly. "Let's talk."

They returned to the kitchen and sat down facing each other across the table. "What are your terms?" said Evan at last.

"We'll tear up the lease, leave Colwyn Court, and never come near you again. Nicola will be completely cured of her infatuation for Tristan—his power over her will have ceased at his death—and she'll only have a blurred memory of the affair. Your father and sister will recover quickly enough from the drugged sleep induced several hours ago to keep them out of the way, and you'll find Tristan's influence over your sister will also be a thing of the past. The twins and Mrs. Shaw are asleep at the cottage. Much as she may want to help you I think you'll find Mrs. Shaw a most inadequate witness. Lucy won't remember anything of the ceremony either but you can rest assured she was quite unharmed. As for Timothy—" She bit her lip. "I could murder that child very easily," she said at last in a brisk voice, "but fortunately for those that depend on me I think commonsense will prevail

218

and I shall leave him alone. He won't be any use to you as a witness either—he was locked up at Colwyn Court during the ceremony."

"In other words," said Evan, "what you're saying to me is this: we'll leave you alone with everyone intact if you leave us alone by fending off any inquiries from the police. However, if you *are* so foolish as to complain to the police you'll find yourself with no witnesses and no evidence which could not be explained away as the aftermath of some wild, but not necessarily criminally obscene party. Am I right?"

"Exactly," said Agnes. "But I would prefer you not to complain to the police. You're a doctor, a man of standing, and your word would carry a certain weight behind it. That's why I'm prepared to concede so much to avoid any trouble."

"When will you leave Colwyn Court?"

"Could you give us forty-eight hours? I think we could manage that."

"I wouldn't let you go before then. I want to make sure everyone makes a complete recovery."

"They will," said Agnes.

There was a silence.

"Very well," said Evan finally. "I agree to your terms. I'll say nothing and you'll fulfill your promises."

"Thank you, Dr. Colwyn," said Agnes.

"All right. Now tell me something. You know, of course, that I lost consciousness this morning and was taken to the hospital. I suppose you claim credit for that."

"Naturally."

"Do you also claim credit for my dazzling recovery?"

"No, you can thank Timothy for that. The wretched child dismantled the spell so recklessly that it rebounded on Sandra who initiated it, and two of the girls are working hard this very minute to try to bring her back to consciousness. She fainted during the homage ceremony."

"I'm not sure I understand. Do you mean—"

"Oh, look it up in Jane Shaw's witchcraft book," said Agnes irritably. "Why should I bother to explain it to you?"

After a moment Evan said slowly: "Do you claim many other such . . . successes?"

Agnes shrugged. "We were responsible for Lisa's death, of course, and Matthew Morrison's. It's remarkable what the powers can do for you when properly applied. But then of course with the Master all things are possible."

"Except the ability to survive when someone yells 'In the name of God, stop!' " said Evan dryly.

"My dear young man," said Agnes, "you don't really think that was what killed Tristan, do you?"

"But then what the hell did kill him?"

"Well, I suppose to be strictly accurate, your invocation did help," admitted Agnes grudgingly. "You destroyed the powers inherent in our assembly and hurled an enormous counterforce at us. It was both very frightening and very overwhelming. I think we all lost consciousness for at least a minute."

"I remember a loud bang—"

"Did the noise surprise you? Your gesture had the same effect as someone who fires a cannonball through a glass window into a china shop. No wonder the result was audible!"

"But what killed Poole?"

"It was only the body that was killed," said Agnes. "Only his fragile mortality was destroyed. That was all."

"But—"

"Dr. Colwyn, you are by no means a believer in my Church although I admit that for a skeptic you're showing an unusual ability to accept the unacceptable. Don't ask too many questions. I've suffered a dreadful shock tonight and an appalling reverse of all my hopes for the future, and frankly I don't want to discuss this further with you. All I'll say in response to your question is that witchcraft can be fought by witchcraft. It's a dangerous thing to do and it can have lethal results. Now if you'll excuse me . . . was that the front doorbell?"

"Yes, it was. Who on earth can that be?"

"Oh, that must be Professor Shaw and the police at last,"

said Agnes wearily. "Tristan had impaired Professor Shaw's memory but as soon as Tristan died no doubt Professor Shaw made a miraculous recovery from his partial amnesia . . . Could you cope with them, please? I'm very tired and I want to be alone. I couldn't face seeing any more people tonight."

"Very well," said Evan, thinking how strange it was that she should look just like a middle-aged housewife suffering from overwork. He even felt a pang of compassion for her. "I'll deal with them. Good night, Miss Miller."

"Good night, Dr. Colwyn," said Agnes, and added, annihilating his compassion with a cold measured contempt: "Oh, Dr. Colwyn, make sure you hold to our agreement, won't you? Because if you don't, I'll certainly kill your sister. Even without Tristan that would be well within my powers."

The doorbell rang far away as Evan stood looking at her. Her green eyes were as inhuman as a cat's. Her plump comfortable frame was heavy with menace, and her mouth was thin and hard as she stared back at him.

"The agreement stands," Evan heard himself say at last. "Goodbye, Miss Miller." And turning abruptly he walked away from her toward the hall, the front door and the police.

II

"So there we were," said Benedict to Jane the next morning. "I've never felt so foolish in all my life. There was Evan, fit as a fiddle, saying there'd been a party on the cliffs but it was all over and everyone was all right. The police poked around up there and found nothing except for some peculiar marks on the ground in the castle which might have been made by a child. Naturally when they heard that the twins liked to play there they assumed—my dear, what's the matter? You surely can't blame me for being cross! All that mumbo jumbo about witchcraft! I knew it was a false alarm."

"But Benedict darling," said Jane, "what happened to

you? Why did you take such a long time to fetch the police? What happened on the way to Milford Haven?"

"Well, it was the most extraordinary thing," said Benedict, polishing his spectacles. "I ran out of gas on a wild road miles from anywhere—"

"Benedict, you took off my gold cross, didn't you?"

"—and then I didn't feel well and decided to have a nap, but after that it took hours to get a lift to the nearest gas station and when I got there I couldn't remember where I'd left the car—"

"Poor darling," said Jane, forgiving him because he looked so guilty and bemused. "Never mind. Everything worked out satisfactorily in the end. I've just been speaking to Evan and he says that the society are leaving Colwyn Court tomorrow because Mr. Poole died suddenly last night, so—"

"Good God!" exclaimed Benedict. "A healthy young fellow like that? What was the cause of death?"

"Evan called in the local doctor and they agreed it was a cardiac arrest."

"Well, I'll be damned," said Benedict, astonished, and was silent. Then: "What did happen in the chapel—if anything?" he inquired sardonically. "What were you doing while this orgy of yours was supposed to be going on?"

"You wouldn't even begin to believe me," said Jane and added regretfully: "Besides I don't remember much about it."

"Why not?"

"Oh . . . I think amnesia must be catching at the moment. Everyone seems to be suffering from it except Timothy and Evan . . ."

Outside the kitchen door Marble was roused from sleep by the sound of their voices and opened one cautious pink eye. Finding himself alone in a patch of sunlight he opened the other eye, unsheathed his claws, and stretched himself luxuriously. It was a long time since he had had the energy to give himself such a luxurious stretch, but for a long time he had felt as if an enormous weight had been strapped to his back. But now the weight was gone. Marble, whose brain was small and memory smaller, did not question the cause of his past malaise or link it with people already half-forgotten, but merely sat up, washed his paws and began to think of his stomach. He found he was exceedingly hungry. Jumping up, he bounded into the kitchen, rubbed himself with a cunning display of affection against Jane's ankles, and began to mew for her undivided attention.

"Marble's looking better today," Benedict commented. "In fact he's looking more like his old self again."

"That's because Tristan's dead."

"My dear, whatever will you think of next!"

Jane laughed. "All right, shall we forget last night and the society and Tristan Poole for a moment? There's something I've been worrying about for ages and I do so want to discuss it with you."

"By all means," said Benedict thankfully, "let's forget the fiasco of last night with all its attendant little mysteries. What is it that's worrying you?"

"Well, darling, it's the twins. You see, Lisa left no will and so they don't have an official guardian and I know they're feeling terribly lost and alone now that both Lisa and Matt are dead, and . . . oh, I'm so worried about what's going to happen to them! Do you think . . . perhaps . . . possibly—"

"Of course," said Benedict. "An excellent idea."

"I know our house in Cambridge will be much too small, but—"

"Well, I was getting tired of it anyway," said Benedict. "It would be nice to have a bigger house and I think we could afford it without too much scrimping and saving. I'll tell you what we'll do. As soon as we get home you can start house-hunting and I'll see our solicitor to find out how we can set about getting a court order of legal guardianship—if the twins are agreeable, of course! You're sure they approve of the idea?"

"I think they've already taken it for granted," said Jane, and smiled at him brilliantly through her tears.

III

"The most peculiar thing of all," said Lucy that same morning as she and Timothy sat on the beach and watched the incoming tide, "is that I can't even remember what Tristan looked like exactly. I just remember thinking he was like Daddy."

"He wasn't a bit like Daddy!"

"Oh, let's face it, Timmy," said Lucy crossly, "we can't even remember what Daddy looked like anyway. If it wasn't for those photos of Mummy's we wouldn't know him from Adam. We'll never really know now what he was like."

"We might," said Timothy. "He might still come home."

"We don't truly believe that," said Lucy. "Not truly. That was just imagining."

Timothy swallowed and was silent.

"Well, it's all very sad, of course," said Lucy, "but it could be worse. You know what Cook always says back at home. 'Look on the bright side, dears, and count your blessings.' "

"I don't see how things could be worse," said Timothy mulishly.

"Don't be dim, Timmy. Supposing there was no Aunt Jane?" Lucy yawned and drew a pentagram on the sand with her toe. "Do you know what that is?" she said, gesturing toward the pattern. "It's an evil sign. At least it can be a good sign, but when it only stands on one point and has two points sticking upward it represents evil. Gwyneth told me. She heard it from Tristan."

Timothy swept the pentagram into oblivion with a circular motion of his heel. "I want to bury all that evil and forget about it. Let's hold the funeral and stop messing around."

"All right," Lucy agreed. "After all, that was why we came down to the beach, wasn't it? I'd almost forgotten."

"Here's your spade," said Timothy, feeling better. "Let's begin."

They began to dig a deep rectangular hole in the sand. "Phew!" gasped Lucy ten minutes later. "That's deep enough, isn't it?"

"I think so." Timothy opened the cardboard box which they had brought down to the beach and carefully lifted out a plasticine figure of a man. The image had the letters T. POOLE inscribed across his chest and was clad in a piece of material which Timothy had cut from one of the suits in the cupboard of Poole's dressing room. The wooden splinter which had once pierced the skull of Evan's image was driven through the left breast where the heart would have been.

"I still don't know how you thought of it," said Lucy admiringly. "How did you know what to do?"

"You poor thing," said Timothy pityingly. "Don't they teach you anything at that stupid girl's school of yours?"

Lucy for once was humbled. "What did you do exactly? Was it hard once you'd made the plasticine figure?"

" 'Course not," said Timothy. "I got the splinter and said: 'Please God, arrange for Tristan Poole to be killed because he's wicked and evil and I don't think You'd like him if You met him.' Then I gave God a choice—just in case He thought Mr. Poole was okay after all and didn't want to kill him. I said: 'But if You want to save him that's okay by me because I know You'll have a good reason. Thank You. Amen.' And then I stuck the splinter through the heart and left it up to God. It seemed a pretty fair way of doing things."

"But does that mean God killed Tristan? I didn't think God ever murdered anyone."

"Maybe God borrowed an evil spirit from hell," said Timothy comfortably. "He must have some arrangement for those sort of circumstances."

"So evil killed evil," said Lucy satisfied. "That's nice." She glanced at Poole's image. "Shall we begin?"

"Okay." They laid the image gently in the deep hole in the sand and looked at it for a moment.

"Rest in peace," said Timothy, not sure what was said at a funeral service.

"Now and forevermore, Amen," said Lucy obligingly. She glanced at Timothy. "Will that do, do you think?"

"I expect so."

225

They shoveled the sand back over the image and stamped on it.

"Well, that's that," said Timothy satisfied. "What shall we do next?"

"Let's go back to the cottage," said Lucy. "Wasn't Aunt Jane going to make fudge again this morning?"

"Aunt Jane's a wonderful cook!"

"The best," said Lucy, and they smiled at one another in satisfaction as they walked off hand in hand over the beach.

IV

"How are you feeling?" said Evan to Nicola, sitting down on the edge of her bed and reaching tenderly for her pulse.

"Very weird," said Nicola frankly. "Did I go mad or something?"

"Or something," said Evan. Her pulse seemed normal. He produced a thermometer. "Let me take your temperature."

"Did I have a nervous breakdown?" said Nicola before putting the thermometer in her mouth.

"Let's call it a nervous suspension from reality."

Nicola took the thermometer out of her mouth again. "What's the date today?" she demanded.

"August the second."

"It can't be!"

"Don't let it bother you. I'll explain everything later."

"Have I been a mental home?"

"No, you've been walking around here and giving a rather distorted semblance of normality. Don't let it worry you, Nicki. It was all entirely natural in the circumstances."

"Was I drugged? Those colors . . . dreams . . . illusions . . . or were they illusions? My God, perhaps they were reality!"

"You were probably drugged some of the time."

"And the rest of the time?"

"Poole had you hypnotized."

"Evan—" Nicola broke off.

"Yes?"

"Did I dream it or did I really—" She stopped again.

"You did," said Evan, "and yet in a sense you didn't. You weren't responsible for your actions."

"Oh Evan, how could I!" cried Nicola, and burst into a flood of tears. After he had managed to calm her she said, distracted: "What can you think of me! Why are you being so nice to me? How can you even bear to talk to me after what I did to you?"

"It served me right for playing around with you for all those months," said Evan. "Don't feel too sorry for me. And as for why I'm acting as if nothing happened, I repeat—you weren't responsible for your actions . . . Nicki, what's the last thing you remember with any real degree of clarity?"

Nicola gulped. "You. Proposing to me. And me wondering why on earth I couldn't bring myself to say yes."

"All right," said Evan, "let's pick up where we left off. Nicki, will you marry me?"

Nicola gulped again. "Evan, you must be the most wonderful man in the whole world and I just don't deserve—"

"Spare me the martyred self-pity. Do you love me?"

"More than anyone else on earth, but—"

"Then you'll marry me?"

"Right now this very minute if I could," said Nicola without hesitation, and saw his taut frame relax in relief as she smiled radiantly into his eyes.